ALSO BY HOLLY SHUMAS

Five Things I Can't Live Without

LOVE AND OTHER NATURAL DISASTERS

HOLLY SHUMAS

NEW YORK   BOSTON

5 Spot
Hachette Book Group
237 Park Avenue
New York, NY 10017

Visit our Web site at www.5-spot.com.

5 Spot is an imprint of Grand Central Publishing.
The 5 Spot name and logo are trademarks of Hachette Book Group, Inc.

Printed in the United States of America

First Edition: January 2009
10   9   8   7   6   5   4   3   2   1

Library of Congress Cataloging-in-Publication Data

Shumas, Holly.
    Love and other natural disasters / Holly Shumas. — 1st ed.
        p. cm.
    ISBN 978-0-446-50477-5
    1. Marriage — Fiction.   2. Chick lit.   I. Title.
    PS3619.H865L68 2009
    813'.6—dc22
                                                    2007048630

Book design by Stratford Publishing Services, a TexTech business

ACKNOWLEDGMENTS

Thanks to my family and friends for their unwavering support. Having you all behind me helps me face down that blank screen.

Tara and Avie, I appreciate your feedback and your friendship. David, your insights into the male psyche were invaluable.

Much gratitude goes to my editor, Karen Kosztolnyik. Karen, I'm so glad you hung in through those early drafts (alternating point-of-view wasn't my finest hour). You really got what I was trying to do, and helped me do it better. What more could I ask for in an editor?

To my agent, Stephanie Kip Rostan — I don't even know where to begin. You are a delight to work with: knowledgeable, approachable, and responsive, with a great editorial eye to boot. Every author should be so lucky.

Thanks to the San Francisco Writers Workshop and the Blackpoint Writers. Tamim Ansary, you're generous and astute and I can't think of a better combination in a facilitator. I knew the book was working when discussion wasn't about the writing itself but about which was worse, an emotional affair or a sexual one.

Thank you, Darrend, for all you are and all you do.

LOVE AND
OTHER NATURAL
DISASTERS

CHAPTER

1

Some years, I gaze around the Thanksgiving table and I feel almost painfully grateful for my own bounty, for the abundance that is my life, for everything that brought me to this moment, with these people, inside this light.

And some years, I just eat turkey.

This Thanksgiving had been off to a promising start. Jacob was at his most adorable, regaling us all with what, at five years old, was a new tale of Pilgrims and Indians and friendship. My husband, Jonathon, was the consummate host, topping off my friend Tamara's and her boyfriend Clayton's wineglasses from the decanter, expertly cuing Jacob whenever he was about to struggle for a word or detail. Jonathon's mother was getting along with mine, meaning Sylvia wasn't openly disapproving of my mother. (Nothing feeds gratitude like lowered expectations.) And I thought, looking down at my swollen belly, about the party crasher inside—boy or girl, we didn't know yet. Jonathon and I wanted the surprise.

My happiness was magnified by this being our first Thanksgiving in our own home. I'd never had a dining room before, let alone a house, having grown up in small apartments in Southern California with my mother and brother, and then living in San Francisco, land of low square footage. Who knew I could get this much pleasure out of a dining room? Who knew I could be so happy living in the suburbs?

When Jonathon and I first had Jacob, we pledged to be urban to the end; we were going to raise street-smart kids who'd osmotically pick up four languages by the time they were ten. We resisted suburbia for as long as we could, mourned the friends who had fallen, and sworn we'd never go to the dark side (meaning, shopping centers perennially anchored by Starbucks and Bed Bath & Beyond). We told each other that we loved the authenticity of our city block—i.e., the smells of sulfurous cooking and urine, the reek of real life—as we seemed to be in the only San Francisco neighborhood undergoing a degentrification. But my bubble of self-delusion burst the day I'd circled twenty minutes to find a parking space, and as we walked along, Jacob asked a homeless man where *his* mommy was and the guy let out a string of invectives that followed us half a block. Since Jon and I couldn't afford a house in any decent city neighborhood, the burbs it was.

The phone rang, and Jonathon said he'd get it, he was already up. From the dining room, I could see into the kitchen, and I didn't expect Jon to reach out and shut the swinging door between the rooms. But it wasn't until he'd been gone awhile, maybe as long as fifteen minutes, that it truly registered as anything out of the ordinary. It wasn't like Jon to disappear when there were people to attend to. What was going on? Could there have been an accident? Or — and fear gripped me most as this thought hit — what if something was wrong with Jon? A doctor calling with test results? A doctor wouldn't call on a holiday unless it was really bad — impending-coronary bad. That was how Jon's father had died, just keeled over at the age of fifty-two. Of course, he'd been married to Sylvia, and that could weaken any man's heart.

When I was pregnant, I was prone to panicked worst-case scenarios. In the later part of my pregnancy with Jacob, and for much of the first year of his life, I turned into one of those people who couldn't watch the news. Jonathon and I developed a little ritual around it where I'd ask him for highlight reels. He'd tell me a bunch of true things and one that was made up and I'd have to guess the falsehood. He started really getting into it, reading different Web sites that specialized in true and wacky news items from around the world. It was surprisingly hard to guess the faux item. For example, there really were two blond twin girls who called themselves Prussian Blue singing perky songs about white supremacy, the Olsen twins of the White Nationalist Movement. Jon and I both loved the ritual, which served to divert me from some truly awful things that were occurring in the world, things utterly beyond my control, and reminded me of the fun and silliness and connection that we shared. It made me feel safe.

But right then, I was picturing Jon collapsed on the ceramic kitchen tiles, gasping for air. (Did people gasp when they were having coronaries?) I excused myself and pushed open the swinging door, relieved to see he wasn't lying prone, but surprised that he wasn't in the kitchen at all. Maybe it's just hindsight, maybe it's too much TV—the "Did I put the dog in the washing machine, or was that on *The Brady Bunch?*" syndrome—but the rest of the house seemed eerily still in that moment and my stomach was pretzeled as I walked down the hall toward our bedroom. I don't think this next part is hindsight, I think it's memory: Though nothing in our marriage to that point indicated that I should, I was moving deliberately, stealthily, like I imagined a hunter would stalk big game. I could hear Jon's muffled voice behind the closed bedroom door. I don't know what made me put my ear up to it, but when I did, I heard Jonathon speaking to someone with great tenderness, saying things like, "Shhh, you're going to be okay. This day will be over soon. And you'll be just fine."

My heartbeat accelerated; I had to remind myself to breathe. There were two options, as I saw it: continue eavesdropping, or open the door. Walking away was an impossibility. If I listened longer, he could say something like, "I love my wife more than anything in the world, and I have to get back to her." Or perhaps, "Henry…" Any man's name would be acceptable. Of course, there were those androgynous names like "Sam." Unless…?

I pushed the door open, and Jonathon looked up, his eyes widening. We held the gaze a few seconds, and then he said into the phone, "Hold on." To me, "I'm sorry this is taking so long. I'll be out in a minute."

Like it was an ordinary call. Could it be an ordinary

call? I wanted to think that it was. But somehow, I didn't. That alone seemed damning, but of whom? Of him? Of me? "Who is that?" I asked.

"It's just a friend," he said. Nothing strange in his tone, but that wording. Does anyone say "just a friend" if someone really is just a friend? Wouldn't you say the friend's name?

But this was Jonathon. He only had just friends. "Which friend?" I tried to make my tone match his, but failed.

He put his hand up to indicate it would be one more minute, and addressed the receiver again. "I need to go now, okay?"

Whoever was on the other end actually kept talking. I could make out a female voice, though I couldn't hear what she was saying. She prattled on at breakneck speed as I stood there waiting. I wasn't just waiting for her to stop talking; I was waiting for him to interrupt her. Who was this woman with the audacity to call my husband away in the middle of Thanksgiving, who hears my voice in the room, who hears him say he needs to go, and keeps talking?

But, I countered, maybe that was what made her harmless. Maybe she had the audacity because she didn't need to fear discovery, she didn't need to fear the wife. She was just a friend who was too upset on Thanksgiving to observe social graces.

I couldn't take it anymore. If he wouldn't interrupt, I would. "We have guests."

Jonathon mouthed the words "I'm sorry" in an exaggerated way, like we were sharing the joke of how some people can't take a hint. "I've really got to go now," he told her. "Take care of yourself, okay?" He clicked the disconnect button on the cordless phone. Then he turned to me and smiled. "Let's get back in there."

I couldn't stop hearing: *"Shhh, you're going to be okay."* It was the intimacy of that *"shhh"*; not how you *shhh* the loud guy behind you at the movie theater, but the way you quiet a distraught lover.

"Which friend did you say that was?" I asked.

"You don't know her. She's someone I know through work. She has a hard time at the holidays. She must have been going through her address book, seeing who'd answer the phone." Was his forehead shiny?

"That's weird, isn't it?"

He shrugged. "I guess she is. I don't know her very well."

I was staring at him, wanting him to say something, do something, anything that would loosen the grip of this terrible anxiety, to expunge all traces of that "shhh" from my memory—some science fiction that would turn back the clock. But that was the problem; it seemed like fiction. "What's her name? Have I ever heard about her?"

He shook his head. "She doesn't work in the San Francisco office. She works out of Chicago."

Okay, that brought some scant relief. Three more factoids like that and maybe . . . "How do you know her?"

"I met her at a conference. You know, that corporate 'Up with People' thing I had to go to last September." He walked toward me. "Aren't you the one who said we have guests?" he teased.

I froze. This was Jon, the man I'd loved for ten years, the father of my child, my children. My hand moved to my belly. Would he really cheat on me, when I would be having his baby in just over a month? Would he really cheat on me, ever? That was the first time I'd actually allowed myself to think the word: "cheat." Jon wasn't a cheater. Jon was a straight arrow, almost to a fault. He mailed back those premade address labels from the Cystic Fibrosis Foundation if he wasn't giving a donation. This was the kind of thing I had chosen to find endearing rather than irritating, the kind of quirk I had chosen to love when I had chosen to love Jon for the rest of my life. Love was a choice that I made every day, quietly. Now that choice was mine again, only it was both thunderous and Technicolor. Would I choose to love Jon? Would I choose to ignore this screaming instinct inside me and believe him?

I nodded, and to Jon, that meant we would get back to the party as he'd suggested. In a thick, dreamlike state, I drifted back to the table with the battle between gut instinct and volitional love continuing to rage inside me. I reseated myself next to Jonathon and sipped my sparkling water and tried to rejoin the conversation like the good host, the loving wife.

Wine. I would have killed for some wine. One glass couldn't hurt this close to delivery; I'd been abstinent for the entire pregnancy, not a single slipup. It wasn't like I was going to marinate my baby in the stuff. It would just be one glass. Maybe my baby could use a little alcohol right about now. Maybe some wine would be good for her heart. Or good for his stress level. I stifled a giggle of hysteria rather than amusement as I pictured our baby swimming around blissfully in a solution of two parts amniotic fluid to one part merlot. I could always explain it later if she (or maybe he) ever found out: "Mommy needed that one glass, sweetie pie. You see, she'd gone a little crazy thinking that Daddy might be cheating, but it turned out Daddy would never, ever do something like that to Mommy, to us. Because that would be really, really fucked up. Not just fucked up, even. We're talking colossally vile, we're talking duplicitous and loathsome. I mean, we're talking *fucked up* here. We're talking about a life that's nothing but a lie. We're talking..."

My hand was nearly shaking as I reached for the decanter, earning me a glare from Sylvia. It was a look that said, "I always knew you were a good-for-nothing baby poisoner who doesn't deserve my son." Which, come to think of it, wasn't actually that different from how she normally looked at me. What I didn't need right then was a confrontation with Sylvia; I wouldn't be responsible for what came out of my mouth. I pretended I was reaching for the sweet potatoes instead, a maneuver that certainly didn't fool sharp-eyed Sylvia.

I tried to concentrate on the lighthearted chatter around me. Clayton (who'd gone to film school with hopes of being the next great auteur, only to find himself a freelance infomercial director five years later) was describing a series of YouTube videos featuring Jacob. The idea was that Jacob was a troubled child star who kept failing rehab.

"So Jake's got his sunglasses on, and he's running to the car, and Tamara's his publicist, trying to hold back the paparazzi, and finally he turns to the camera, all mournful-like, puts out a hand and says, 'No press.' Show them, bud," he instructed Jacob.

To the laughter of the table, Jacob instantly adopted a world-weary expression and recited, "No press."

I forced a smile and looked at Jonathon, who was obviously doing the same. The fact that Jon seemed off-kilter was not comforting to me. If he really had been talking to a friend—a friend his wife didn't know about, but just a friend nonetheless—would he seem shaken afterward? Noticing my scrutiny, he steadied his rickety smile and reached for his sparkling water. He never drank alcohol around me during my pregnancies in a show of solidarity. Was that all we were? A show?

At that thought, I hoisted myself to my feet. "Excuse me," I said. "Jon, could you come with me, please?"

"And cut!" I could hear Jacob exclaiming as I left the room. He loved directorial lingo.

Jon followed me to the bedroom and closed the door behind us. I remained standing for two reasons: the first was that I was hoping this would be fast, I wanted to get my reassurance and get out; the second was that my pregnancy hemorrhoids had been acting up all damn day. I refused to sit on my special pillow in front of company.

I squared my shoulders. "I'm asking you, please don't lie to me," I said. "Please don't."

He nodded, eyes filled with concern. Whether it was

the concern of a cheater about to get caught or of a man whose wife was cracking up was as yet unclear.

I took a deep breath. "Are you cheating with that woman on the phone?"

"No," he said immediately.

"Then who was that on the phone?"

"I told you. A friend."

"A friend who knew she could call you on Thanksgiving, and that you'd talk to her?"

"What was I supposed to do? She was crying. She needed help." He raked a hand through his hair. "I'm not cheating. I wouldn't cheat."

He looked so earnest. He looked so Jonathon. But I'd heard the way he talked to her. It didn't add up. "So who is this woman, exactly?"

"I told you. A friend." There was something almost hypnotic in his repetition, and his tone was so soothing.

Wait a minute! He was soothing me like he'd soothed her. "I heard you earlier. The way you were telling her it would be okay. You were talking to her like a lover."

"I'm not her lover." His eye contact never wavered. "We talk on the phone sometimes, that's all. I'm sorry I never told you about her. We met at the conference, we went to lunch a few times, we exchanged e-mail addresses, and that was it. She's just a friend."

There it was again, that "just." I knew he was lying. It was so strong, this sense, strong enough to override all that I'd known for the past ten years. Strong enough to override what I wanted so desperately to believe. "So you met her over a year ago, but she still calls you?" He said nothing, as if it had been a rhetorical question. I suddenly felt like I was cross-examining a hostile witness. "How often do you talk to her?"

That's when he broke eye contact. "We don't talk all that often," he said.

"I can get phone bills."

"We've been talking more lately," he amended.

Oh, God. "How often?"

"She gets depressed at the holidays, I told you. She needed someone to tell her she'd be okay, and that's what I did. That's all I did."

"How often?" I pressed, my voice tight with anger. I had begged him not to lie, and here he was, lying to my face.

"Lately it's been once a week. Sometimes more."

"That's more than you talk to Clayton!" Finally I had proof of something, but I didn't yet know what.

"She's been lonely lately. We mostly just send e-mails."

"How often do you e-mail?"

He looked immediately sorry he'd opened up the e-mail line of inquiry. "Sometimes."

"I asked how often, and don't lie. Because if I have to get your computer hacked myself, I'll find out."

"Pretty much every day," he said reluctantly.

"Every day?"

"But there's nothing physical between us. I wouldn't do that."

I actually believed that. But I was thinking about how Jon used to write me long, hilarious e-mails filled with the minutiae of his day, and how much I had loved them. I hadn't had a digest like that in months. They were all going to her. "What's her name? The other woman. What's her fucking name?"

"Laney."

"Are they long?" He looked confused, so I added impatiently, "The e-mails."

"Sometimes."

"Like the ones you used to send me."

He finally had the decency to look fully abashed. "Yes."

"Is Laney pretty?"

He clearly didn't want to answer that, which meant yes.

"Do you want to fuck Laney?"

"I told you, I wouldn't—"

"But do you *want* to fuck Laney?"

His silence answered again. Then he pulled himself together enough to say, "I only want to be with you. With you and Jacob. And with—" He reached for my belly, and I moved away reflexively. I could tell that hurt him. Good. *Reach out again and I'll hurt you some more.*

"I just want to make sure I understand," I said. "You e-mail this woman every day, you talk to her at least once a week, you comfort her on holidays, and you wish you could fuck her. But she lives in Chicago, so you can't." I paused. "Did I leave anything out?"

During the staring contest that ensued, I found myself wondering how we had landed here. Just the week before, we had finished our birthing classes. With

Jacob, I'd gone the epidural route, but this time, we were going natural. We'd chosen the Bradley Method instead of Lamaze because it focused more on the husband's coaching. Also, with Bradley, you learned to go through the pain rather than simply distract yourself. I pictured us in class, how Jon had doodled cartoons for me during the boring parts. I remembered the first day, when we were asked to rate our commitment to a drug-free birth—0 being no commitment and 10 being absolute commitment—and we each wrote our number on a three-by-five card, and when instructed, we presented it to the other like we were on *The Newlywed Game*. When we saw that we had both written 4, we whooped and high-fived, and then laughed at the uneasy smiles of the other couples, who had rated themselves 9s and 10s. How could Jon do this to me? I couldn't handle this much pain. Didn't he remember I was only a 4?

"I don't want any other woman," Jonathon said. "I mean, if anything, you should feel sorry for her. She's thirty-three and single and she would kill for what you have."

"Oh, my God!" I exploded. "Have you lost your mind, saying that to me? You want me to feel sorry for her?"

"I want you to have some perspective here. I didn't do anything with her."

So Jon had turned into Bill Clinton. Or, at best, that other one...Which president was it who said he'd been unfaithful only in his heart? My husband was unfaithful in his heart for over a year. He deliberately hid Laney from me, and he gave her the things that should have been mine, the things I had always assumed were mine. I thought of all the moments of excitement we had shared during the pregnancy, and all the while, he had Laney. Maybe the night we conceived our baby, he'd been thinking of her.

Before I knew it was happening, I vomited. All over my shoes, all over the carpet. I started crying wildly, with shame, outrage, fury, sadness. I crumpled to the floor; I didn't have the strength in my legs to keep standing.

Jonathon sank down beside me and pushed my hair back. It was such a tender gesture—the kind I was used to—and I needed it, even though accepting any ministration from him right then felt tawdry. It felt weak. "I'm sorry," he said. "I'm so sorry." There were tears in his eyes.

"You can't stay here tonight," I said.

He looked surprised. I guess he had thought that the weeping and vomiting had reduced me to a state of pure vulnerability. "We just need to talk more," he said. "I'm sorry for what I did. I'll cut her off. It's done. Okay?"

"You're asking if it's okay?" I drew myself up to my knees, willing myself to stand. Just a few more seconds and I'd be able to stand.

"No, I'm not saying what I did is okay. I'm saying—"

"I can't be around you right now. So you can't stay." Finally I was on my feet, and feeling a strange calm. An out-of-body calm.

CHAPTER

2

There are two kinds of pain. I don't mean physical and psychological. Those are just categories. I'm talking about pain with a purpose, an end point, a reward (childbirth being the obvious example), versus pain that only takes away. I know there are hundreds of inspirational memoirs to tell me that the latter can turn into the former, that losing a breast or a leg or a husband can ultimately make my life richer than I ever dreamed it could be, but that night, I was in no mood to believe them. I mean, isn't the lesson of those memoirs always to appreciate every moment we have with the people we love? There I'd been, in midgratitude, damned near in love with my life (without benefit of alcohol, I might add), and then, *splat*. I'm convinced that's the kind of pain — cruel, purposeless, ironic — that kills if you don't just check out for a while.

So that's what I did. *This must be what's called shock. It must be what's called survival*, I thought, almost marveling at my capacity not only to make it to the dining room, but to announce with dry eyes and a steady voice that I'd gotten sick suddenly and I was so sorry, but everyone would need to leave.

Because I was elsewhere, I have trouble remembering what came next with any specificity. I know more must have been said—Jon must have tried to make things seem normal; Sylvia would have wanted to make sure my mysterious ailment wasn't going to affect the baby; Tamara and my mother would want to look after me—but mostly I see faces. I have reaction shots without transcripts, as if the projectionist inside my head couldn't work under these conditions. It's like that trick they do in movies, where they'll capture, say, a wedding day in still images as if we're viewing the photo album later, with picture upon picture of the bride and groom kissing, friends and family clapping and, later, dancing, the happy couple laughing as they feed each other cake, and if the director's feeling especially sappy, maybe the receding limo with "Just Married!" soaped on its back windows. The whole thing is a wonderful confection, this distillation of images tells us. It tells us all we need to know of their story, where it begins and where it ends.

Here's my photo album of that night:

The red-walled dining room—I'd always thought the red was so sophisticated, never before had it seemed garish, like the scene of a crime—still full of holiday levity. I can see everyone assembled around the table with forks halfway to smiling mouths in that split second before they take in my reappearance.

Faces of fairly uniform concern and surprise before I start to speak...

Then, afterward, their expressions become more separate, distinct: my mother's frightened, like that of a child who knows there's more than what's being told; Sylvia's eyes go to Jon, and suspicion vies with worry; Clayton just hopes I'll feel better tomorrow; Tamara's mouth drops open as she immediately, instinctively, grasps the terrible import; Jacob looking to his left and then to his right, trying to understand what it means through the others.

After I pull Tamara aside — after I tell her that Jon's having an affair and I can't be a mother that night, I just need to be a wife, no, just a woman, and could she please take Jacob overnight? — her eyes are filled with tears.

Tamara hugging me, my body rigid.

Jacob's outstretched hand. He's excited and wants us to go to his room and pack for Tamara and Clayton's.

Jon slouched in the doorway, watching, speechless, motionless, not seeming to realize he's blocking us.

Jon backing away, letting us pass.

Jacob, hyper, jumping around, bouncing up and down on his bed, singing songs as I fill his backpack with senseless objects that I hope are the right ones. Pajamas. I know I gave him pajamas. But I didn't ask if he wanted these or those, fire engines or Mickey Mouse. There was no illusion of choice that night, not for any of us.

The dining room again: Jon sitting in a chair now, looking up at me, saying nothing, begging. He didn't want to leave, I couldn't let him stay.

Me hugging Jacob, fiercely enough for him to protest.

Tamara and Clayton walking to their car at the end of the drive, Jacob between them, chattering upward, Jon trailing behind.

Jon leaning inside the car as he buckles Jacob in, touching his forehead to Jacob's, lingering there for a long minute.

That's when I turned away.

I sat down on the living-room couch, just feet from the front door, suddenly dizzy. Sylvia and my mother were still in the dining room. I couldn't imagine what they were saying to each other. I didn't want to imagine. I closed my eyes and thought, *This actually happened. Jon has another woman.*

I repeated those phrases and even tried some new ones, calculated to cause agony. Like, *Jon's in love with her, he doesn't care about you. He's just been pretending all these years. He's a liar, and a cheat.* It was like punching myself in the face after Novocain. I was trying to feel something, but I couldn't.

I heard the front door open; then I felt Jon's weight beside me on the couch. I kept my eyes closed.

"Eve," he said softly.

"Don't talk to me," I said, but without feeling.

"You're right, we shouldn't talk anymore tonight. I'm going to a hotel."

I said nothing.

"Please know that I'm sorry, and that I love you. Please know that."

I didn't open my eyes.

Did I believe Jon loved me? Yes. But the value of his love—our love—changed that night. And what do you do with devalued love?

I had a certain story about my life with Jon, a story I liked, and it didn't fit anymore. Worse, maybe it never had.

I met Jon when I was twenty and he was twenty-one. It was the beginning of my junior year at Berkeley, and his senior. I'd been unhappy, and then I wasn't. Four years later, we were married. Then we had Jacob. We bought a house. We got pregnant again.

Those were all the facts I had left.

But here's the story I used to tell myself:

During my senior year of college, I worked part-time as a receptionist in a doctor's office. The waiting room had a large tank, well-stocked with colorful, exotic fish. But my favorites were the plainest. Long, thin, and dull silver, they circled each other constantly. One would remain stationary while the other orbited around him/her; then they'd reverse. All day long, they'd circle. Jon joked that maybe they had OCD; I thought it was love. Compulsive, no doubt. But a love that was about purpose and constancy. Those were two committed fish. They never circled any other.

One day, I came in and one was floating, and I saw the difference between stationary and motionless. The other fish was still circling, and there was a frantic quality to it that I'd never seen before. I knew I couldn't just leave the dead fish in the tank (it would be a bad subliminal message to send in a doctor's office, for one thing), but I hated to think of the other all alone in a sea of prettier, flashier fish. Finally I got the net, and did what I had to do. For the rest of the day, the remaining silver fish tried to circle other fish. I don't know if it was their apathy or that he/she just figured out that some beings are irreplaceable, but by the next morning, circling had become spinning. Then it became nothing. Within a few days, the second silver fish was dead.

I didn't have grandparents that loved each other for fifty years, and after one died, the other's heart gave out. The fish were it for me. Corny, macabre, or just plain strange as it may seem, they were my love story. The day I flushed the second fish, I went home and cried, and Jon held me and not one thing about him said, "But they were *fish*." I was twenty-one, and I wanted to circle him for the rest of my life.

CHAPTER 3

I applied carpet deodorizer four times, waiting the requisite ten minutes before each vacuuming, and still, it was like my Thanksgiving dinner was sitting there winking at me. I'd thought motherhood had sucked all the squeamishness out of me, but I was wrong. As they say, the learning never stops.

I wished I weren't alone, that it wasn't just me and the white noise of the vacuum. If I got really hard up for company, I could always go wake my mother. She was in the office/guest room, adrift on sleeping pills with her ears plugged. Earlier, after Jon left for the hotel, I told her the truth, that he was having an affair. She started wandering around in such an obvious state of bereavement that I said she should take her pill early. I didn't mean for it to come out so harshly, and I hated that she just nodded and followed instructions. Sometimes she seemed like a puppy that had been kicked too often; she was always ready to roll over and show her belly.

That was a mean thought. Why have mean thoughts about my mother? This wasn't her fault, unless her tendency to pick rotten men was genetic and my birthright had finally caught up with me.

But it didn't make sense. In all these years, I'd never had occasion to doubt Jon's love and fidelity. It was like suddenly finding out you've been living in someone else's marriage—someone else's bad marriage. I mean, these sorts of things don't happen in good marriages, do they?

We had a good marriage. *Have* a good marriage, I corrected myself. So maybe he could spend all that time e-mailing and talking to Laney and have it be friendship, nothing more. She could be some lonely, needy woman he felt sorry for; she could just be a habit or a distraction, a way to get through a boring day at the office. It was possible. He was Jacob's father. I was carrying his second child. It had to be possible.

I could check his e-mail and find out.

At first it was a rogue thought, immediately and easily dismissed. But it just kept bobbing to the surface. It wouldn't be denied. I'd never contemplated something like this before, but how else could I get the truth? At the very least, Jon had lied by omission for a year, and right to my face this very day. Besides, I opened Jon's mail all the time. We shared a bank account. We (usually) shared a bed. I could read the e-mail, he'd be exonerated, and we'd laugh about this later. *Oh, remember the Thanksgiving when I vomited all over my shoes and then broke into your e-mail?* Hilarity would surely ensue.

I turned off the vacuum and padded into the guest room. Fortunately, there was some light seeping in from the hallway, enough to guide me to the desk. I didn't touch the overhead light, for fear of waking my mother. She was lying on the futon, her back to me, and she didn't stir. I silently thanked the makers of Ambien as I settled myself at the desk and booted up the computer. It seemed an interminable wait. My heart was beating madly. It knew before I did that this was one of those moments from which there's no turning back. Whatever I read, I couldn't un-read. I couldn't un-know.

A few clicks of the mouse, and I was staring at the log-in screen for Jon's e-mail. I was pretty sure I knew the password. Jon used the same password for everything. He was trusting that way.

For a long minute, I sat there, battling my conscience; then I typed in "redwood53." Obligingly, his in-box filled the screen. Along with various spam for penis enlargement and wet Russian girls and cum-ing that would go on for days, there was a message from Laney in bold, meaning he hadn't read it yet. "Happy Thanksgiving!" was its subject heading.

J,

I don't even think I remembered to tell you happy Thanksgiving when we talked, I was so busy blubbering! So here you are. Also, I wanted to apologize for pulling you away from your family. I know it was selfish of me to call, but I felt like yours was the only voice I wanted to hear. ☺ I didn't mean to get you in trouble with Eve.

Talk soon?

L

Exclamation points and emoticons. *J* to her *L*. She was nauseating, but there was nothing that screamed "more than a friend" about it. The fact that his voice was the only one she wanted to hear could just mean that she was a big loser and had no other friends. I liked that idea.

I looked at the folders on the left, and saw that there was one named Laney. I couldn't help noticing that there was no folder called Eve. Being more interested in what he'd written to her than what she'd written to him, I zeroed in on the Sent folder. But first, I covered my tracks, marking the Thanksgiving e-mail once again as unread, in bold.

The Sent folder went back only about six months, probably because it was so overstuffed with missives to Laney. He must have written a million gigabytes to her. Or was it megabytes? He'd said the e-mails were daily, but sometimes there were two or three over the course of a day. I tried not to think about the instant-messaging possibilities.

Steeling myself, I opened the earliest. To the untrained eye, it seemed innocuous enough—he was giving her advice about whether to fly out for a friend's wedding, telling a cute anecdote about work—but what shattered me was that I could hear him as if in voice-over. The warm conversational tone was so similar to the e-mails he used to send me that if I hadn't known better, I would have thought they were mine. Jon didn't woo with overt flirting or romance; he wooed with charming asides and attention to detail, with responsiveness and empathy. You felt understood by him; you thought you knew him completely.

Every day, he was wooing Laney with the stream-of-consciousness details of his past and his present (in one e-mail, he started out riffing about his penchant for overly sentimental sports movies, then went into a self-deprecating description of his one glorious season as a high-school shortstop, and ended on his excitement over Jacob starting T-ball next year). Laney was a fixture in his life. He was her *J*, and she was his *L*, and the affection he felt for her couldn't have been clearer.

And where was I? Pretty much nowhere. After reading ten e-mails full of stylized ramblings, I started obsessively skimming message after message, trying to find myself. Over the course of months, I got four mentions. It seemed like a sure sign that Laney wasn't just a friend; she was the other woman. I couldn't think of any other explanation for my conspicuous absence.

Then there was what he chose to tell her about me:

> Eve reacted just like I said she would, like I was hoping she wouldn't. I know she gets really stressed out, with it being early in the pregnancy, but sometimes I just feel like I'm walking on eggshells around her.

I looked at the date and tried to figure out what could have happened the night before. It wasn't the day of an ultrasound, not that I could recall. Just an ordinary day, except that whatever I'd done, it was bad enough to tell Laney about. Not bad enough to tell me, though. Walking on eggshells? I'd never heard him use that phrase. Since I wasn't featured in any nearby e-mails, he could only have made his prediction on the phone to Laney, which meant he'd bashed me on the phone to the other woman.

Blinking back tears, I clicked on the next e-mail, and the next. Twenty or so later, I found this:

> Eve and my mother bad-mouth each other a lot.
> When Eve says something about my mother, I want to
> defend my mother. When my mother says something
> about Eve, I want to defend Eve. How hard can it be
> to just get along?

Okay, that was nothing new. He'd said that directly to me before; just as he'd chosen to do earlier tonight, I'd always chosen to take it as rhetorical. Only Laney probably had an answer. She was probably the type to nod and smile politely even through one of Sylvia's back-handed compliments. Maybe she wouldn't even notice it was backhanded.

In the next e-mail mention I got, after talking about Jacob's great personality:

> A lot of it's Eve's doing. She's a really good mom.
> I know she has a temper, but she manages to keep
> that away from Jacob.

Talk about your backhanded compliments. You'd think I spent half my life breaking dishes over Jon's head, the other half smiling beatifically at Jacob. Laney probably thought I was schizophrenic.

Was this really how he saw me?

At least when he was describing our family trip to Disneyland (when he wrote her every day but one), I rated a "we," as in "We took Jacob on every ride he was tall enough to go on," but maybe that was just accidental. I mean, he was "we"-ing all that week. "Should we do this?" "Should we go there?" But there was no "Eve."

While I hated that he'd said those things about me (some being things he never said *to* me), it was my absence that hurt the most. So many paragraphs of him discussing his impending second fatherhood, and I wasn't mentioned in any of them, as if I were an incubator. He'd just rubbed me out of his life, in order to forge a second, imaginary life with Laney.

I wanted to stop reading, but I couldn't. I was a glutton for truth, hungry to know Jon and my marriage. Yet as I continued reading, it was like I was finding out everything about his life (sometimes down to his thoughts on dry cleaning) and nothing at all. There were no grand confessions. I knew the old stories and anecdotes. It wasn't as if Jon kept important things from me and told them to Laney (eggshells notwithstanding); Laney was the only important thing he'd neglected to tell me.

Midway through an e-mail that found him musing about chicken salad sandwiches, I felt an unexpected flash of sadness at just how boring Jon's life was. He worked in financial services, he'd been with the same company since college, and he was a fairly typical suburban husband and father. Even having an affair was typical, when you thought about it. The unique thing was that his was cyber, not sexual, and that was getting less unique all the time.

Maybe this was just the sign of an early midlife crisis. He was trying to pump himself up, see himself through Laney's eyes. I could almost understand that. (I was having his baby. That was a pretty big incentive toward understanding.) What I could understand, I could forgive.

But then I read an e-mail from about two months ago:

L,
I can't wait to see you either! Fortunately, there were still tickets left for the Giants game on Saturday. You and me, kid.
J

That's when the tenor of the e-mails changed. The next two weeks' worth were feverish with exclamation points. You could practically read the hard-on. Then, after they must have seen each other, he wrote this:

L,
I feel horrible about what happened. Can you forgive me?
Love,
J

Oh, God. There it finally was. I went on to the next e-mail of his, but scrolled down to read what she'd written first.

J,

You're married, you have a baby on the way. I shouldn't have pushed like I did. I thought I could handle things and I guess I couldn't. I'm in love with you, but you already knew that. I've never been this humiliated, but I know it's my own fault. The only thing is, you love me, too.

L

L,

You're right about some things. I do feel love for you, and I am attracted to you. You're a phenomenal woman. If I'm honest with myself, I sensed that right from the first night, and when the bar was closing down, I should have gone back to my own room. That would have been the safest thing. But I didn't, and that was one of the best nights I've ever spent with a woman. The way we talked, and the way we laughed... I hadn't felt like that in I don't know how long. I was buzzing just being near you.

I can still laugh just thinking about us nominating the worst songs of all time, you explaining why "Take A Letter, Maria" is worse than that piña colada song (you said, "He's blowing off his wife for her, but she still has to take dictation," and I said, "How hard is it really to find someone who likes...piña coladas and sex on a BEACH?") and then we were both singing and laughing until we could barely breathe. It was perfect, there's no other word for it.

But tempted as I was, I didn't want to have an affair, not then and not now. I want to be married. I want to raise my kids with their mother. I can't give that up. Last week, when you said it would be enough for us just to spend a night together, I didn't believe you. And even if it was enough for you, it wouldn't be okay with me. I can't live that kind of a double life.

I've looked forward to you, to telling you things, having you tell me things. I looked forward to seeing you more than I let myself realize. Somehow you became the easiest part of my life. But that changed when I had to lie to Eve's face so we could go to the baseball game, and then afterward, in the car, when I had to tell you no, the way I had to say it twice, once while prying your hand off my jeans.

Things are different now, and the reason I went all the way back to the beginning, to those feelings I couldn't admit to myself, is because I want you to know how fantastic you are. I want you to find love with someone who'll see that and love you back and marry you and give you a family. He's not me.

J

P.S. I've rewritten this e-mail five times. I've never had to do that before with you, do rewrites. It's always been so effortless. Can it go back there? The answer's probably no, but I have to ask the question.

That brought the count to four. Four times he'd mentioned my name. *I had to lie to Eve's face.* How many times had he done it today? Every time he'd said Laney was just a friend. When he talked to her, I had no name; when he talked to me, she had no name.

But that wasn't the most chilling part. No, the worst was that he didn't say he wanted to be with me, he didn't call me the woman he loved; no, he wanted to be married. He wanted to be with the mother of his children. I just happened to be that woman. He never said he was in love with Laney, only that he "felt love" for her, but it wasn't at all clear that if the playing field was level, he'd choose me over her.

I didn't want to—Lord knows I didn't want to—but I resumed reading. I had to know the next chapter.

I could tell he and Laney weren't the same after the visit. Occasionally they skipped a day in their correspondence, and some of the lightness was gone. I got the impression that she sometimes cried to him on the phone. She was afraid she'd always be alone, that she'd never love someone else the way she loved him, and that no one would love her the way she believed he could, if he'd only let himself. He never told her he loved her again, at least not in print.

I caught up to the present. There were no more secrets, at least none that could be discovered this way. Turning off the computer, I didn't know if I'd ever been so exhausted. But my mind wouldn't stop. I was fighting to reconcile the type of man who would redact his own wife for another woman with the notion of my husband, the father of my children. Most terrifying was that he could carry on like that for over a year and act entirely normal with me. He should have felt guilty every time he looked at me, every time he looked at Jacob. He was betraying our family.

If I hadn't overheard him tonight, how long would he have continued behind my back? And how far would it have gone? He'd resisted Laney once, but he hadn't ended their relationship. At the word "relationship," I felt a bout of nausea. It worsened as I thought of Jacob and the baby inside me. I'd always believed I was giving them the best man I knew for a father.

I was back in our bed, and nowhere close to understanding, when the phone rang. It could only be him.

"Hello," I said, my heart at a canter.

"Eve, let me come over. Please. Can I come over?" Jon said in a rush.

"No."

"Please. I'm right by the house."

"That's not the point. How close you are isn't the point."

"You're right, okay? I've been an asshole. Worse than an asshole. I don't want to be away from you, from our life together. I'm sorry. Can I come and tell you in person how sorry I am?"

He'd put me in a position where I couldn't believe him anymore. I felt the tears starting. "No, you can't come here."

"Please, Eve. Please." He sounded like he was about to cry, too.

"I can't believe you right now. Should we talk when I can't believe anything you say?"

"Yes."

"I can't even look at you."

"Yes, you can. Please, Eve. For Jacob. For our baby."

"Don't bring her into this!" I nearly shouted, and as I said it, I knew it was true. We were having a girl.

He was silent. I was silent. Then he said softly, "You know it's a girl, too. I just realized it a little while ago."

At that, I wept too hard to talk. I buried my face in the pillow and let the phone drop beside my head. He didn't speak for a few minutes; then I heard my name over and over. I lifted the phone to my ear.

"Please let me come over," he said.

How could we recover from this? Six weeks ago, he'd spent the day with Laney, he'd signed off to her with "Love." He was a liar and a cheat and possibly in love with another woman, and possibly not in love with me and . . .

I exhaled, and surprised myself. "Okay."

CHAPTER

4

He wasn't kidding about being right by the house. Five minutes after we'd hung up, he was knocking on the front door. It wasn't enough time to develop a decent game plan, so I was operating on one principle only: *Don't tell him what you know. Don't tell him you read the e-mails.*

I felt shame at violating his privacy, which felt like my own violation of our marriage vows, but perhaps most shameful, I knew that if I showed my hand, I'd never be able to check up on him again. He'd change his password, knowing I was the kind of person he had to guard against. I hated that we'd arrived here, that neither of us deserved to be trusted anymore.

I looked at myself in the full-length mirror affixed to the bedroom door. Wavy auburn hair (my natural shade, no hair dye during pregnancy) with a halo of frizz to frame my face, blotchy skin, wearing the rhino-sized flannel pajamas that were my greatest comfort outside of chocolate. And, normally, Jon.

It had been a long time since I'd really considered my appearance and what Jon might think of it. The truth was, I didn't look that much worse right then than I looked normally. I lived in those pajamas. I put them on as early in the day as I could get away with, sometimes cooking dinner in them. My skin was often broken out during pregnancy, and I couldn't easily recall my last haircut. But I wasn't supposed to spend my life worrying whether my husband found me attractive. I wasn't supposed to have to worry whether there was a Laney somewhere, pretty and thin and woe-is-me-ing her way through the holidays. In Jon's mind, maybe I was one of those hearty women who can squat down in the field and have their babies and then get back to plowing, and Laney was off being a damsel in distress with a perfect manicure and a blowout.

He was knocking again, insistently. He probably thought I'd changed my mind about letting him in. If that's what he was thinking, he wasn't entirely wrong.

I quickly tied my hair back in a ponytail, walked to the front door, and opened it. Jon and I looked at each other with wariness, his tinged with sadness, mine with . . . damned if I knew. There was no word for this maelstrom.

"Can I come in?" he asked with a note of hesitation.

I stepped to the side by way of answer.

"Do you want to talk in here?" he said, indicating the living room.

I shrugged and settled myself on the couch. He sat on the opposite end, his feet flat on the floor, leaning forward. He was getting ready for a pitch. It couldn't have been clearer if he'd had a PowerPoint.

"I know you're angry," he said. "I mean, obviously you're angry."

"I don't know what I am," I said.

"I should have told you about Laney a long time ago."

"Why didn't you?"

"I didn't tell you about meeting her at the conference because it wasn't a big deal"—(Lie Number 1)—"and I didn't think we'd ever talk again. Then she e-mailed me, and I e-mailed her back, and it still wasn't a big deal. Then we were e-mailing more often, and she wanted to talk on the phone, and at some point, I decided not to mention it to you because I hadn't mentioned it sooner."

"So you decided to start officially lying to me."

"It didn't seem like a lie. The thing is, in my mind she was completely separate from you. She didn't really have to do with you. I'm not saying that was the right way to see it, it's just the way I saw it."

"And now how do you see it?" I said.

"I see that I shouldn't have been writing to her and talking to her so much, that it's disrespectful to you and to our marriage. I understand that now and I won't do it anymore." It sounded canned, rehearsed.

"You had feelings for her. You must still have them. I mean, you were talking to her this afternoon." If he said he had no feelings, that was another lie, maybe a lie that indicated just how strong his feelings actually were; if he said he did, then I had to listen to my husband talk about another woman. Double-edged swords as far as the eye could see.

"She was my friend. I would never do anything physical with her. This wasn't an affair, Eve."

"It's an emotional affair." I closed my eyes in disgust.

"I can't believe I just said that. You've turned me into an episode of *Oprah*."

"I'd go on *Oprah* with you, let the audience stone me if that's what it took."

"You went outside our marriage for a year. You were giving Laney things and getting things from her, and it makes me sick."

"I understand how this looks, and how bad you feel, and I feel terrible about that. I'm not saying I can make it up to you overnight. I can sleep in the guest room until you're ready."

"My mother's in the guest room."

"I'll stay at the hotel until Barbara leaves, and then I'll stay in the guest room for as long as you want. I know I have to earn your trust back."

"I can't stand this! I can't stand how we've learned to play these parts. It's like you know just what to say because every man before you has said the same things. We've seen it all on TV and this is how it's done. Next you're going to say we can go to marriage counseling." He looked away. "Am I right? Was that your next move if I didn't go for the 'guest room/building trust' thing?"

"I'd do counseling, if you wanted," he said carefully. "But I'm not playing a part here. I love you. I'm not saying that because it's in the script." He was gaining intensity as he spoke. "I'm saying it because I have never in my life loved someone like I love you. I have never wanted to marry anyone but you. I have never wanted to have a life with anyone but you. That's the truth, Eve."

I wanted to be moved; I wanted his speech to turn me around. But if what he'd said was true, and he could feel all that for me and still write those things to Laney, what did any of it really mean?

"You've only e-mailed and talked on the phone? You haven't seen her since the conference?" I asked, willing him to tell the truth.

He didn't answer right away. Then, hesitantly, he said, "A couple months ago, she was in San Francisco."

The correct answer was six weeks. But at least he was close. "She came out to see you?"

"She'd always wanted to see San Francisco...," he trailed off. "Yeah, she came to see me."

"And what happened?"

"Nothing. We went to a baseball game. That's all."

"You're saying she flew out here so you could go to a baseball game, and nothing else?"

"Maybe she had a crush on me. But like I said, nothing happened."

"Were you tempted?"

"What does it matter, Eve? I would never cheat on you. I love you."

"And what do you feel for her?" My eyes bore into his and, for a second, I thought, *We can survive this if he just tells the truth right now.*

"She's my friend, that's all."

"How can you do this? How can you just lie like this?" I burst out.

"I'm not lying! She's my friend."

"That's not a feeling. Friendship isn't a feeling."

"It is a feeling. I have friendly feelings toward her."

"Jesus Christ, Jon. What do you take me for?"

"I'm telling the truth."

What scared me was he seemed to believe it. "Then something's wrong with you. If you'd deceive me for a year for someone who doesn't even matter, then something's wrong."

"I told you how that happened."

"I think you're either lying, or you're too afraid to admit what she really means to you."

"There is a third possibility, you know."

"I don't think there is." I paused. "I want you to go to therapy so you can figure out who you are and what you want."

He snorted. "Come on, Eve."

"I'm serious, Jon."

He studied my face. "We'll go to marriage counseling and figure it out together."

"No. You go to counseling by yourself."

I felt a certain grim satisfaction in watching Jon squirm. I'd done tons of therapy in my life; it was always a given between us that he never needed it. I was the fucked-up one, even if it was in remission.

"Fine," he said. "I'll go to counseling."

"I don't want you to come home until you've figured some things out."

"Where do you expect me to go?"

"I'm sure you can stay with your mom."

He was looking at me with disbelief. "You're kicking me out for this? For writing e-mails?"

"If that's all you think you've done, you really have some figuring out to do."

"I know you want to punish me, but what about Jacob?"

"This isn't about punishment. It's about what I'm feeling. Would it help Jacob to see us hating each other?"

He winced. "You're saying you hate me? You're capable of hating me?"

"Just—you can't come home. Okay? Can't you understand that?"

"Look, I know you're hurt, and sometimes it's easier for you to be angry—"

"Fuck you, Jon. This isn't my character deficit we're dealing with."

He visibly took a deep breath. "I knew this wasn't going to be easy, and I'm prepared to deal with your anger. For as long as it takes."

"Do not patronize me."

"I'm not patronizing you. I'm trying to be with you. I know you don't have to make that easy for me, but can you at least admit that part of you, a small part of you, wants me home, too?"

"A lot of me wants you home. If you'd asked me this afternoon...but you hid another woman from me, you told her all sorts of things..." *Careful.*

There were tears in his eyes as he said softly, "Please. I'm begging you. Let me come home."

I started to give way, but then I felt a hard pellet inside me. I couldn't say the size or the location (my head? my stomach? my chest?) but it said, *HE CANNOT COME*

HOME. It said, *DIDN'T YOU HEAR ME? I SAID HE CAN'T.* And I suspected that pellet was me. It was who I was. I had to listen to it, even if it tore me apart. I had to trust myself, if I couldn't trust Jon.

"I can't," I said.

"I think you are just trying to punish me," he said.

"I don't think I am."

"But even if you are, I'll do anything to come home. If it takes therapy and living with my mother, that's what I'll do."

"It's not a promise. It's not like, 'If you do therapy, you get to come home.' I mean, who knows what you'll find out." I got butterflies saying that. I suddenly realized anything could happen. Of course, anything already had.

"How about two sessions, and then I get to move back into the house? Into the guest room. Your mom will be gone by then."

"Don't you think it's a little soon to negotiate, 'Mr. I'd Do Anything'? Not twelve hours ago, you were sitting in our bedroom, telling another woman, 'Shhh, it'll be okay.'"

"You're right, you're right. I'm sorry." He reached for my hand, but I wouldn't give it to him.

"I don't want you touching me right now."

"Fine. I understand."

"I need you to give me some space."

He shifted on the couch.

"No, not physical space. Well, that too. But I mean, don't call me, I'll call you. That kind of space. And time."

"How much space? And how much time?"

"I don't know."

He sighed. "I truly am sorry. I'm not just saying that. I mean it."

"What are you sorry for?"

"For hiding Laney from you." Seeing from my expression that wasn't near good enough, he added quickly, "Even though I would never do anything sexual with her, the whole thing was wrong."

It was the kind of dialogue I had with Jacob after he'd misbehaved, my attempt to teach him morality. I realized what a bad technique it was—coercing apologies, complete with a recitation of sins—since Jacob was only trying to avoid punishment and, really, so was his dad.

CHAPTER
5

That night was a kaleidoscope of feelings, a truly dizzying assortment. When I was a kid, my brother, Charlie, and I used to get giddy over a trip to the ninety-nine-item salad bar. Some of it was nasty, like three-bean salad. But ninety-nine items! Well, this was like that, only all ninety-nine sucked.

After Jon left, I did not sleep. Not one minute. No matter how much I begged the powers that be to let me go, to let one hour pass in painless slumber, I was held hostage. Of course, I was my own captor. That's the worst part of insomnia. You're holding the gun to your own head.

I watched the room lighten incrementally for hours, sometimes through eyes gone vacant with exhaustion, often through a fresh round of sobs. No matter how I tried to spin it, Jon's version just didn't fit the story those e-mails told. I wasn't sure which was more painful: his defection with Laney, or that he had become so comfortable lying that he could deny everything right to my face. That was how little he thought of me and our marriage. I could only hope that I'd be able to believe in him again before our baby was born. If not . . . I didn't even want to think about that.

There were a lot of things I didn't want to do. I didn't want to get out of bed, I didn't want to lie there any longer staring at the oversized Paul Klee print on our wall (*Blue Night*—a cubist jigsaw puzzle of tonal blues and black that had started to seem like a Rorschach test). If this had happened years ago—before marriage, before Jacob—I would have stayed in bed for days. That kind of wallowing wasn't an option anymore, which seemed like both a blessing and a curse.

It was Black Friday, and not just for me. The heaviest shopping day of the year, it was downright un-American not to spend, spend, spend. Huge chain retailers were opening their doors at 6 A.M. Jonathon and I had originally planned to get an early start and combine baby shopping and The Holiday shopping (The Holiday being our family's hybrid of Christmas and Chanukah, with its own idiosyncratic rituals that, to my perpetual delight, made Sylvia want to shit bricks). Knowing I needed to do something, anything, I decided to follow the plan. Jon might not like that I'd done it without him, but I couldn't give him a say right then.

After taking a shower and putting on my elasticized maternity jeans and a sweater, I went down the hall to the kitchen. I could hear the dishwasher running, and my mother was standing at the sink, scouring a pot. She'd cleared away most remnants of Thanksgiving. My eyes watered.

I leaned against the counter and for a second studied

her up close in the morning light. My mother insisted on dyeing her hair a deep, unnatural red, but she did it so irregularly that it was shot through with gray and dull brown. I could see new furrows on her forehead, like birds flying in V formation.

"Thanks," I said.

She seemed flustered by my arrival. "It's the least I could do, right?"

"No, you could do less."

I'd been kidding, but she looked around skittishly. She was always ready for me to dig at her, and, somehow, the fact that she expected it made me do it. We both wanted it to go differently, but our relationship had always been one big self-fulfilling prophecy.

"I want to try to get some shopping done today," I said.

"With Jon?" she asked hopefully. She laid the pot in the dish rack. I picked it up for drying, while she started a ferocious scrub-down of the turkey pan.

"No, just me. Do you think you could watch Jacob? You two could stay here, or walk to the park. I don't know if children's museums are open today, but you could always see a movie."

"What about Jon?"

"I don't know what he's doing today."

"I mean, maybe I should go shopping with Jacob, and then you could spend the day with Jon."

"I don't want to spend the day with Jon. At the moment, the absolute last thing I want to do is spend the day with him."

She looked worried and hesitant. "How are things going to get better between you if you don't—"

"It's too soon, Mom, okay? I need more time." I reminded myself that she was trying to help and softened my tone. "If you don't feel like watching Jacob, maybe Tamara could do it. I was just thinking it might be nice for you to spend some time alone with him."

"No, I want to be with Jacob. I'll watch him."

The bruised way she averted her eyes made me feel like I needed to apologize. "I'm sorry. I just didn't sleep at all last night."

"You could try one of my pills tonight, if it would help."

"That's probably not a good idea for the baby."

"Right. That was stupid of me."

My head was throbbing violently. "I'm going to call Tamara and Clayton and check on Jacob. Did you eat yet?"

She nodded. "I finished off the pumpkin pie. That was good. Who made that?"

"Jon."

Now her expression was apologetic, but she didn't say anything.

Was Jon's name going to become a dirty word now? People might try to stay neutral, but ultimately they were going to have to take sides. Wasn't that the way these things worked? "I'll be back in a few minutes," I said.

I returned to the bedroom, shut the door, and dialed.

"Hello?" Clayton said.

"Hi, Clayton. It's Eve."

A brief pause, a search for the appropriate remark, then realizing there was no such thing: "Hi, Eve."

"Hi." I perched on the edge of the unmade bed. "How's Jacob?"

"He's got us making pancakes," he said.

"He loves pancakes." I heard Jacob chirping happily in the background. I felt a rush of relief that last night hadn't touched him, and I missed him sharply. I was about to ask to talk to him, but Clayton was too quick for me.

"Hey, Tamara's right here. Hold on just a second."

From the speed with which he extricated himself, I guess I knew whose side Clayton was on. "Eve," Tamara said. "I was thinking about you all night."

I almost laughed, thinking what kind of night Clayton must have had. Tamara tended to be rather vocal about her feelings.

"Are you all right?" she asked. "I mean, of course, you're not, but are you . . . ?"

"I'm still breathing. I'm still walking around. So for our purposes here, let's just call that all right."

"I just couldn't believe it. I mean, this is Jon we're talking about."

"I know."

"How did you find out? I mean, one minute we were all enjoying Thanksgiving, and the next, you're white as a ghost and kicking us out."

"I heard him talking on the phone."

Shocked silence. "He took a call from his mistress on Thanksgiving?"

"That he did."

"Wow, that's more balls than I thought Jon had."

"You and me both." I started to laugh, in spite of myself. Tamara joined in a few seconds later, as if she'd been waiting to see if it was permissible.

"What was he saying?"

"He was telling her it'd be okay, like she was crying."

"Don't tell me. She was crying about being alone on Thanksgiving."

"That's my guess."

"Well, that's what happens when you date married guys. You don't get holidays. Booty calls, but not holidays."

"Did you just say 'booty calls'?"

"I did."

"Oh, so now it's 1992. You're a teacher. I'd think you'd at least know what they're calling them these days."

"I'll ask my third period." Tamara laughed. "You sound like you're holding up a lot better than I would be. And I'm not pregnant."

That's when the lightness died. I couldn't speak.

"I'm sorry, Eve. I was getting punchy there. Like I said, I didn't sleep last night, I was so worried about you. I thought of calling, but I figured you knew you could call anytime you needed me. I mean, you *can* call anytime. Really. Day or night. And you can say anything you want about Jon."

"Thanks."

"So where did he go last night?"

"To a hotel."

"He's getting a love nest out of this?"

"No. He and Laney haven't had sex."

"Oh." She sounded confused.

"It was an emotional affair. They've been talking and e-mailing for over a year. He says he never intended to have sex with her, and I believe him, actually, but I know he wanted to."

"Oh."

"What?"

"Well, that's not as bad, is it? I mean, that's easier to work out."

She'd understand just how bad it was only if I confessed to reading the e-mails. I wasn't prepared to do that, not even with Tamara. "Not for me, I guess."

"I don't mean that it's okay. I just meant that it changes things a little. I'd just assumed he was sleeping with someone else."

"Don't take this the wrong way, but you've never been married. I'd probably understand him having sex with someone else before I'd understand him sharing private jokes with another woman, sending her long e-mails about his day. I mean, sex fades in marriage; it's the other stuff that's not supposed to." I started to cry. "He's supposed to be my best friend. How could he do this? Why would he do this to me?"

"Oh, Eve. I'm so sorry. I'm really sorry."

Finally I said, "I should get going. I need to go to Costco."

"It'll be a madhouse. No. I'll come over. I can bring whatever food you want, and some movies."

"No, I need to shop."

"You hate to shop."

"But I need to keep moving."

"Well, I'll come with you then."

"To Costco?"

"Sure. I'll buy stuff I can't even get through the door of our apartment. I'll just store a giant vat of pickles in the hallway. For guests."

I laughed. "Are you sure about this? Don't you and Clayton have plans?"

"I told him last night that I was going to clear the weekend. Anything you need, I'm at your service."

"You're amazing. Thank you."

"Don't mention it. Now what time should I come over? I'm sure Clayton could watch Jacob today, if that'd help."

"No, my mom's going to spend the day with him."

"Okay. I'll bring Jacob over, and then Middle America, here we come."

Costco was a nightmare, as expected. But somehow, it was just the right kind of nightmare. The massive labyrinth of consumerism—with shelves as high as Jack's beanstalk, and aisles clogged with people who somehow seemed more aggrieved and agitated than I was—suited me.

Tamara hadn't been inside one in years. "It's like the Astrodome in here!" she said, gaping. "Nothing is to human scale. If one of those light fixtures fell, it's good-bye, Cleveland!"

"It'd be a pretty undignified way to go."

"Crushed under the rubble of a hundred thousand

potpies. No, no dignity there." She looked around, push-ing her straight blond hair behind her ears. "Where should we start? Toys for Jacob, or stuff for the baby?"

"I don't know. I don't even have a list," I said, suddenly feeling helpless. "Jon and I didn't make a list."

"Spontaneity is great for gift buying. We'll just walk down the aisle and see what screams Jacob."

"But what about the baby?"

"We'll just go down each aisle slowly, okay? And if we forget anything, you've still got over a month, right?"

I focused on my breathing, childbirth-style. "Over a month," I repeated.

"Exactly. Let's tackle Jacob first." She steered me toward the toy section, pushing the cart slowly. I walked beside her, docile as a child. Not my child, but somebody's.

"Jon thinks we're having a girl," I said.

"What do you think?"

"I don't know. I'd like a girl." I'd never said it out loud before. "I'm like everyone else. If I had my choice, it'd be one of each. I like the idea of Jacob having a little sister. Maybe he'd feel more protective than competitive."

"Was that how it was for you and Charlie?"

"I felt like I had to take care of him. I mean, I did actu-ally have to take care of him." I stopped, looking at the toys for young girls: pink tea sets, pink grooming sets with a brush, comb and hand mirror, pink fairy princess dress-up kits, tiaras. "Ugh. How sexist is this stuff?"

Tamara had picked up a jewelry box with a pink ballerina on it. "Five years old, and they're already accessorizing?"

My cell phone rang. "It's Jon," I said, glancing at the

ID window. After a few seconds of internal debate, I answered the call. "Hello."

"Hi," Jon said, his voice subdued. "I wanted to see how you are."

"I'm at Costco."

"Oh. I'm sorry." When I didn't say anything, he went on, "I just wanted to tell you how bad I feel about everything, and how truly, truly sorry I am. I'm willing—"

I asked him for space, and he couldn't even give me that much. "I don't need you calling every day to tell me the same things. You should feel bad. You got caught having an affair and you got kicked out of your house." My voice was rising, and the throngs of people closest to me glanced over furtively. Costco performance art, that's what I'd become.

"What am I supposed to do here?" he asked. "How do I make this right if you won't talk to me?"

"I'm taking care of myself right now. It's all I can do. Look, I've got to go." I disconnected the call. With deep concentration, Tamara was pretending to study a children's fudge-making kit. "Do you think I was too hard on him?"

"I'm not stupid enough to answer that."

"Shit!" I said. I wasn't supposed to be here, not like this. When people turned to look again, I fought the urge to shout, "What are you looking at?" But whatever I was, I wasn't the "Crazy What-Are-You-Looking-At Lady." She was the worst.

"We don't have to do this today. We can sit down and make a list first. Then I'll come back with you next weekend, or by then, maybe things will be different."

I shook my head. "No, I have to do it now." I started pushing the cart resolutely down the aisle.

Two hours later, we were in line, the cart piled high with presents for Jacob and baby paraphernalia (onesies, crib sheets, car seat, ointments, that blue bulb that sucks the snot from those improbably tiny nostrils). I was congratulating myself on not having broken down even once when I had one horrifying clarion thought: Sylvia. This was all supposed to go to Sylvia's house.

When I was pregnant with Jacob, Sylvia told me about the Jewish tradition of not bringing anything for the baby into the home until after the birth—to do otherwise would be to tempt fate. Jon said it was superstition, not tradition, and what were we, Romanian peasants from the 1600s? Should we boil some sheep's dung to ward off the evil spirits, too? Besides, he argued, I wasn't even Jewish. But Sylvia knew what she was doing, telling a nervous first-time mom something like that. And there was a loophole: we could buy everything and store it at her house and then bring it home after the baby was born; we could even preorder the furniture for the baby's room so long as it was delivered later. Sylvia had it all worked out for us.

I'd decided during my last pregnancy that there was no harm in following the tradition, and Jon eventually went along. This time around, I'd planned to do it again. But now, a trip to Sylvia's house was fraught on multiple counts: having to see Sylvia, and possibly having to see Jon. (I'd gotten off the phone too quickly to find out if he had already checked out of the hotel and gone to stay with her.) Maybe Jon was right the first time and it was a stupid tradition. We had a garage. Maybe the demonic forces would only search the house.

See, that's how ridiculous this whole line of thinking was. Did I really believe there was a search-and-destroy mission for my baby? Of course I didn't. But what if—God forbid—something happened to her? I'd forever wonder if it was because I had the hubris to put the onesies in my garage. That was the problem with adhering to a superstition the first time. Next time around, you think, *If there's even a one-tenth of a percent chance that that's what kept Jacob safe and healthy . . .*

"What's wrong?" Tamara asked.

"Could I store this stuff at your apartment?"

"It seems like you have more storage space at your house," she said carefully, as if I'd developed Alzheimer's.

"No, I have room at my house. It's just that we can't store it there. It's a tradition."

"What tradition?"

"It's a Jewish tradition, not bringing any baby stuff into the home until after the birth. Otherwise, it's bad luck."

"What did you do with Jacob?"

"Kept everything at Sylvia's."

"Do you think she's too angry to keep your stuff?"

I shook my head. "I don't like the woman, but she wouldn't jeopardize her grandchild's safety. She really believes in this crap."

"I'm sorry, I don't have that kind of room."

We moved up a few feet in the line. Only ten carts ahead of us.

Keep the call brief, to the point, I counseled myself. Businesslike. It's not like Sylvia enjoyed small-talking me under the best of circumstances. This wasn't for me, this was for her grandchild.

"Hello." Damn it, it was Jon. "You've reached 510-555-6434." On Sylvia's answering machine. The widow's home-protection system, having a man record her outgoing message. "Please leave a message, and we'll call you back at our earliest convenience. Have a good day."

I felt an involuntary pang for him, that the fraudulent "we" of Jon and his mother was coming true.

"Hi, Sylvia. It's Eve. I just bought a batch of things for the baby, so I'm going to come drop them off now. They'll be stacked by the back door, unless you're home by the time we get there." I paused. "Well, thanks."

Other daughters-in-law would have keys. Jon had a key, of course. But Sylvia never let me forget that I was his choice, not hers.

Still, I had to be grateful for small gifts, like not having to deal with her directly. "We should head straight to Sylvia's," I said to Tamara. "Hopefully, she'll still be out."

A half hour later, we were on our way in Tamara's overstuffed car. I held a bag in my lap, with another sitting on top of my feet.

"You're doing really well, you know," Tamara said, her eyes on the road. "I'd be a wreck."

"I am a wreck."

"You spent three hours in Costco without a tear. Not even when you held up those little undershirts with the sailboats on them. I almost cried then."

"You want a baby, don't you?" I asked. Outward directed conversation, that was the way to go. We were on the lower deck of the Bay Bridge, headed toward Berkeley, and I could hear the noise of the city-bound cars overhead. Their direction had the view.

"You know I've always wanted a baby." Tamara changed lanes carefully, peering over the cargo in the backseat.

"But it seems like you want it to be soon."

"Well, not too much later, if I can help it."

"How does Clayton feel about it?"

"He wants kids someday. He loves having Jacob around." She cast a quick glance my way. "Don't think I'm sick or anything, but watching him with Jacob is incredibly sexy. They'll be working on one of their little videos, and, I swear, I want to have him right then." She added, "I wouldn't actually do it in front of Jacob or anything."

"No, I know what you mean."

Suddenly I flashed on an image of the last time Jon and I had sex. *No, don't think about that,* I cautioned myself. Don't think about the fact that the last time, Jon had an orgasm with all the intensity of a burp and you didn't have one at all, and then with him still inside you, the two of you started talking about the Iraq War. Animatedly. Possibly with greater energy than had been expended in the sex act itself. Don't think about how you thought nothing of this at the time, how you didn't think it was the death of romance or a troubling indicator of the state of your union, but rather, if you'd bothered to think about it, you would have interpreted it as the height of intimacy, with intimacy defined as comfort, safety, security, the knowledge that there would be a million other orgasms that surely would offer ample opportunity for the simultaneous blowing of both your minds.

No, don't think about that.

I asked Tamara for all the gossip she knew, celebrity and otherwise, and she obliged by keeping up a running stream. The distraction was incomplete, but it was something. "Which exit is it?" she asked.

"The next one," I said. With my luck, Jonathon and Sylvia would be in lawn chairs on the front yard. It would be a regular family reunion.

Tamara took a right off the freeway. "You'll have to direct me."

Jonathon's father had been a math professor at Berkeley, and Jon had grown up in an idyllic neighborhood in the hills above campus. Tamara and I drove up steep, winding streets, with houses that ranged from unpretentious Craftsman bungalows to facsimiles of Italian villas or Spanish farmhouses (Sylvia's was a three-bedroom Tudor). On a clear day (and most days were clear up in the hills—the fog would roll in below and I imagined it was like living in a castle on a cloud), you could see the Bay Bridge and the more celebrated/less traveled Golden Gate, with San Francisco between them. I knew Jonathon loved it there, but the vista was wasted on his parents. His father had been obsessed with work, and his all-consuming interest in the quantifiable rendered views irrelevant; Sylvia—given that her favorite game is Spot the Flaw—has always found the appreciation of natural beauty something of a trial. But despite that, Jon had grown up privileged and happy. He bested me on both counts.

"That's the one." I pointed to the house. "The Tudor on the left."

"Not bad." Tamara parked the car and looked around admiringly.

"Sylvia's car isn't here," I said with relief. "Let's get this over with before she comes home."

We started unloading onto the curb as quickly as possible. I realized how silly I looked, a massively pregnant woman dashing up the path and around the side of the house like a thief in reverse, clutching a boxed car seat. In spite of myself, after I set the box down and looked at the view, I couldn't help thinking about a childhood spent gazing out at what must have seemed the whole world.

CHAPTER

6

This time, we'd had a plan. This time, my pregnancy hadn't been the result of a broken condom but a well-orchestrated series of efforts. This time, Jon and I had known what we were getting into, and we both wanted it. We wanted her.

But when I was twenty-four, before Laney was a twinkle in Jon's eye, we were living together in a railroad apartment in San Francisco and my normally clockwork period was a week late. Jon and I bought the pregnancy test at night, but it said morning urine was best, so we decided to wait, "do this thing right," as Jon put it. He wanted to talk that night about babies and families and options, but I said I couldn't do it. See, Jon always thought he'd have a family, but I never did. It sounds so melodramatic—remember, I was twenty-four—but I just never thought I was worthy of one. I wouldn't have admitted that. I told myself I didn't want a conventional life, I had too many wild ideas and dreams, but hindsight tells me what I didn't want to see: I didn't think I was capable, or deserving. Jon never had that worry.

Jon fell asleep with his hand on my stomach, something he'd never done before, a sort of subconscious wish. I stayed awake, except for one patch of sleep during which I had one of the most vivid dreams of my life. I was in a meadow—the kind you see in commercials for panty liners or dryer sheets, the kind that evokes freshness—and I came across her. A little girl named Lavender, of all things. She was about three, with Jon's brown eyes and my auburn hair, and she reached out her hand. I took it, and knew we belonged to each other. I was her mommy, and in the dream, it was all I wanted to be.

I shook Jon awake and said, "I need to know now. I'm taking the test." It was 4:38 AM. That had to count as morning.

"Okay. Do you want me in the bathroom with you?" he asked drowsily.

"No. I want to pee alone."

"That sounds good," he slurred. He rolled over and immediately fell back asleep.

I read the instructions twice. Not sure about my aim, I decided to pee in a glass and dip the stick in, rather than "holding it in my urine stream." My hands were shaking as I returned from the kitchen bearing a shot glass emblazoned with the word "Jägermeister." I could be carrying the baby of a man who had a Jägermeister shot glass.

But what had me shaking was that I felt I had seen my little girl, and how could I abort her now that I'd seen her? I'd always expected abortion to be my choice if faced with the decision, and now I thought I'd have to choose her.

Two pink lines would mean I was pregnant. One pink line meant no baby, no choice. I wished for it fervently.

I had a ten-minute wait. After a few minutes, I squatted next to Jon's side of the bed and said softly, "The clock's ticking. Seven minutes, and we'll know."

He stirred, opened his eyes, and caressed the side of my face. I tilted my head into his hand. "I love you, Eve."

"I know," I said.

He sat up and shook his head almost violently. I was still on my knees, and then he was on his knees beside me, taking my hands in his. "Oh, wait, it's supposed to be one knee," he said.

"Jon—are you...don't..." Not like this.

He adjusted. "Maybe you should sit on the bed. No, I think you should be standing. This doesn't seem quite right."

"It doesn't seem right because it's not right."

"I know you never thought you'd get married, never thought you'd have kids, blah-blah. You've been telling me for years. But, lady, I want you to be mine. My wife, the mother of my children, I want you to be all of it."

I shook my head, my eyes tearing. "I don't think I can."

"That's just crazy talk. I won't hear of it." He looked into my eyes and softened his voice. "I'm asking you to marry me. Whether you're pregnant or not, whether we decide to have the baby or not, I want you to marry me. My life is with you."

I was crying. "What if I can't be a mom? You want kids. What if I never do?" But I knew that was impossible. I already did. Maybe not now, but someday, I'd want Lavender. I wouldn't name her some hippie-dipshit name like Lavender, but I wanted her.

"You will."

"What if I don't?"

"Then you don't," he said. He smiled at me, and brushed at my tears with his fingertips. "Eve, will you marry me?"

If that night had never happened, would Jon still have proposed? He'd said kids or not, his life was with me, but maybe that was just the romance of the moment. What if there had been only one pink line? He could have back-pedaled, said we were too young, that we needed a long engagement. Sylvia could have gotten to him; he could have reconsidered. But with Jacob growing inside me, there was no turning back.

In the forty-eight hours since I'd found out about Laney, my mind had been awash in alternate history. My life suddenly seemed like a Choose Your Own Adventure book, with Jon turning the pages.

I found myself creating timelines: When he met Laney, had we still been in discussion about having another baby, or already trying? I remembered how gung ho Jon had always been about having a second child, but in one conversation, he'd asked if we should try to travel more first or if I might want to go back to school. I'd assumed he was just considering from all angles, but now I wondered if his attraction to Laney had given him pause. Maybe he'd thought I'd be easier to leave if we had only one child together.

I was flooded by moments from the past year that I'd given no weight and now they were clues. I could hear snippets of conversations, see images of him looking distracted, remember times he'd left the room to take a call. I saw myself kissing him before going to bed as he sat at the computer, saying he was just going to finish up one more e-mail. But there were no lipstick stains on the collar, no sudden changes in grooming habits. I never smelled Laney on him. Our sex life seemed ordinary. If you trust your husband and believe in him, if you know that in any long relationship some days you'll be closer and some days further apart, it just looks like marriage.

Jon left me alone on Saturday, as I'd asked. I called him that night. Much as I wanted him to say something that would make forgiveness come easily, I couldn't imagine what that would be. It seemed more likely that I'd catch him in another lie and everything would become more unforgivable. I decided to focus only on what had to be said.

"Hey," Jon said, his voice soft and tinged with modulated hope.

"Hi," I said. "We need to figure out how we're going to handle things with Jacob."

"Oh. Sure." He seemed slightly disoriented by the

absence of niceties; I wondered how that could be. "How's he doing?"

"He seemed happy after he talked to you last night. He's under the impression that you'll be back any day now."

"I'm hoping that's true. A little time and space and who knows how you'll feel?" When I didn't answer, he went on. "I just wish you would consider working this out with me back at home. I'd still go to therapy."

"Let's not go over this again, okay? I just want to talk about Jacob right now." I took his silence as agreement. "I want him to understand that you might be gone for a while. I don't want him asking every day when you're coming back." My voice faltered a little as I said, "I wouldn't be able to take that."

"What is it you want to tell him?" he asked with a note of resignation.

"I think you should be the one to tell him that it might be a while, but that you're going to talk to him every night, and we'll work out a visitation schedule so he can predict when he'll see you. You know, give him reassurance. That's better coming from you than me."

"A visitation schedule. That sounds formal."

"I'm not talking about lawyers. I'm just talking about you and me figuring out what days and how much of the weekend you'll spend with him. Predictability will make this easier on him. And on us." I paused. "So I was thinking that you could see him at least two weeknights. You can take him out to dinner, or if you want to hang out and play with him at the house, I'll go out for a while. And he could do an overnight with you on the weekend."

"So no family time is what you're saying. It's just Jacob and me."

"Yes."

"Eve," he said, "I'd really like to be with both of you."

"That's not possible right now," I said, fighting to keep my voice neutral despite the imminent threat of tears.

"I just don't see how you're supposed to warm up to me if you're not willing to be around me."

"You need this time to figure out why you were with Laney. Maybe you want to be with her. Maybe you just thought all this time that the right thing was for you to be with me and the kids, and I'm not really the one for you." The tears had started in earnest. "I'd never keep you away from your kids, no matter what happens with us."

"Eve," he said tenderly. "Please don't keep me away from you. I already know the answer. I want to be with you."

It was just what I wanted to hear, and that's why I hung up.

CHAPTER

7

My brother, Charlie, would have been a witness to the Thanksgiving festivities, but he'd canceled his trip at the last minute. He said it was because he'd like us to have more alone time, not so many people around, and since he wasn't working, he could come up any weekend. My mother let slip that one of his friends was having a party that was supposed to go all weekend, a "rager" that had the potential to be "historic." I should have been insulted, but I knew it was just Charlie. Besides, it was better this way: I wouldn't have wanted him to learn about the affair when Jon was within swinging distance.

Sometimes it was hard to believe I was only four years older than Charlie. My mother has a story she likes to tell about how when I learned she was pregnant, I marched around the house for days shouting, "I'm a big sister now!" and insisted she throw out all my childish accoutrements. Since she couldn't afford to buy it all again, she just hid it. But my point had been made. I took big sisterhood seriously.

Even as a kid, I could set limits and hold them in a way my mother never could. I always knew my mother loved us a lot, but it seemed like no one had ever told her that it's better to stand firm and be wrong sometimes than to buckle at the first sign of resistance. Sometimes when I was a teenager, I would tell my mother she was undermining my authority with Charlie, and I wasn't kidding. "I said no parties on school nights!" I would say to her, after she'd told Charlie he could go "just this once." He'd come home drunk and puking when he was fourteen and my mother would just shrug as if to say, "Kids! What are you going to do?"

My mother barely graduated high school and she'd always had low-paying jobs, so you would have thought she'd encourage us to excel in school. But she thought C's were good enough. "Just graduate," she'd say. "I'll love you no matter what." It infuriated me. She seemed to have no standards: not for her kids, not for the men she dated, not for herself. It was a deadly combination, having no bullshit detector and no backbone.

I was bent on going to Berkeley from the time I was twelve, and while it wasn't too hard to be valedictorian at our neighborhood school, I spent most of my time studying and reading anything I could get my hands on while wearing black, listening to punk music, and dreaming of the days when I'd be understood. Charlie's organizing principle was fun, and his world was filled with friends, sex, pot, and speed metal. I believed that nothing worthwhile comes easy or cheap, and sometimes it just never comes at all, no matter what we do. By turns, I was a nihilist, a fatalist, a Marxist—but never an optimist. Charlie believed it would all work out for him in the end,

and if it didn't, well, at least he'd loved the ride. Sometimes he frustrated me; sometimes I envied him; but I
loved him ferociously from the first time I held him, as
he lay swaddled in the receiving blanket that had been
mine.

When Charlie called later that night, I knew he'd
been tipped off by my mother. "Hey there, Evie," he said.
"What's up?"

I had to laugh at his false casualness. "Oh, not too
much. It's just another dull Thanksgiving weekend."

"You want to talk about it?" he asked.

I sighed. "I've spent a lot of time talking. And I don't
seem to be getting any closer to forgiving Jon."

"Why should you forgive him? He cheated on you
when you're about to have his kid. The guy's scum."

Sometimes the simplicity of Charlie's world view was
refreshing; I wasn't sure if this was one of those times.
"But that means the father of my kids is scum."

"Our fathers are scum, and we did all right."

He was using a pretty liberal interpretation of "all
right." I mean, Charlie was twenty-six, living back at
home with my mother because he'd lost yet another job,
and seemed to have no future direction at all. And let's
not get started on me. I'd spent half the day resisting the
urge to hack Jon's e-mail. I did resist, but barely. I wasn't
sure I'd be so lucky next time.

"Well, no matter what happens with Jon and me, I
know he'll stay involved with Jacob and the baby."

"How do you know that?"

"Because he's Jon."

"Hey, men leave, go on and have second wives and new families. Third wives and new families. It happens all the time."

I didn't know how to explain that no matter what Jon had done with Laney, he wouldn't abandon his kids. Charlie was still living in Orange County — not the OC of soapy prime-time TV with its beautiful homogenized people and oceanfront property, but a small, working-class town inland. When I went away to college and lived among the other half, Charlie stayed put, barely finishing high school. He didn't know people like Jon, who might have affairs, but they don't leave their kids behind. While I believed Jon loved Jacob profoundly and couldn't imagine him not wanting to love the new baby the same way, I couldn't help thinking that one of the reasons he wouldn't sever ties was because he couldn't stand the world knowing he was that kind of man. A man like my dad, and like Charlie's. Deadbeat dads. I'd never thought before about that word: "deadbeat." I guess it was reserved for men whose hearts were so dead that they could fail to love their own children. My mother had managed to get pregnant by two men with dead hearts.

My silence must have thrown Charlie, because he said, "I'm sorry, Eve. I didn't mean to upset you. Forgive him if you want."

"I do want to, I just don't know if I can."

"If it were me, I'd call the bitch. I'd tell her she doesn't know who she's messing with."

I laughed. "Yeah, I'm a real threat to her in Chicago. I'm so pregnant I can't even get on a plane." His comment made me realize that I hadn't even gotten mad at Laney. Maybe I should work myself up. Maybe that was one of the steps to healing. Try it, call her a bitch. No, it just felt forced. Silly. This wasn't high school.

"What's she doing in Chicago?"

"Living there. She works at the Chicago office of Jon's company."

"So he's been flying off to see her? You should get all that plane fare back in the divorce settlement."

"Hopefully, there won't be a divorce. And no, I don't think he's flown to see her. I mean, I'm pretty sure he hasn't. He hasn't been anywhere this past year."

"So she flies in to visit him?"

"I don't want to think about it." Thinking about it conjured the image of Laney's hand on Jon's crotch.

"Well, when does he—you know—do the deed?"

"I don't think he has."

"What am I missing here?"

"He e-mails her all the time, and talks to her a couple of times a week. He's been hiding her from me for the past year."

"So she's his friend."

"That's more intimate than friendship."

"But it's a whole lot less intimate than sex."

"Charlie, you don't know anything about this."

"That's why I'm asking questions."

"Betrayal is betrayal." It sounded like I was part of a crime family, like Jon was about to get whacked.

"If you say so."

"I do."

"I'm just trying to help."

I knew he was. I knew he'd stand by me no matter what, and even if sometimes he didn't say the right things and he surely didn't do the right things (drinking too much, quitting or getting fired from jobs, mooching off my mother), loyalty was about all I was prepared to ask of anyone right then. "You are helping."

"So there's that," he said. "What else have you got?"

After hanging up with Charlie, the desire to get into the e-mails intensified until it was like a physical craving. I'd never been a smoker, but I imagined this was what it was like when people first quit, when nicotine seems like air. I needed a hit, just a little something to get me through until morning. So I bargained with myself. I was allowed to check only the recent e-mails to see if he'd written to Laney and told her it was over. Much as I wanted more—to see a picture of her, for example—that was all I could have.

I was antsy for the rest of the night, waiting for my mother to take her Ambien. I didn't want to risk going into Jon's e-mail while she was awake. *That's because you shouldn't be going into it at all,* I scolded myself. *It was supposed to be a onetime thing.*

The baby was moving again. She'd been moving almost constantly—I remembered that from late in my pregnancy with Jacob—but it was so frenetic right then that I wondered if it was in support or reproach.

Finally, after an episode of *Law & Order* that seemed

as long as *Gone with the Wind,* my mother gave me a hug and said she was going to bed. I followed her down the hall and went into my bedroom. From there, I could hear her nightly bathroom ritual. Why did she have to be such a dedicated flosser? It was cruel, what she was doing to me.

Ten minutes later, she was out of the bathroom and settled on the futon. I waited five minutes, then tiptoed to her doorway. When her breathing became even and regular, I pounced on the computer.

Remember, just the Sent folder. That's all you get.

But I wasn't prepared for what I found. Which was nothing. It appeared he hadn't responded at all to her Thanksgiving e-mail. Did that mean he'd called her instead? Or was it possible that he realized what I was doing and wasn't using this account anymore? Had I driven him underground? Or had he decided to have absolutely no communication with her, not even to tell her it was over?

Of all the possibilities, the last one (my favorite) seemed the least likely. It was just too mean. Not Jon's style. Besides, if he had done that, there probably would have been e-mails from Laney asking what had happened to him.

That meant he'd called her, which was just plain out of my jurisdiction. I couldn't know if he'd told her they were through, or to lay low for a while, or that they'd have to keep it to the phone from now on. Well, I couldn't know that night. If I kept checking the e-mail, I might find out something in a few days or a week. He might write an e-mail to someone else saying what had happened, for example.

Unless he suspected me.

No, he wouldn't suspect me. I wouldn't do anything like this. I wasn't this kind of person. Jon knew that.

I hurriedly shut off the computer. I'd done all I was permitted to do that night. There was no sense sitting there and inviting more temptation. Anything else would have to wait for another day. My mother was leaving tomorrow, and I'd have the room all to myself.

There was a red terror alert at the airport, which meant we'd slowed to an absolute crawl. My mother was departing from the farthest terminal.

"I can just get out and walk," she offered, reading the tension in my face.

"No, don't do that," I said. "I'm sure it'll clear up soon." I was not at all sure of that, but Jacob was with Jon for the day, so I had nowhere to be. "Is Charlie picking you up at the airport?"

"He's supposed to. But you know Charlie."

"I know Charlie."

"Are you working tomorrow?" she asked. She was digging in her purse, finally producing a pack of Juicy Fruit. She thrust it toward me; I shook my head no.

"I work every weekday. I just work shorter hours. You know, Jacob's school hours." I'd worked the same job with the same hours for two years now. She'd always been bad with details.

"That's nice."

We had actually stopped moving completely. I put the car into park.

"My casserole didn't come out right this year," my mother said. "People left a lot on their plates."

"It tasted fine to me."

"If I come up next year, maybe I should make something else. But that casserole used to be your favorite thing when you were little. I think Tony was the first one to make it for us."

Ah, yes. Tony, the drunken philanderer. But he did like to cook for us, which was a greater kindness than any of her other boyfriends ever paid her. "Why did you and Tony break up again?"

"He went back to his ex-wife. I just came home one day and he'd left me a note. 'Gone fishing,' it said. 'With Meredith.' And I knew."

"How?"

"Because he'd never been fishing in his life."

Thankfully, I didn't have to come up with a reply because traffic started up again. I shifted into drive and lurched several feet.

"Jonathon called me," my mother said.

It wasn't surprising. He had to get his side of the story out. Couldn't have all those people thinking he was like Tony.

"I told him I'm staying out of it," she added.

"I appreciate that."

"But did you know he didn't sleep with her?"

"Yes, Mom." So much for Switzerland.

"I just wanted to make sure you knew."

"I knew."

We had almost reached the pedestrian walkway. Some people dashed across, their rolling suitcases clattering behind them, while others sauntered with duffel bags thrown over their shoulders. Fully half of them were talking on cell phones, with varying degrees of excitement and animation. We were trapped, unmoving, while their lives were rushing on. My legs felt itchy. I'd barely walked all weekend. Except for my time at Costco, I'd either been home in a state of torment or driving somewhere in a state of aggravation.

"This is the last thing I'm going to say," my mother said, "but I believe Jon loves you very much and would never do anything like this again."

As if my mother were any judge of trustworthy men.

"Sometimes men do stupid things. It doesn't mean they don't love us," she continued.

I realized I was in the same boat my mother had been in time and time again. That was one boat I'd never wanted to board.

I didn't say anything, and she didn't know where to go in the face of my silence. Finally I pulled up in front of the terminal.

"They only let ticketed passengers go to the gates," I said. "Security. Otherwise, I'd come in with you."

She nodded. "Just because I never seem to say the right thing, it doesn't mean I don't love you. I'd do anything to make you hurt less."

Unhooking my seat belt, I reached across the divide and hugged her. "I know that. I love you, too."

She gave me a hard, quick squeeze, then released. I was surprised to find myself wishing that she'd held on longer, and tighter.

CHAPTER 8

When I got home from the airport, I put my pajamas back on and crawled into bed. Not long after, there was persistent knocking on my door. No one I wanted to see would come by without calling. I don't mean just because of the current state of my life; I've never had one of those houses where friends can drop by anytime. I like to know when things are going to happen.

There was a pause; then the knocking started again. Since it was Sunday, it wouldn't be the UPS guy (not that he'd have enough invested in my signature to knock that long anyway). The religion peddlers would have already left what they euphemistically called "literature" and gone on their way. Jon wasn't due back with Jacob for hours. If that was Jon, changing the plan without calling, he'd better be wearing body armor.

I stormed down the hall and yanked the door open to find Lil and her son, Luke, waiting there. Shit. I'd forgotten to cancel Jacob's play date.

Lil was the unflappable type, so her smile never wavered despite seeing me in my pajamas at one in the afternoon, my puffy face transforming rapidly from fury to embarrassment. She was, as always, dressed in form-fitting designer clothes, long blond hair in gleaming waves down her back. She never looked thirty-eight.

"Where's Jacob?" Luke asked impatiently, through his slight lisp. "We've got things to do." He's a ballsy kid, like his mom.

"He's not here," I said. I looked at Lil apologetically. "I'm so sorry I didn't call. I got mixed up on the day. He's out with his father."

I don't know if it was my appearance, that I said "his father" instead of "Jon," or the fact that I never mixed up days, but Lil gave a brisk nod and said to Luke (who was loudly broadcasting his disappointment), "I don't think Jacob's mom needs that right now, Luke. I think she needs you to take this like an adult. Now try. Try right now." I watched in amazement as Luke screwed up his little face in concentration, trying to summon his inner resources. Then to me, "Maybe Luke could play in Jacob's room and you and I could talk awhile?"

Lil used to be an ER nurse. What was happening with Jon and me wasn't even close to a crisis for her, something I simultaneously appreciated and resented. "Let's give that a try," I said.

Lil and I were friends, but not what I'd call close. I met her through Jacob. Luke and Jacob were, mostly, best friends. They could both be headstrong, and every now and again, Jacob would march into the kitchen—with Luke trailing behind—hollering that he didn't want Luke coming over anymore, while Luke shouted that he didn't want to come over anyway. According to Lil, this routine was repeated at her house, only Luke was out in front. Lil and I had become masters at mediation, and that was the common ground on which we'd forged a friendship.

But Lil and I were hardly kindred spirits. She's the type of person who tells you the first time you're having coffee that her marriage ended because she was too sexually audacious, someone who'd detail her latest conquest in whispered tones during a PTA meeting. She was the only woman I knew who dabbled in the "Casual Encounters" section of the Craigslist personals, the only woman who had STD testing at least three times a year ("Whether I need it or not!" she said cheerfully) despite buying her condoms in bulk at Costco. I appreciated Lil's fearlessness, and that she was so completely herself in every setting. But she wasn't my first choice of confidante.

We sat down at the kitchen table. It was funny, that we went to the kitchen instead of sitting on the living-room couch, which was closer. It was like we just knew that women had been having these sorts of conversations in the kitchen since time immemorial.

"Where's Jon?" she asked. The directness of that opening was vintage Lil.

"He's out with Jacob." She continued to look at me, saying nothing. "He's staying with his mother."

"What did he do?" There was nothing accusatory in her tone. She barely knew Jon, and she wouldn't have been shocked if she knew him better; nothing men did surprised her. What I admired about her was that she was matter-of-fact rather than bitter. She thought women had to be prepared for certain realities when it came to men, and the sooner they learned it, the better. "I wish I had a little girl," she'd said once. "Luke's great, but he's going to turn into a man no matter what I tell him. But my daughter would turn into a woman who never, ever let her self-esteem rest on a man."

"He's been involved with this woman Laney for a little over a year." Her name was like instant indigestion. "She lives in Chicago. No sex, but he tells her everything. Lots of e-mails and phone calls."

Lil nodded. Without inflection, she said, "That's bad."

I felt a tsunami of gratitude. That was all I'd wanted, someone to get that it wasn't a question of relativity. It wasn't about whether sex would have been worse. This was just bad.

"That's worse than sex," Lil said. "He's attached to her."

I stared. I didn't want it to actually be worse. "What do you mean?"

"Well, sex can warp the mind. And let's face it, sex with the same person can get boring. Sex after marriage and a kid?" She waved a hand. "If he was having sex with this woman, you could chalk the whole thing up to novelty. It could be that he was so overcome by lust that he lost his mind for a while. You could even say he was so hot for her that he mistook it for love, and once they go thinking it's love, well, everything's fair game. But a year of e-mails and phone calls—that's about his mind and his heart, not just his dick. Call me crazy, but I always think the dick's preferable."

I was dumbfounded. Finally I stammered, "You really think it's worse?"

"Oh, exponentially. Look, I know sex. And I'd rather have my man fucking someone else any day than telling her everything." She leaned in. "I'm not saying this to be harsh. I'm saying it because I think the best thing one woman can do for another is not bullshit her. Leave the bullshitting to the men."

"What do you think I should do, then?"

"Well, what are you doing now?"

"I told him to go to therapy and figure out who he really is and what he wants."

Lil nodded approvingly. "And you take this time to figure out who you are and what you want. If you wind up wanting each other, you can try to fix this. But maybe this is your opportunity. Maybe you never thought you'd get a second chance and now you have one."

"But I didn't want a second chance."

"If you knew then what you know now about him, maybe you would have."

"What about my kids? Don't I owe it to them...?" I trailed off.

"To sacrifice your happiness? To live with a man you can't trust?" She shook her head. "My ex and I split up when Luke was barely two. I knew it was right, and that's all Luke ever saw from me. If you show your kids you're doing what's best, they believe you."

"I don't know what's best."

"Look, you're still young, you're cute—"

"I'm pregnant," I cut in.

"Unless you're planning on carrying that baby around for another twenty years, you could be back in the game like that." She snapped her fingers. "If that's what you want."

I was dubious, but at least I wasn't crying.

I should probably mention that Jon's the only man I've ever been in love with. He wasn't my first boyfriend, or my first sex, but I never fully understood the point of either boyfriends or sex until Jon.

We were introduced at a "Take Back the Night" rally. It wasn't a fix-up; he just fell in step beside my friend Jennifer as we marched through the streets, decrying violence against women. We called it marching, but it was really just walking. He shook my hand; then he and Jennifer started talking. I couldn't hear him all that well, given the chanting around us, and I wasn't trying hard. I wasn't particularly struck by his appearance: dark hair, slightly big nose, oversized polo shirt on a thin frame. He was cute enough, but innocuous. He was an everyman.

I was surprised when Jennifer later said he'd asked about me. She said he "liked my energy." I didn't know what he meant, but I was flattered in spite of myself. I wasn't the surly adolescent I once was, but I never thought of myself as the kind of girl with good energy. I also didn't really see myself dating the kind of guy who'd use the phrase "good energy," but Jennifer vouched for him and I hadn't had a date in months. Sometimes you just need to exercise the muscle.

Jon picked a Vietnamese restaurant near campus for our first date, and when I walked in and saw him, my heart went into free fall. I was suddenly sure no good could come of this meeting. Jon's hair was sticky with gel and he was wearing a plain white T-shirt and jeans. I was no style icon, but at least I understood that first-date clothing was a chance to say something about yourself. I wasn't impressed with Jon's blank-canvas look.

The food was greasy, the lighting was too bright, and our table featured a glass overlay and a single red carnation wilting in a blue ceramic vase. And Jon was a business major, for heaven's sake, which Jennifer had neglected to mention.

Slowly but surely, though, he won me over. He seemed to sense that initially I wanted out of there, and he was prepared to wait me out. I didn't know what in his life had imbued him with the confidence to believe that I'd come around—or why he seemed so certain I was worth waiting for, I wasn't sure of that myself—but somehow the combination of dogged and sweet worked for me. He didn't try to dazzle; he was just curious and interested and, eventually, funny. I was charmed in spite of myself.

I'd spent a lot of time in and out of depression in my life, and with Jon, I found an easy happiness that I'd never experienced before. Around him, I felt lighter. I hadn't realized that I carried this tension inside me all the time until it disappeared. I don't know if Jon loved me first, but of the two of us, he was the one to throw himself into it. He was the one to name the experience "love."

I was skittish where love was concerned (I'd never seen good love in operation), but once I let myself love Jon, I felt the most incredible joy. We became That Couple. You know the one: talking in restaurants until the floors are being mopped, always touching each other as if magnetized. Of course, now, so many years later, I realize that pretty much everyone has a stint as That Couple. For ten years, I thought of Jon and me as That Couple, the one worth envying, the one worth emulating. Maybe I'd ignored all evidence to the contrary. I mean, obviously, I'd missed something. But I never saw things change. I never saw him fall out of love with me. We still held hands at the movies; we could still talk until closing. It wasn't like I'd been in a state of continuous bliss, but I'd been happy and assumed he was, too. How could he appear to love me so much, and be so invested in another woman? How could he have broken down all my defenses, gotten completely inside of me, only to give himself to Laney?

We were That Couple, all right, the one where the husband's cheating and the wife's saying, "But just last week, he was kissing my belly and telling me he loved me." I wanted to forgive him, I wanted us to get back what we had, but how could we? It suddenly seemed like a figment of my imagination.

"Just wanted to let you know we're on our way back. With no traffic, Jacob should be home in a half hour." There was a slight crackle on the line, but Jon's voice seemed almost normal. It was too early for normal. Unless normal was the new abnormal.

"Fine," I said. Brusque was the new polite, as far as I was concerned.

"How do you want to handle the drop-off? I'd love to see you, but I understand if you just want Jacob to knock and then you'll let him in."

"It's been a long day. Let Jacob do the knocking."

I was about to hang up, when he said, "Eve? I booked my first therapy appointment." He continued, seemingly unfazed by my silence. "Also, I had an idea for a system. If I really need to talk to you about something—say, about Jacob, or finances, or the baby—I could call you on your cell phone, but the rest of the time, I'll call on the home phone and you can screen me."

"You want me to screen you?" I said flatly.

"That way, I could call, say what's on my mind, and then you could listen and decide if you want to pick up or not. If you don't, that's okay. That way, you get your space, but I'm not in Siberia. What do you think?"

"We can try it." I did miss Jon's voice.

"Great!" he enthused. "Well, bye!"

"Bye."

As I hung up, I realized: Jon had gone to Plan B. He was big on Plan B's. And C's, if necessary. He was strategic, I'd give him that.

Forty minutes later, I heard Jacob knocking at the door. I opened it, and even though he'd been gone only for the day, it was a thrill to see him standing there, zipped up in his puffy blue jacket, cheeks flushed with happiness or cold or both. He was holding a rolled-up tube of paper.

After I'd hugged him, I looked outside. Jon was parked along the curb, his window rolled down, watching us. He lifted his arm in a wave; I waved back. As his car pulled away, I wished I'd let him come in. Then I shut the door.

"Look!" Jacob said. He was struggling to unroll the paper. Together, we spread it out over the living-room carpet. Once unfurled, it was the size of two poster boards put together. Across the top, it said "Jacob's Calendar." Jon had made neat, even squares in Magic Marker, with dates for the next month. He had written in all his upcoming visits with Jacob and the activity they would do together, and it appeared Jacob had done the supporting stickers, sometimes indiscriminately. There were blue, red, and silver stars everywhere. This week, Tuesday was "Jacob and Daddy Movie Night," while on Thursday, they'd go out for pizza. The weekend marked the "First Ever Jacob and Daddy Sleepover!" The accompanying sticker showed two frogs snug in a double bed together; a silver star danced above their heads. The final calendar square said "Jacob Gets A Sister (Or Maybe A Brother)!" surrounded by stickers of balloons and, of course, stars.

"I made it with Daddy."

"I can see that," I said. I reached out and patted his hair, still flyaway from the cold. The way he was looking at the calendar made my heart hurt. I didn't want him to lose anything, ever. "It's beautiful. It must have taken you all day."

"We ate lunch, too. We had room service."

"Oh, you were at a hotel?" I asked, surprised. I'd assumed that Jon had already moved to Sylvia's.

Jacob nodded. "I could hear the planes going by. I ate a lot of French fries. It was fun."

"We can hang this on your wall," I said, smoothing out the calendar, Braille galaxies beneath my fingers.

"That's the whole point!" he said.

I looked in on Jacob before I went to bed, like always. It was strange to think that soon, I'd have two rooms to look into, two little people that had been created by Jon and me.

Jacob had a snore like his daddy's. I was glad he was young enough to just accept that Jon was living in a hotel, and to sleep so undisturbed. It made me realize that Jon and I had done a good job of making Jacob secure in the world. He didn't know to fear change.

I caught sight of the calendar on the wall, and was reminded of all the times I'd seen Jon hunkered down with Jacob as they did an art project together. And for the moment, I didn't care what Lil had said; I didn't care what Jon had done. He was, simply, the man I loved. He was Jacob's father—an amazing father, at that—and for all I'd known for so long, he was a wonderful husband, and who was to say that there was more truth in those e-mails than in all the years of looking into his eyes? Maybe his dealings with Laney really didn't mean anything, just like he said.

He was probably fifteen minutes away, at most, since his hotel was near the airport. If I called him, he would come, no questions asked. Didn't that mean something? Before I could stop myself, I dialed his cell.

"Hello," he said, sounding groggy.

"It's me," I said. I tried to ignore the voice inside my head asking, *How can he sleep at a time like this?*

"I'm so glad," he said.

I started crying. "I want you to come over. Can you come over?"

"Of course. I'll leave right now."

"Okay. See you soon."

"Thank you. God, Eve, just—thank you."

After I hung up, I fought my second thoughts. I didn't want to think how just days before, Jon had been the one calling late at night, and how the things he'd said had been contradicted by the e-mails. I didn't want to think about Laney. I wanted to just think about Jon and me, and the lives we'd created together.

The shower seemed the perfect place to block everything out, and afterward, I was in a robe, drying my hair, when Jon came up behind me. I jumped as he touched my shoulder.

"Sorry," he said. "I guess you didn't hear me at the door."

I'd imagined opening the door and throwing myself into his arms. That would have circumvented the awkwardness. But now, I had to turn off the dryer, and the bathroom light was way too bright.

"It's okay," I said.

He backed out of the bathroom into our adjoining bedroom, and stood waiting for my cue. I went and sat on the bed. The only light came from the lamp on the nightstand.

"I want to be able to get past this." I looked up at him. "Do you think we can?"

In a few quick steps, he was on the bed beside me. "Yes. Of course we can." As soon as I felt his arms around me, I was racked by sobs.

"It's going to be okay," he whispered, kissing the top of my head. "I'm so sorry, Eve. I am so, so sorry. I love you. I love you, Eve."

I believed him, and now I was crying with relief. We could do this. We could make it through anything.

"It's going to be okay. Shhh."

That was when my blood ran cold, so cold that the crying stopped. Everything stopped.

I pulled away. "I don't think it is."

"What just happened here?" He looked at me steadily.

"I thought I could just overlook everything, like we were bigger than this thing with Laney. We're not."

"Yes, we are. I love you, and I love this family. What could be bigger than that?"

"You jeopardized all that for Laney."

"I didn't see it that way at the time."

"No, you thought you could have it all." I stood up so suddenly that my robe threatened to fall open. I retied the belt securely around me. "I shouldn't have let you come over. This was a mistake."

"It's not a mistake." He moved toward me and cradled

my face in his hands. "Let me stay. Or let me leave and come back tomorrow. But don't do this indefinite thing. Don't just send me out there with nothing."

I shook my head and his hands fell away. "I'm sorry, but you need to go."

"Can I come back tomorrow? Or the day after that?"

"I don't know. I can't tell you that right now."

"If I call you tomorrow, will you answer?"

"I don't know."

"I'm going to call. Every night, just like I said."

"I might screen you every night. I'm not saying that to be mean, I just want you to be prepared. I don't know how to do this, Jon."

"Let's do it together," he said, his eyes an appeal.

"I don't know if we can." I didn't know if I'd ever said "I don't know" so many times in one conversation. I did know I'd never been so lost.

CHAPTER
9

The next day, somehow, we resumed our lives: I dropped Jacob off at school and headed to work. When I was about two blocks away, I found myself driving in the outer lane, easing my foot from the gas pedal. I had little desire to arrive. I worked with nice people, concerned people, intuitive people. They'd take one look at me and want to help, but the exposure would only make it worse. I didn't want the world knowing my life was in shambles. The more people who knew, the realer this would get. I was already up to my neck in reality. I was drowning in it.

I worked as an academic counselor at a community college with kids primarily from lower and working-class backgrounds. I liked the kids well enough, and there was often a certain comfort in the easy administrative tasks, as if my mind were just idling for a few hours. Hired with no qualifications two years ago, I'd been idling ever since.

Mindlessness was the only appeal of the job that day. What I wanted was to get to the cell that passed for my office and focus on everything that wasn't Jon and me.

But given the layout of the Student Services office, I figured I'd at least have to interact with Chad—the department's admin, barely twenty-one and a free spirit who claimed he lived in the Bay Area only because his car had broken down and he couldn't be bothered to get it fixed—and Dyan and Melinda wouldn't be far behind. I most wanted to avoid Dyan. She was the mental-health counselor, and nothing got by her.

When students first came to the department office, they encountered a perpetually sticky mauve front counter, with Chad seated at a desk beyond, surrounded by various office machines and filing cabinets. Branching off from the main area was the break room and the four individual offices, one being unoccupied and the others belonging, respectively, to Dyan, Melinda (the department supervisor), and me. I knew Chad sometimes used the vacant one for a lunchtime catnap; he'd emerge with renewed energy and his normally buoyant curly hair matted on one side. Melinda knew about the naps, too, and the fact that she didn't mind was one of the selling points of the job, as far as I was concerned. In terms of workplaces to have a public breakdown, I could do worse than this one.

I pushed open the door.

"Hey, Big Momma!" Chad called out immediately. He'd recently taken to calling me that, and it was proof that you really can get used to anything. He was sitting at his desk, wearing a short-sleeved polyester shirt whose placket revealed part of a rather concave chest. Neither Melinda nor Dyan was in sight.

"Hi, Chad," I said. I was trying not to talk too loudly, lest the others materialize. Dyan, in particular, liked to pet me as if I were a cat. Women tend to get tactile with pregnant women, I'd noticed—men, not so much. There's information in that, I'm sure.

"How was your turkey day?" he asked cheerfully. He was vegan (a step beyond vegetarian, he wouldn't eat dairy or wear leather shoes) and liked to underscore the animal-murdering aspect of the holiday. At other times, he liked to highlight the Indian murdering. Needless to say, he didn't celebrate.

To my pleased surprise, I felt perfectly steady and technically honest as I answered, "The turkey part was good."

He put a hand to his chest, mock-wounded. "Have I taught you nothing?"

"Yes."

He laughed. "I bet it'll be slow today."

"Next week it'll be crazy, with everyone gearing up to register for spring semester."

"We should enjoy it now."

Somehow, inexplicably, that did it. I found myself getting teary. "I'd better get to my office," I said, moving quickly past him. *Just get inside and close the door,* I thought. *That's all you have to do.*

"Okay," I could hear Chad saying slowly, obviously confused. I figured he was more likely to assume pregnancy hormones than my husband was having an emotional affair.

Once seated in my windowless office, through concen-

trated breathing techniques and sheer force of will, I managed to pull myself together. I consulted my schedule, and
saw that I didn't have any appointments or meetings until
the afternoon. Fortunately, there was busywork. The job
had a surfeit of busywork.

Two hours later, submerged in minutia, I was jarred
by the ringing phone. I'd been doing my damnedest to
become one with the transcripts.

"This is Eve," I said.

"Hey, Eve. Just checking in," Tamara said.

"Are you at school? It sounds so quiet."

"I'm in my car. It's my free period."

"Oh. Thanks for calling."

"Nothing to it. Tell me how you are."

"I'm unpredictable." I sat back in my pleather office
chair, wincing slightly as I recognized the consequence
of my unfortunate ergonomic choices. "Chad just made
the most benign remark and I had to run in my office so
I wouldn't cry in front of him."

"Well, sure," she said, as if it were the most normal
thing in the world. I loved her for that.

"Jon made this great big calendar for Jacob's wall with
all the days they're going to see each other and what
they'll do. He decorated the last square with balloons
for the baby's birthday."

"That's sweet. I guess," she added, trying to straddle
the fence.

"And then I let him come over last night." I didn't want
to admit that I'd invited him over.

"Really? How'd that go?"

"At first, I thought I could get over it; then I remembered everything and I asked him to leave. I just can't wrap my head around Laney. The Jon I know wouldn't do that. Not if we were having the relationship I thought we were having."

"Did I ever tell you my stuffer theory?" she asked.

"I don't think so."

"You know how I had that string of nice guys who seemed really into me, sometimes even in love with me, and then they weren't anymore?"

"Yeah. There was Chris and Jeff and—"

"Hey now. We're talking about you."

I laughed. "Sorry."

"I decided, based on my ex-boyfriends and the evidence from the exes of friends, that there's this class of guy called a stuffer. Stuffers are these seemingly great, nice guys who stuff their anger down rather than expressing it, which is why they seem so sweet all the time. They don't even know they have all these negative feelings because they're out of touch with themselves, and then, because they don't know, they never release the feelings. They just keep stuffing them, so it's layer upon layer of old anger, which turns to resentment, and eventually it gets so they can't feel love like they used to. It's like getting a blockage in their arteries.

"Meanwhile, the woman has no idea; she only finds out when something dramatic happens, like she's suddenly dumped or you've got a Laney on your hands. And because the guy never expressed anything, the woman never got a chance to do anything differently. It's like, he gives her the rope to hang herself. Remember how Chris only told me at the end that when I thought our sex life was so tender and cuddly, he thought it was boring? So that whole time, I'm sitting there thinking we've evolved to this higher plane and he's wanting a blow job. But he doesn't *say* he wants a blow job. He doesn't say anything until he's dumping me. That, my friend, is a stuffer."

"You've had a theory about Jon all this time and you never told me?"

"No. I had a theory, but it never occurred to me that Jon fit the profile. He flew right under my radar."

I felt faint. "Do you really think he has ten years' worth of resentment stored up against me?"

"Maybe not ten years," Tamara backtracked. "I mean, it's just a theory. It might not fit Jon at all. It might not even be a good theory."

"No, I think it's a good theory," I said. "I've always thought he was mellow, that things didn't bother him, but maybe he just wasn't telling me. Like you said, maybe he didn't know himself. Maybe he just gradually stopped loving me, and then he found Laney . . ." I started to cry.

"Oh, Eve. I'm sorry. I didn't mean to make things worse. I don't know what I was thinking. You know how I get. I like to puzzle things out. You do, too. I thought maybe if you had a theory to explain how this happened, it'd help somehow. But I'm probably completely wrong about Jon. I'm sure I am."

"What if you're not? What if Jon's a stuffer?"

"The difference is, he didn't dump you. He wants to

be with you. Maybe stuffers can be reformed. I've never seen one try."

"Wouldn't that take, like, years?" I sniffed.

"I don't know. He's starting therapy, right?"

"Yes."

"He still loves you, I know he does."

"Just not as much as he used to."

"We don't know that."

"Yes, we do!" I said. "If he loved me like he used to, he wouldn't have been with Laney."

"He wasn't *with* Laney."

"If this was the old days, he wouldn't have been talking to Laney. Or maybe he would. Maybe he never loved me like I assumed he did. Maybe he never loved me like I loved him. Like I still love him." I was sobbing uncontrollably.

There was nothing anyone could say to that.

"Hi, Eve. It's me." Jon's voice was nervous as it broadcast through the tinny answering-machine speaker. "Testing, one, two, three. I don't know how long I get before the machine cuts me off. I guess I'm about to find out. Or maybe you'll pick up, who knows? I just realized the flaw in my plan is that I'm going to spend every second hoping you'll pick up, and you might not even be listening.

"Even though it didn't turn out the way I wanted, I was happy just to have that time with you last night. I'm going to keep trying. I'm not going anywhere, Eve.

I mean, other than my mother's." He lowered his voice. "Not that you should feel sorry for me or anything, but, man, this is not the place you want to be exiled to. I'm finding out all sorts of disturbing things. I had no idea how much cottage cheese that woman eats, for one thing.

"I'm trying to be funny. It's going badly, I know. I'm not funny right now. Earlier I was trying to compile a list of things to tell you, sort of a highlight reel, but the truth is, it was a shit day. And I did that thing where you get a song caught in your head and you can't shake it loose. It was that old Replacements song, the one about saying good night to an answering machine. And I realize that's all I want to say to you. Just regular stuff. I'm sitting here auditioning, performing, whatever, and I'm flopping." He stopped talking for a few seconds. "I don't think you're picking up. I think I can talk till this tape runs out, but this just isn't going to be my night. So...sweet dreams, Eve. I love you."

I was listening, of course. After talking to Tamara, I'd sat in meeting after meeting dazed and mute, then picked up Jacob and some takeout, and watched DVDs with him until his bedtime. As soon as he was down for the count, I retreated to my bedroom to release the torrent that I'd been holding back for hours. That's where Jon's voice had found me.

The whole time he'd been talking, the baby had been moving energetically. I rubbed my belly, apologizing that she was getting to hear her daddy's voice only on the machine. I wished our voices were a duet for her. For Jacob, too. I didn't want this to be the end of our family.

I thought of the days and weeks before Jacob's birth, when it seemed like Jonathon and I were nearly vibrating with love: for each other, for the life inside me, for the life we would all have together. But maybe those vibrations were just nerves. Maybe what I'd assumed was love was something else. Laney's existence had called everything into question. There wasn't one memory that was beyond reproach.

I could picture Jon's face when we'd made love, or when we were laughing together, and I'd assumed I was seeing the depth of his feelings for me. But if that first night he spent with Laney was one of the best he'd ever spent with a woman, his not touching her may have meant more than our whole last year together.

"I'm sorry," I said to my little girl. "I wish he could come home, too."

CHAPTER
10

Nothing seemed easy anymore. It wasn't easy to sleep, or to wake up, or to eat, or to take care of Jacob. It wasn't easy to talk, or to remember, or to forget. Every choice—no matter how piddly it would seem to the untrained eye—became daunting. I didn't want to make any more wrong moves, so I did the minimum. I made my life small. I went to work and I came home; I did my best to shield Jacob and keep him happy; I talked to my belly; I sent apologetic e-mails to friends, revealing nothing, blaming my elusiveness on the last month of pregnancy. I figured if everything worked out like it was supposed to, and Jon came home, I could tell them the story later. It would become an anecdote. If he never came back, then they'd all have to know. But I didn't want to be an object of pity until I absolutely had to be.

Since I was a big believer in setting limits, I only allowed myself to hack Jon's e-mail every other day. It wasn't like the e-mails actually made me feel better (nothing did), but since all I could do was wait for Jon's therapy to offer some sort of explanation, reading them seemed like the only action I could take. I was so emotionally and physically exhausted that sometimes I could barely muster guilt.

I'd finished reading all of Jon's back e-mails to Laney, so it was time to move on to her correspondence to him. I wanted to answer the question that had been dogging me, lying just beneath my consciousness, for days: *what does Laney have that I don't?*

The Laney folder didn't offer any plot twists: I already knew she was going to fall in love with him, and about their failed rendezvous in the third act. I knew she'd go on to grab my husband's crotch in a parked car and that he'd refuse her, but she'd soon get at least some of what she wanted: the admission that he "had love" for her. The boldness of her crotch grab aside, Laney's letters made her seem edgeless, like an ordinary, not unintelligent woman who relied way too much on my husband (and on emoticons) to get her through the day. If I never saw another colon/parenthesis combination or an "LOL," it would be too soon. I learned Kahlua is the secret ingredient in her famous French toast; she'd live in Seattle if it weren't for the rain; she liked *The Love Boat* but not *Fantasy Island* (she used to have nightmares about Tattoo); she had a perfectly normal, middle-class family; her last boyfriend was sweet but "not the one"; she worried that she'd never get to have kids; she hated panty hose. It was clear that she adored Jon and seemed to think everything he said or did was brilliant, hilarious, and/or charming. Was that all it took? I kept waiting for her to be fascinating, insightful, funny. But she wasn't, at least not in e-mail form. So what did that make me, that I could be upstaged by her?

Years ago, Tamara saw pictures of her then-boyfriend's stunning ex-girlfriend. After exhaustive analysis, we came up with the following axiom: You never want the exes to be too good-looking (you feel inferior) or too homely (then you worry you're actually in that league). You want them to be in the ballpark of your own attractiveness—only you're obviously better. Tamara and I agreed that we always wanted to be Version 2.0. Since I couldn't find a picture of Laney attached to any of the e-mails, my biggest fear was that she was beautiful, and that beautiful ultimately took all.

My low point was calling the Chicago office and pretending to be a client who needed Laney's last name. The receptionist gave it to me so easily that I felt even smarmier. Laney Castle. I shit you not. I went to Google, set it to search for images, and typed in her name. Nothing. I thought briefly about ways to get a hold of Jon's wallet, just in case he carried a picture of her. The truly disturbing part was that in this particular scenario, I was hoping that my husband was carrying a picture of the other woman on his person.

Jon's e-mail did finally give me confirmation that he really had broken it off with her right after Thanksgiving. She'd sent two e-mails since then: the first asking if he was sure there was absolutely no room in his life for her, and the second wishing him well and telling him that if he ever reconsidered, she'd love to hear from him. According to his Sent folder, he never wrote back.

Still, I was haunted by that open door. Even if Jon and I got back together, I'd always know that if he was feeling neglected or angry or misunderstood or horny — or any one of a million other emotions that had made Laney so appealing the first time around — the possibility existed that he'd go back for seconds. After all, it wasn't his conscience that had stopped him; it was getting caught. Sure, he'd halted contact with her now, but who knew how long that would last? It was a thought that kept me snooping despite the diminishing returns. Man, I hated the word "snooping." It was just so preteen. *Dear Diary, Today I got my period for the first time and snooped on my husband!*

One time, Jon called for his nightly screening earlier than expected and I could hear his voice faintly in the other room as I was logged into his e-mail. I couldn't make out his words, only the tenor of his voice. The innocent warmth I heard there was punishing. After thirty seconds, I turned off the computer and followed him to the bedroom.

"...it's kind of surreal, all the ways I have to listen to myself these days. On these messages to you, in therapy. I haven't spent this much time just with myself in I don't know how long. I don't like it. I mean, part of that's the fact that I'm pretty bad company these days. But the other part is that I like myself better when I'm with you and Jacob. So I don't just miss you — though I miss you something crazy, don't get me wrong — I miss me with you. To state the obvious, I miss us.

"And you know I haven't been pestering you to let me

come home. You've wanted space and I've respected that. But I think it's time for us to at least get in a room and talk, because I've realized a lot of things. I've had three sessions of therapy and not to toot my own horn here, but I'm making progress. Maybe you could meet with me and see for yourself? If you're there, could you pick up so we could talk about it?"

As he paused, I reached for the phone, but then I stopped myself. I didn't want to talk to him just then, when I felt so unclean. My heart was pounding triple time with the painful hope that I could forgive him. Every night, I'd listened to his messages and felt the terrifying swell of love.

"Maybe you're not there, or you just need time to think it over. If you decide you're not ready to meet up yet, could you at least send me an e-mail so I won't wait for a call that's not coming?" At the mention of e-mail, shame struck anew. "Well, good night, Eve. You're in my heart."

The next morning, I told Jacob there would be a change in his schedule. That night was normally his night with Daddy, but instead, it would be mine. Jacob clearly wasn't happy about the disruption.

"It's 'Jacob and Daddy Movie Night,'" he said, pointing to the calendar. He had just finished getting dressed for school in his jeans and favorite blue long-sleeved T-shirt, the one that he insisted on wearing despite the paint stains on one arm.

"But now 'Jacob and Daddy Movie Night' will be tomorrow. See?" I gestured toward the blank square next door. "We can just draw an arrow..." I began, reaching for a marker.

"No! Tonight!"

I sat down on his bed and patted the space next to me. He was having none of it.

"Tonight!" he said again, glaring.

"I know you're disappointed. I know you really wanted to see your daddy tonight. But you're going to see Aunt Tamara and Uncle Clayton instead. You always have fun there."

"No! I want to see Daddy!"

"I bet Aunt Tamara and Uncle Clayton would watch a movie with you. I bet they haven't seen—"

He started crying, that furious full-body crying that always makes you embarrassed for parents at the supermarket, the kind that makes you think, *They should give that little boy less sugar,* or *Why don't they discipline him?* Despite my best efforts, the past weeks had been hard on Jacob, and it was heartbreaking to see him turning into that boy.

"I'm not going! I hate them!" he said through his tears.

"Jacob, I know you're upset, but that's not nice. And it's not true. You love Aunt Tamara and Uncle Clayton." I moved toward him and kneeled so we could be eye to eye. He wouldn't look at me.

"You can't take Daddy away," he said.

"You'll see him soon. Tomorrow." But my voice lacked conviction. I was wavering.

While I knew a parent should never give in to a child

having a tantrum, I found myself considering it. Every morning and every night, Jacob looked at that calendar on his wall, as if something might have changed during his hours away or asleep, as if he might suddenly find that there were no more "Jacob and Daddy" days. The truth was, Jonathon and I could talk tomorrow night just as easily. I was being selfish, desperately wanting a "Jonathon and Eve Talk About Whether He's Made Enough Progress to Come Home Night." And I wanted it ASAP. I'd deluded myself into thinking that Jacob would take the rescheduling in stride. Everyone would have you believe motherhood is the end of selfishness and I tried—I really did try—and for the most part, I succeeded, but maybe just this once, could I have this? I didn't want to wait another day to find out what was going to happen to me, and to this family I loved.

Jacob seemed to read my uncertainty, and his crying let up. Like a hunter sensing the vulnerability of his prey, he said again, loudly, "I will see my daddy tonight!"

I'd been swaying, but that tone put me back on solid ground. If I taught Jacob that all he had to do was plant his feet and outlast me, things would only get worse. "You're not seeing Daddy tonight. You're seeing him tomorrow night. Now it's time for you to eat breakfast so you won't be late for school."

"No-o-o-o," he wailed, jumping up and down. "No breakfast! No school! Nooooo!"

"Jacob—"

"No!"

"Come in the kitchen—"

"No Aunt! No Uncle! Daddy! Daddy! Daddy!" He shouted it over and over in a frenzy, and I couldn't take it. I put my head down and shut my eyes. I needed this moment to end. I needed this day to end. I needed this life—this post-Laney life—to end. And finally, mercifully, he quieted down. I felt his hand on the top of my head. "Mommy?" he said tremulously.

Looking up at his face, I didn't see any trace of anger anymore, just fear. I held out my arms.

I didn't think time could move any slower than it had for the past several weeks. But it could. Time moved so slowly that day that there ought to have been another word for it. Something with more syllables.

Finally, late that afternoon, I dropped Jacob off at Tamara and Clayton's with a backpack laden with his favorite DVDs. All signs of his earlier resistance were gone, and he was happy to see Tamara when she opened the door. She gave me a hug, whispered in my ear, "Go get 'em, tiger," and then I was off.

I tried to put myself in a mind-set to forgive Jon. I told myself over and over, *He didn't have sex with her. She was right there in front of him and he resisted.* That had to mean something. Everyone except Lil thought it did. But I kept getting stuck on the image of Jon and Laney in the car together, with him struggling mightily against himself. He might not have touched her sexually, but he must have at least entertained the possibility. Not to mention, he could very well be in love with her.

If only I could have stopped at that first thought: *he didn't have sex with her.* Or, better yet, *he's really in love with me.* But every thought led inexorably to the next, down this rabbit hole of betrayal, and in my mind, it never ended well, much as I tried to force it. Finally I just tried to think as little as possible, staying busy right up until Jon knocked at the door.

As we stood at the threshold, I felt curiously shy and expectant, and I saw that in Jon's face, too.

"Hi," he said. His voice had a faint crack in it, like when you haven't used it in a while and aren't sure what will come out.

"Hi," I said, sounding soft and girlish. It surprised me. "Come in," I added, now more like myself.

"Okay." He laughed. "You want to step back then, sister?"

I laughed, too, realizing I'd been barring his entrance. I moved aside sheepishly, and he came forward.

"Couch?" he asked.

"Couch," I affirmed.

We settled ourselves, both laughing slightly at the shared absurdity of being so nervous around the person you knew better than anyone. *Thought* you knew better than anyone. My laughter dried up immediately.

"So, hi," he said, smiling.

"Hi," I said, not fully returning the smile.

He realized it was down to business. "Well, then," he said. "I guess I'm supposed to give you a progress report."

"I guess so."

"Have you been listening to my messages?"

"Yes."

"That's good. I wondered sometimes if you were just deleting them."

"I wouldn't do that."

He looked at me with affection. "No, you wouldn't."

I had to look away. His gaze was too intimate. It pulled too hard.

"What do you think of the messages?" he asked.

"What do you mean?"

"I guess I just want to know where I stand before I start talking. I mean, if it's okay for me to ask that."

I felt flustered. "I just — I don't know how to answer."

"You don't seem as angry as you did. Am I reading you right?"

"Sometimes I'm still angry, but on the whole, I'm just upset. Confused. Disappointed. Scared about what's going to happen to us."

"Well, we're feeling a lot of the same things, then. That's a good thing, right?" His expression was hopeful.

"Maybe."

"You wanted me to go to therapy to figure out why I did what I did. And I think I have."

"So fast?" I couldn't help but ask.

"I have a really good therapist. You'd like her. She doesn't let me get away with anything."

"What are you trying to get away with?"

"It was a figure of speech. Maybe the wrong one, given what's happened between us." He hesitated. "Can I touch you? Maybe hold your hand?"

Again, too intimate. "I don't think I'm comfortable with that yet."

"That's okay. My therapist said this is going to take time. She said that I'll probably have to reassure you a lot, and accept that you might not be reassured for years. I might have to keep answering the same questions, and living with your doubt, and with the fact that you might not let yourself really trust me or love me completely for a long, long time. I want you to know I'm prepared for that."

"This feels kind of like a sales pitch."

"Does it? Sorry." He leaned forward, then rocked back. I realized how much adrenaline had to be coursing through him. This was it, the bottom of the ninth inning. He reached into his bag and pulled out a book. "My therapist recommended this." He held it up so I could see the cover. At the top, in foolishly ornate script, was *The Touchless Affair,* and below was a picture of a couple obviously in turmoil, the woman crumpled against one side of a door, the man—imploring—on the other side. Along the bottom, *How to Survive Emotional Infidelity.*

"Have you finished reading?" I noticed that his bookmark was only about halfway through.

"I didn't need to. The reason my therapist wanted me to read this is because when I showed up at her office, I didn't really understand what I'd done. I was minimizing it. She wanted me to read the book so I could get that an emotional affair is as bad as a physical one. I get that now." He opened to a page marked by a Post-it. "I got it when I read this: 'Attending to someone outside of the marriage robs your partner of the intimacy they deserve.'"

"You needed a book to tell you that?" I wished I could believe his conversion, but it seemed a little too convenient and showy, like something you'd find in a revival tent.

"I'm not proud of it, but yeah, I guess I did." He turned to the next Post-it. "'Sex isn't the essential ingredient in infidelity; secrecy is.'" He closed the book. "I was hiding Laney from you. And that was really wrong of me. I'm sorry."

Weeks of waiting for this, for my husband's epiphany that he shouldn't lie to me for a year.

"You want to know why I was with Laney. Not *with* Laney, just—"

"Yes, I want to know why."

"The thing is, it doesn't really make sense. I mean, I have this great wife and this great family, and Laney—well, she's a nice woman, but that's all. Why would I jeopardize all I have for her?" He paused. "It's got to be because I was scared. Nothing else makes sense."

"Scared of what?"

"It turns out that transitional events often kick off affairs because of all the anxiety they bring up. So I must have been scared about becoming a father." He paused. "Again."

"You were scared about becoming a father," I repeated, "for the second time."

"I met Laney around the time we were trying to conceive. Maybe I was thinking about how much my life would change. Maybe I wanted to recover my lost youth."

"Maybe you were thinking that, or you *were* thinking that?"

"I wasn't thinking it consciously. Here, listen." He opened the book to the third Post-it note. I was really starting to hate those fucking things. "I read this, and I thought, 'We're a lot like Bill and Gina.' 'Bill, twenty-eight, and Gina, twenty-nine, were a doctor and a house-wife living in an upper-middle-class home. Bill was used to their orderly life, and to getting a certain amount of affection and attention from Gina. While pregnant, Gina shifted her focus from Bill to the baby inside her. This was threatening to Bill, who found himself more drawn to a *coworker* named Catherine." I was pretty sure the emphasis on *coworker* was Jon's. "'At first, Bill started to confide in Catherine more while he was at the office. Then, they began meeting for drinks after work—'"

"So you're saying that you were threatened by the idea of the new baby? Were you threatened when I was preg-nant with Jacob?"

"Maybe a little bit of both," he said. He looked so earnest. What Jon was peddling, it seemed he was also buying.

"So you felt neglected by me when I was pregnant with Jacob?"

"A little."

"And when we were trying to have another baby, you

were worried that you'd lose even more of my attention?"
I couldn't keep the incredulous note out of my voice.

"That's part of it. You didn't let me finish reading the
vignette. Bill isn't just threatened about losing attention,
but anxious about the change in role from husband to
father."

"What change in role? You're already a father!"

"It's different to be a parent to two kids than one. And
to be a parent to a girl instead of a boy—that's a whole
different ball game."

"Jon," I said.

"What?"

"Give me that book."

He handed it over, and I paged through, my distur-
bance rising. I saw that he'd highlighted sentences for
the most part, not even entire passages, and all of them
seemed calculated to make his case about a generally
faithful, upstanding, loving husband who has one aber-
ration in his life. I flipped past his bookmark and began
to scan. "What about this chapter?" I demanded. "What
about how affairs are often about a lot of unacknowl-
edged hostility toward your partner? How people who
can't express anger sometimes channel it by acting out?
Maybe, for example, by doing things like talking on the
phone to their girlfriends on Thanksgiving with their
wives in the next room."

"I didn't read that chapter."

"Oh, you didn't?"

"I didn't have to, because that's not what it was about.
It was about my new role."

"It wasn't a new role!" I said heatedly. He was lying to me again. I'd asked him to take some time, to dig deep, and he brought me a book and some self-serving pop psychology. He was treating me like an idiot, just like he had for the whole past year.

"Look, I understand that it's hard for you to trust me. I'm prepared to ride all that out—"

"Fuck you!"

I could see that my anger was only making him calmer, more confident somehow. He said, "I'm sorry, and I'll keep saying that for years if that's what it takes."

"It takes honesty. It takes strength of character. Two things you clearly don't possess. I want you to leave." I stood up and walked to the door.

He followed me slowly. "No more minimizing, Eve," he said with a seeming sincerity that made me want to vomit. "I'm here to accept the consequences of my actions, and to deal with your anger."

"And what about your anger, Jon? Where does yours go?"

"I'm not really an angry person, Eve."

At that, I yanked open the door. "Oh, bullshit! We're all angry!"

It was the dynamic we'd played out for years, writ large: He was sane, and I was crazy. He was calm, and I was angry. I didn't want to live in that ever again. I saw his belief in his own superiority, even as he pretended to prostrate himself, even when he was the one who'd had the affair. The touchless affair. Was that bile I was tasting?

"I'm sorry I couldn't say what you wanted to hear. But I was honest. I'm trying to give you time, but there's not much time until the baby comes."

I didn't say anything, and finally he brushed by me and out into the night.

CHAPTER
11

Jonathon and I had been together only about a year when his father died. I barely knew the man, but I don't think that would be any different if he were still alive. After all, Jon barely knew his father and he had a twenty-year head start.

David Gimbel was, in a word, remote. When Jon first took me to dinner at his parents' house, David didn't make an appearance until we'd already finished the salad course. He didn't apologize, and neither Jon nor Sylvia made any comment. It was a given that David's work came first. Once at the table, he ate quickly, efficiently, speaking only when asked a direct question. He seemed completely oblivious to the social purpose of a shared meal, especially one with his son's new girlfriend. At the time, I was slightly offended by his refusal to appraise me (though it was soon apparent that Sylvia was judging me enough for the both of them). A few years ago, I was reading one of my parenting magazines and came across an article about autistic children. It detailed their disinterest in human interaction, their inability to read social cues, and their complete focus on a narrow range of activities. I gave it to Jon to read, and we agreed that David had been autistic before his time.

So maybe there was nothing strange about the fact that Jon didn't cry when he learned his father had died or at the funeral. David was buried in the Jewish section of a grand, parklike cemetery in Oakland. It was a beautiful spot, surrounded by pine trees and Grecian-style monuments and panoramic views of the Oakland hills. If ever a final resting place deserved to be called lush, this was it. During the funeral, Sylvia alternated between complete composure and helpless sobbing. She clutched Jon's arm and said, "He's gone — can he really be gone?" Jon said, simply, "Yes."

I kept watching Jon for changes. I thought losing a parent was supposed to ripple through your life. But there was nothing I could detect. A year after the funeral, we returned to the cemetery for the unveiling, which was when David would get his headstone. Jon actually joked that morning, "See, for Jews, everything's earned. You've got to be dead a year before you even get your headstone."

Again, we stood graveside, and again, I saw little in Jon's face. But when we made love later that day, there was a different level of intensity, and I was relieved to feel it.

I don't know if my own father is alive or dead. I've spent exactly one day with him. When I was about Jacob's age, he took me to a pool hall. I remember that I sat on a bar stool and drank Shirley Temples and the bartender did card tricks for me, and men called to my father as he worked the room and took everyone's money, "Hey, is this your kid?" and my father said with what sounded like pride, "Yeah, she is." I remember feeling happy. I might have invented the pride part, but I think the rest of it's accurate. Of course, when my mother heard about the pool hall, she wasn't too pleased. I don't know if she would have said anything to my father about it if he'd come back around, but he never did. I guess he realized I wasn't for him, or he wasn't for me. My mother said later that it was probably for the best because if he thought a pool hall was the place for a five-year-old, who knew what he'd do with a twelve-year-old? I still prefer not to think too deeply about that remark.

I guess my point is, some people think presence is always better than absence when it comes to parents. I've never subscribed to that. Sometimes it's better to keep things simple, not to muddy the waters too much. Maybe that's why I was able to even consider what some people would call unthinkable: not having Jon in the delivery room.

It was early evening when Charlie pulled up in his ancient Datsun. (Is there any other kind of Datsun, post-millennium?) He'd planned to get on the road by 7 AM, arriving by midafternoon, but I never really expected that to happen. Charlie had a way of getting sidetracked.

I could hear the Datsun from what seemed a half a mile away. It emitted irregular wheezing/clanging noises, not unlike those produced by a really unskilled kid practicing a band instrument. Just when you thought you could predict the next note, it changed. Charlie said the car owed its life to a welding torch and a prayer; he said it with pride. He was pretty ingenious when it came to that car. It was hard to get some of the parts, so he'd pioneered his own modifications. I'd encouraged him to become a mechanic, and he'd tried for a while, but the boss didn't seem to appreciate Charlie's virtuosity (or his low threshold for actual work). Charlie's gift was for distraction. He could distract himself from nearly any focused pursuit (work, relationships), and then when occasionally he'd start feeling down about the wreckage of his life (no work, no girlfriend, living with his mother), he was able to distract himself from even that. He could distract other people with the force of his personality, which was, I think, the final nail in his coffin at the garage.

I was standing on the doorstep waving as he leapt from the car. "Evie!" he said with a grin. "You're one good hug away from popping!" With that, he wrapped his arms around me and lifted me up.

I protested laughingly as he spun me around. When he finally set me down, I said with a grin of my own, "Traffic, huh?"

"I could have crawled here faster," he said, still ear to ear.

"Right." I looked toward his car. "Do you want to bring your things inside?"

"It's just a bag. There's no rush. Why don't we take a ride?"

"In your car? I don't think my neighbors could handle it."

"No, let's take your car and head into San Francisco. Let's drive the Golden Gate."

"You want to go to Marin?"

"If that's where the Golden Gate takes us, then yeah."

I looked at him uncertainly. There was no real reason why we couldn't go anywhere we wanted. Jacob was doing an overnight with Jon at Sylvia's house. But somehow it seemed wrong. That wasn't what adults did. Adults sat down at the kitchen table, drank coffee, talked about the drive up. An adult guest, upon arrival, "got settled." Whatever that meant, it usually didn't involve a spontaneous jaunt with a pregnant lady about to pop.

"Just because you're pregnant doesn't mean we need to stay in tonight," he said. "It means you shouldn't eat raw fish, or drink alcohol, or sit in a hot tub. But other than that, the sky's the limit."

"How do you know about sushi and hot tubs?"

"I've been reading. If I'm going to be Jon's understudy, I've got to learn the part, right?"

I hugged him. "You really are something, you know that?"

When I released him, he said, "I'm kind of pulling for Jon, though."

"Pulling for him to what?"

"I don't know, whatever he needs to do to make things right between you."

"I don't think they'll be right anytime soon. The best he can hope for is to be in the delivery room. And that's looking like a long shot."

Charlie squinted at me. "See, this is just what I was trying to avoid. This is what you've got your girlfriends for. So you can talk about your *feelings*. Me, I'm here to help you forget. It's not going to be easy, what with the ban on alcohol. But I'm going to do my best."

"Why don't you come inside and we'll figure out what we want to do?"

He shook his head emphatically, making his thick, dirty-blond hair bounce. "No way. Bodies at rest stay at rest. You get me in the house, we sit on the couch, and next thing we know, we're watching *Terms of Endearment* or some shit. You and me, Eve, we are going to be bodies in motion tonight. When's the last time you were a body in motion?"

"I've been doing my pregnancy yoga tape four times a week." I mimed a downward dog.

He looked toward the sky. "Suburbs, what have you done to my sister?"

It wasn't an entirely unfounded question. The way I was reacting to his Golden Gate suggestion, you would have thought he was proposing we drink a fifth of Jack while joyriding. "So you're saying we just get in the car and go?" I asked.

"Well, you can put shoes on." His eyes scanned me. "And a brush never hurt anyone." He laughed as I pretended to punch him. "I'm just saying, it's a big world out there, you never know who you're going to meet."

He'd stumbled onto the reason for my hesitation. I didn't want to venture far from home. Scary things happened when you didn't even leave, so why tempt fate?

"Eve," he said, "it's going to be okay. I'm here with you."

I immediately burst into tears. Lately, that's what kindness did to me. You know your life has gone hideously awry when kindness is like jalapeños in your eye sockets. "Come in the house," I sobbed.

Charlie was way off. We found *There's Something About Mary* on cable, and we didn't talk about feelings once.

I'd started to believe that talking about feelings wasn't all it was cracked up to be. Exhibit A was Jon telling me he *maybe* felt jealous of our unborn child, and *maybe* was frightened of being a father (again). Exhibit B was when, later that night, I tried to tell Tamara how sick I felt about Jon lying to me for over a year and then lying to me once again, using that Bill and Gina crap, and after five minutes of concerned nodding, she actually suggested that maybe Jon and I really were like Bill and Gina. When I didn't go for it, she defended Jon, saying that he was just desperate to come home and was grasping at straws. She'd never been married, she had no kids—what the hell did she know about betrayal on this scale?

I wondered what she would have said if she'd seen the e-mail Jon wrote to Clayton the next day. I'd never read a non-Laney e-mail before, but there it was, in the Sent folder, with the subject heading "The Big Talk."

It was bad. Really bad. I read that book my therapist suggested, and I thought maybe it would help things, but it didn't. I went in there all prepared—it was like

when you cram for a test, and you give what seem
like the right answers, only the grading's all messed
up. It was like whatever I said, she was going to blast
me for it. I took responsibility for what I did, what more
does she want? I feel like she's just pummeling me.
And the worst part is, maybe she enjoys it. Maybe she
likes getting to punish me. I don't know what I've done
to her all these years for her to like it so much. I don't
know what anyone's done to her.

There it was, in black and white. I couldn't believe he'd
been able to sit in front of me, pretending to understand
the depth of his betrayal and expressing his willingness
to pay any reparation, and then turn around and say
those things about me. He thought I could enjoy this?
And that line about what someone had done to me . . . Jon
thought I was damaged to the point of sadism. My husband actually thought that about me. I was having the
baby of a man who believed I was a monster.

That e-mail had been the last straw. I'd decided I
couldn't do it anymore. I couldn't be alone in the house.
The possibility existed that I might actually crack up and
have a good old-fashioned nervous breakdown, complete
with yowling sobs and smashing objects. That's when I
called Charlie and told him I needed him right away, and
that I might need him in the delivery room, too, with
that last part momentarily fazing the usually unfazable
Charlie. "But I don't know how to be anyone's coach," he
said. "I didn't go to any of those classes."

"Oh, don't worry. I've changed my mind. Nothing's

natural anymore. I'm getting the epidural. If I could, I'd be on one right now."

He hesitated, then asked with great solemnity, "What can be done so that I never—and I mean never, not for an instant—see your hoo-ha?"

I laughed, even harder because he clearly wasn't kidding. "I bet we can arrange that. You can do the 'hand-holding/brushing my sweaty hair back from my forehead/saying comforting things' part. Oh, and cutting the umbilical cord. Definitely that." I waited for the laugh that didn't come. "That thing about the umbilical cord was a joke."

"I knew that."

A few days later, he was here. Indefinitely.

He'd arrived just in time, because for the next week, my exhaustion verged on paralysis. I was calling in sick every other day. My obstetrician assured me that the baby was fine, but it was hard to believe. How could my baby be immune to this? I tried to think happy thoughts so that her last days inside me would be pleasant ones. I didn't think I was fooling her, but I hoped.

I'd envisioned Charlie's role as one of moral support, but he slipped into a far more domestic one without complaint. He'd always been the "fun uncle"; now he was helping Jacob get ready for school or for bed, keeping him entertained, whatever I asked. He pitched in on grocery shopping and cooking; he even ran interference with Jon, working out the scheduling for Jacob's visits, handling the pickups and drop-offs. Every time I tried to express my inexpressible gratitude, my eyes misted up and he tried to get out of the room as quickly as possible.

One evening, when Tamara stopped by with DVDs, Charlie was wearing Jon's apron with the tuxedo print on it and preparing a casserole. He escorted her to the bedroom, where I was sitting upright against the headboard. "Do you need anything?" he asked. "Dinner will be ready in about an hour."

"I'm great, Charlie," I said, smiling at him. "Thanks."

"Are you cool?" he said to Tamara.

"I am," she said, sitting down on the bed. "I'm very cool." As he started to leave the room, she said, "There's a word for you, you know."

"Yeah?" He looked a little wary, like her statement was usually the preface for an insult.

"Avuncular," she pronounced.

"Huh. What's that mean?"

"It means 'uncle-like.'"

"That's the whole definition?" he asked.

She nodded.

"Weird. So that's a compliment?"

"In this case," she said.

He hung in the doorway an extra second. "But what about those pervy uncles, you know the ones, like, 'Hey, don't leave the kids alone with Uncle Harvey, he's just a little too avuncular'?"

We all laughed, and he left the room, shutting the door behind him. Tamara looked at me. "You weren't kidding."

"I told you, he's really taken to this whole thing. Yesterday I caught him humming while he was making Jacob's lunch. I think it was Metallica or Slayer or something like that, but still."

"I'm glad he's here for you."

"Me too."

She lifted a tote bag onto the bed. "So I brought the first season of *Weeds*."

"That sounds perfect." We'd been careful with each other since the heated talk about Jon. Pop culture was generally a safe topic, and Tamara had mentioned the other day that Mary-Louise Parker had gotten dumped for another woman while she was pregnant and then went on to win an Emmy the following year. I'd decided to worship at the altar of Mary-Louise Parker, at least while I was on semi–bed rest.

There was a knock on the door. "Come in," I said.

"Sorry to interrupt you guys, but I meant to give you this earlier." Charlie laid an envelope on the bed.

I glanced down and recognized the handwriting. It wasn't an accident that Charlie was giving this to me now. He wanted me to read it with Tamara here. It occurred to me that he was giving his all to being a housekeeper and playmate because he knew he could handle that; he wasn't sure how to talk to me about pain, especially when his own life was largely structured around its avoidance. "Now's a good time," I said, giving him a smile.

I picked up the letter as Charlie withdrew. I was nervous to read it with Tamara, and nervous to read it alone.

"What's been happening with Jon?" she asked, some-what gingerly. Either she'd read Jon's handwriting, or my face.

"I haven't had a talk with Jon since—you know. And he doesn't do the call screening thing anymore, which is a relief." Well, it was mostly a relief. "It's strange to get an actual letter anymore, isn't it? Sort of anachronistic."

"It seems old-fashioned. Romantic." She looked like maybe she'd said something wrong.

"How should we do this? Should I read it out loud? Or should you?"

"Why don't you read it to yourself, and then let me know if you want me to read it?" she suggested.

I looked at her gratefully. "That's a good idea."

Dear Eve,

 I feel like we misunderstood each other the last time we spoke. I'm not trying to go back over the same ground, but I wanted you to know—in case there's any confusion—that I was really happy when you were pregnant with Jacob, and despite the current circumstances, I'm really happy that we're about to have two. When I said I was threatened, that just meant I had worries, not that I wanted to have it any other way.

 Here's the thing, though. When you were pregnant with Jacob, I just felt more distant. I touched your belly and I felt excited, but it felt like the whole thing was more yours than mine. I mean, naturally, biologically, you just had so much more of a relationship with him.

But when I was there in the delivery room, it was like I
saw him transform from an idea into an actual person,
and this dam just burst. There was all this love I hadn't
even fully recognized just exploding as I held him.
Now that I know what it's all about, now that I've seen
it happen, it's like I can already love the hell out of our
little girl. She's not just an idea. It's like this love I have
for her, it's real, but it's love as an act of imagination
and as an act of faith, and that's all we have to go on
right now. I love you, Eve, and I love our little girl, and
I don't want to be away from either of you.
Please, talk soon,
Jon

P.S. In the interest of full disclosure, this was my
therapist's idea.

I laid the letter against my stomach and closed my eyes.

After a minute, Tamara asked, "Do you want me to
read it?"

I looked at her. I could see that she wanted what
was best for me, but if she read the letter, she wouldn't
understand what I was feeling. She didn't know what Jon
had written to Clayton. She wouldn't understand why I
thought it might be just a beautiful manipulation. That
stuff about the delivery room—he was no fool. I hadn't
told him I was thinking of keeping him out, but he knew
what was at stake. He probably did believe what he'd put
in the letter, but only because he needed to. If he didn't
love me, he wasn't going to admit that even to himself.

It was how he'd convinced himself that we were Bill and Gina. Necessity was the mother of self-delusion. As much as I wanted to believe the letter, I couldn't allow myself to.

"No," I said.

CHAPTER
12

I took the easy way out. I'll be the first to admit it. I should have sat Jonathon down in advance and told him that I'd be more comfortable with Charlie in the birthing room this time around. Maybe I could have added an apology, but it would smack of "I'm sorry you feel that way," and no one likes those. The problem is, there's no good way to tell a man that he's unlikely to attend the birth of his child. If only it was thirty years ago when it was assumed that the man was insignificant to the proceedings and should be in the waiting room with a box of cigars at the ready.

This wasn't a decision born of anger. I just truly couldn't imagine having Jon there, feeding me ice chips, fluffing my pillows, whispering in my ear that he loved me, that I could do it, that "We're having a baby, can you believe it? We're having a baby." Having him there, but as a stranger, would be heartbreak. My baby would enter the world with heartbreak palpable in the room, surrounded by what had been lost. I wanted to spare her that.

I've heard that it's easier to get forgiveness than permission, and I hoped that would be true. But if Jon never forgave me...well, the feeling might be mutual. Strange as it sounds, though, even as I made my decision to exclude Jon from the delivery, what I wanted most was for us to find forgiveness.

Tamara didn't approve of the choice, that was obvious. She assumed it had something to do with what was in the letter, and I let her believe that. But she also believed that Jon had a right to be at the birth, no matter what he'd done, or what any letter had said. I suspected that what bothered her most was not telling Clayton. Clayton knew only that once I went into labor, he and Tamara would be watching Jacob (mostly Tamara, since she had just started winter break and had her days free while he was filming an infomercial for a revolutionary new work-out system that combined Pilates and Tae Bo), but he thought that was because Jon would be with me.

Two days before the due date, the contractions started. It was textbook perfect: a contraction about every ten minutes, lasting thirty seconds. With Jacob, early labor had gone on for hours, with me lying on the bed and Jon at my side holding a stopwatch so he'd know precisely when we should drive to the hospital. We'd been determined to do everything right, to earn our A's in labor and delivery.

Things usually move a whole lot faster the second time around, so just as soon as I established that I was indeed having contractions and not gas pains, I toddled down to the kitchen, where Charlie and Jacob were baking cookies. They were sitting at the table, and Jacob—flour dust in his hair, so he looked like the world's oldest boy or the world's youngest old man—was carefully imprinting dough with a shot glass. He looked up at me and grinned. "It's the head!" he said, indicating his handiwork.

"Snowmen," Charlie added. "And women. They don't have gonads, so, really, it's all in the frosting."

"Uncle Charlie and I might have to finish those up, sweetie," I said to Jacob.

"Why?" he asked, squinting at me.

"Remember the plan we talked about? That when the baby's just about here, you're going to stay with Aunt Tamara?"

Jacob nodded, his expression neutral. It was Charlie who was suddenly wild-eyed with understanding. He jumped to his feet.

"So we need to drop Jacob off and get to the hospital," he said rapidly. "Do we have time to drop him off? Do you need an ambulance? You can go to the hospital while I drop him off. But then you'd be alone. I mean, not alone, you'd have the paramedics, and they'll know a hell of a lot more than I do. Sorry," he said, looking at Jacob. "I mean heck. Is it okay to say 'heck' around him?"

Charlie's panic inspired calm in me. I laughed. "We have plenty of time before we need to go to the hospital. But we should get Jake over to Tamara's, just in case." I glanced at Jacob, who still appeared impassive. "Aren't you excited? You're going to have a little brother or sister soon."

He pursed his lips in the facial equivalent of a shrug.

"Well, maybe you'll be more excited when you can see her. Or him. It could be either." But in my heart, I still thought it was a girl. Maybe it wasn't intuition, only hope, that told me that. "You need to get ready to go."

I recognized his look of escalating defiance and expected him to refuse, but then he turned to Charlie. Charlie gave the slightest of nods, and Jacob got up and left the room. I was rendered momentarily speechless by the sight of my brother, the Preschool Whisperer.

"How do you feel? Are you okay?" Charlie asked anxiously. "I didn't want to ask with the kid here, just in case."

"I feel fine. At this point, it's kind of like cramps."

"Don't those hurt?"

"It's more like a twinge. A reminder that something's going to happen soon." I added quickly, "But not too soon."

He nodded earnestly, like he was committing my every word to memory. "How far apart are the contractions?"

"About ten minutes apart."

"And we're waiting for contractions that are five minutes apart and last about a minute each, right?" He'd done his homework.

"Right. After an hour of that, we go to the hospital. No ambulances needed." It was funny, how easily I slipped into big-sister mode, and how soothing it was. It created the illusion that I knew what I was doing, and I needed that. I'd be strong for Charlie. For the moment, it was just good to have a focal point. The real fear was yet to come, when I wouldn't know where to look.

*   *   *

"Are you sure you don't want me to call Jon?" Charlie asked. We were settled in the birthing room, and he was trying not to pace. I'd asked him not to pace.

"If I change my mind," I said grimly, "you'll be the first to know."

Jon and I had picked out this birthing room together after touring area hospitals. With Jacob, I'd gone from the hospital room to the delivery room and back again, while the birthing room would allow us to stay in one place throughout. This one had seemed homey, like a child's nursery: the pale-blue-and-yellow color scheme, the duck-patterned curtains for the window, the rocking chair beside my bed for Jon, the infant warmer just waiting for her arrival. "It's like nothing can go wrong in a room like this," Jon had said, squeezing my hand.

The catheter was already inserted in my spine and the epidural administered, but the pain was still acute. It was extremely irritating to go against all the Bradley Method/natural-childbirth brainwashing and still be in pain. I'd sold out, and I wasn't even reaping the benefits. I let out a moan that was half-exasperation.

"What am I supposed to tell you?" Charlie asked. "Work through the pain, be the pain, go into the light, pant like a dog, what?"

I laughed in spite of myself. "There are exercises, but you don't know any of them."

"Teach me."

"I'm not going to teach you. That's what a coach is for."
I felt a sudden flare of anger. "Fucking Jon!"

"That's right. That's how you got into this mess in the
first place," Charlie joked. I shot him an irritated look.
"Hey, it's not my fault. And I'm here with you, even though
I know something no one likes to talk about. The unmen-
tionable." I couldn't help looking at him with some interest. "Oh, sure, we all know the miracle of life is a messy
thing. I've watched ER. But you and I both know that at
some point in this process, you're going to shit yourself.
I'm going to have to bear witness to my sister shitting herself. You think that's going to be fun for me?"

"You know, Charlie, I just hadn't really thought about
that."

As a contraction overtook me, I bit my lip and tried
to remember how to relax. Twelve weeks of that course,
and I couldn't summon up one trick just then. Nothing
I told myself in my head, no breathing technique, could
change the fact that I was having the baby of a big fat
liar. A big fat cheating liar. A big fucking fat cheating liar.
A big fucking fat cheating asshole liar. A big fucking...

I rode that hypnotic, rhythmic wave until the epidural did the rest. When the nurse checked on me next,
she said cheerfully, "It shouldn't be too long until you're
holding that baby in your arms."

"That sounds nice," I said. Nothing had ever sounded
nicer, in fact. I suddenly ached to hold my little girl. Oh,
let it be a girl.

Charlie crossed the room and sat by my bed, taking

my hand. We were smiling into each other's faces. "I'm going to be an uncle again."

"You're good at it," I said.

"I'm trying."

"I know."

Suddenly I heard Jon's aggrieved voice. "How could you do this?" I looked up to see him at the foot of my bed. His eyes were red and his hair stood up in tufts. "How could you not even call me?" What struck me was that his tone was more plaintive than angry. I'd never seen such sorrow in him.

"I'm having a baby," I said dumbly.

"Our baby. She's ours, Eve. Doesn't that mean anything to you?" He was on the verge of tears.

"Look, man," Charlie said, standing up protectively. "She's been through it. I mean, she's going through it. Don't make things worse for her."

"Worse for her?" Jon said, his voice rising. "I'm the only one trying to make things better! She doesn't talk to me, she won't forgive me. What the fuck am I supposed to do? What am I supposed to do?" He dissolved into tears, then full-blown sobs. As he turned away, ashamed, I started to cry, too.

Charlie was standing awkwardly between us. He looked at me. "Do you want him to leave? Should I leave? What?"

"I don't know," I said. "I can't feel anything. The epidural . . ." I was sobbing now. I wanted to tell Jon to come sit beside me. I could imagine his face against my hand, the feel of his wet, stubbly cheek.

I don't know how long we stayed that way, but it startled the nurse when she came in to check on me. "I need to get the doctor," she said, looking back and forth between all of us. "You're about to deliver the baby."

Then the doctor and the nurse were there, and Jon was beside me, and Charlie, too. I was surrounded. I was numb below my stomach. I didn't know what was happening with my mind or with my body, either, courtesy of the epidural. The doctor was telling me when to push and I was trying, but I felt so distant. With Jacob, despite the epidural, I'd still felt the urgency of the uterine contractions. They weren't just pain, they were propulsion. It was a pain that told you what to do.

Charlie later told me that Jon was coaching me almost under his breath, but I didn't hear him. A half hour after I started pushing, the baby was lying on my stomach, hot pink and mucosal. It was a girl. My little girl. Jon whooped with joy, and I started crying hysterically. I could tell from the reactions of the nurse and the doctor that it wasn't the way mothers usually cried. There was something primal in it, like she was saving my life.

Charlie was in the rocking chair closest to the bed, and Jon had stationed himself in an armchair nearby. We hadn't spoken directly since before the delivery had begun in earnest.

Charlie asked, "Is it okay if I take a walk? That was kind of intense."

"Sure, I'll be okay," I said. I was still holding my girl.

I didn't want to let go of her. When I looked at her, I smiled, I cooed, I knew what to do. I was her mother. When I looked at Jon, I felt lost, confused, bereft.

Charlie left us alone, and Jon moved into the vacated rocking chair. "Can I hold her?" he said.

I nodded, but it was another minute before I could actually relinquish her. Once out of my arms, I felt her absence like a phantom limb.

Standing up, with our baby in his arms, Jon was the one to find himself. "Baby, baby, baby," he sang softly, looking into her face, slowly circumambulating. It hurt to watch.

After a few minutes had elapsed, he turned to me. "Have you thought about names?" he asked tentatively.

"A little," I said.

"Me too." I waited for him to tell me what they were, but he was immersed in her again.

"I'm sorry," I said. I was surprised to say it, more surprised to feel it. "For not calling you."

He acted like he hadn't heard me, but I knew he had. Finally he said, "That was a lousy thing to do, Eve."

"I didn't do it to be lousy."

"Why did you do it, then?"

"I'm not going to be able to make you understand."

"Join the club. It seems like I can't make you understand anything, either." He was still jiggling her a little bit, but his attention was on me.

"That's the problem, isn't it? We don't understand each other at all. We don't know each other, Jon."

"That's not true. How can you weigh a bunch of e-mails heavier than ten years of us being there for each other?"

"Not now, okay?"

We were both quiet. Then he said, "I was thinking of Olivia."

"Olivia," I repeated.

"I could picture this little girl, with light brown hair in curls, and we'd call her Liv."

"Olivia Gimbel," I said experimentally. "Liv Gimbel."

"You want her to have my last name?" he asked.

"Of course." It hadn't occurred to me that it would be otherwise.

There were tears in his eyes. "So what do you think? Do you like it?"

"I do."

"In English, the origin is 'elf army.'" He was smiling.

I laughed. "I don't see how I can refuse now."

"But what did you have in mind? You said you'd thought a little bit, too."

"I didn't get too far, really." I held out my arms. "Let me try something." He brought the baby to me. "Olivia," I said, gazing into her eyes. They were so blue that it was hard to believe they wouldn't stay that way. In six months, we'd know the permanent color. Who knew where we'd all be in six months? "Olivia." She blinked up at me with what I would have sworn was recognition.

Jon was standing by the bedside, smiling down at both of us. "What do you think?"

"I think she's Olivia."

What a tableau we made — mother, father, baby — for just an instant. "Let me come home, Eve," Jon said.

Olivia let out a little cry. "Shhh," I said. "It'll be all right. Everything's going to be all right."

CHAPTER
13

Just days after Liv was born, we spent The Holiday together as a family. We ate our traditional five-course meal consisting entirely of desserts; Jacob tore open presents with his usual sugar-fueled zeal; Jon and I smiled at each other in a pantomime of parental connection. I was grateful for Charlie's presence and his willingness to play the court jester, to say, "Hey, don't look at the mess that is your marriage, look over here, I'm pouring high fructose corn syrup directly on my Pop-Tart!" He loved me enough to try to be the pink elephant. I cried when I hugged him good-bye just after New Year's.

Right from the start, Olivia was so different than Jacob had been. It takes a while for babies to smile, but with Jacob, it was like I could tell that he wanted to from so early. There was a lightness to him while Olivia seemed so solemn. She didn't cry as often, but I wasn't sure that was a good thing. Maybe she'd absorbed my distress while in the womb, like radiation. It was a terrifying thought, and one I didn't share with Jon, as hard as it was to bear it alone.

The fact was, Jon and I didn't share much at all. He was

spending a lot of time at the house, but the children were the focus of almost all our attention. If I wasn't holding Olivia, Jon was; if Jon wasn't tuned into Jacob, I was. For the next few months, we went through the motions of family, minus the intimacy of marriage. Once the kids were asleep, Jon and I talked about them or about practical matters; we did household tasks (he would clean up the kitchen, I would fold yet another load of laundry) and kept the TV on so awkward silences wouldn't hurt too much. Eventually he'd say he should get going, that it was a long drive across the bridge. The saddest part was that we both knew we were a pale imitation of ourselves, but neither of us said it. I don't know about Jon, but I was hoping that if I kept acting the part, eventually I'd feel the right accompanying emotions. It's the reason movies have soundtracks, I suppose, in the hope that emotion can be induced.

Jon continued to half-ass his way through therapy, occasionally tossing a faux insight my way, like a scrap to a dog, and I held my tongue. I tried to convince myself that Jon's affair was a thing of the past and that he wasn't stupid enough to repeat it. I wanted to believe that the *why* of it didn't matter, only what he *would* or *wouldn't* do. The visual of Jon sobbing against the wall in the birthing room was one I recalled frequently to remind myself just how much he loved this family, but by February, I was pretty desensitized to it. And sick of the pretending.

I was still reading Jon's e-mails. Every time I did it, I felt low and slimy and just a little demented. But I'd discovered the Drafts folder, and I'm sure no jury would convict me.

The Drafts folder contained the e-mails Jon had written (or half-written) and never sent. It was like having a direct line to his id. I know, I know. It's wrong to peek into someone else's subconscious. In my defense, I never did it before. I guess I foolishly assumed I knew what was in there.

Some of the drafts were actually addressed to me. Like this one:

Eve,
You haven't said anything about the letter I sent you. Maybe it never arrived? Or it arrived and you chose not to read it? Or it arrived, you read it, and you're thinking it over? There are a lot of scenarios going through my brain right now, and maybe

That was it. He never did finish it, or send anything like it. But at least it confirmed that he was worried and that he cared, and while I should have been able to take both of those as givens, nothing seemed so clear-cut in a post-Laney world.

I wasn't learning anything new from the e-mails, but that wasn't the point anymore. In fact, I wanted to be bored. If I could be greeted every day with a bulletin saying "No change," I probably could have forsaken the e-mails altogether. They were reassuring because of their very dullness. The only problem was, I didn't know when it was all going to change. After all, I'd never seen

Laney coming. I felt like I had to stay vigilant, even if it was turning me into a person I didn't much respect.

Then one day, in the Drafts folder, there she was again.

> Laney,
> I know it's been a while. I hope things have been going well for you.
>
> A lot's happened for me. I have a little girl now. We named her Olivia. She's so pretty. And tiny. So tiny that it amazes me, every day.
>
> Eve and I are trying to work things out. I'm staying with my mother right now, and I don't know when that will change. Slow and steady wins the race, is that how the saying goes? I'm hoping that it's true.

My immediate thoughts: Why her? Why now? Maybe it would never be over, this pull toward Laney. Of all the people in the world he could tell about his new baby and working on his marriage, he wanted to tell her. As we hid behind the drone of the television night after night, instead of thinking of things he could say to me, he must have been thinking of her.

I was tired of being jealous of Laney. There, I'd admitted it to myself. I had two children by this man; I shouldn't have had to feel jealous of anyone. I should have had a secure place in the world. I shouldn't have had to wonder why he'd stopped writing that e-mail, if he planned to finish it later, or if he'd just gone ahead and called her instead.

I don't know how long Jon and I would have continued

in our state of suspended animation if it hadn't been for that draft, and for Olivia herself. I thought that if what she'd absorbed in the womb had been bona fide sadness, what she was absorbing now was forced happiness. I didn't want her to grow up thinking that life is about just pushing on and pretending it's good enough. It seemed like Jacob was learning that. At first, he would say things like, "Daddy, hug Mommy!" because he noticed that we didn't spontaneously touch each other anymore, but now he accepted things as they were. No wonder Olivia didn't feel like smiling.

I'd seen a flyer for a postpartum support group and on a whim decided to go. I thought a group of sympathetic, impartial strangers with their own set of problems might be good for me. But the women gathered in the meeting room at the community center weren't exactly what I had in mind. I don't even remember any of their names, except for Alix — "Alix, with an 'i,'" she said, with a tight little smile that didn't reach her pale blue eyes. Everyone seemed to have gotten the memo to dress up — by which I mean wearing pants with hems and shoes that didn't have rubber soles — except for me. I was wearing yoga pants and my snazziest Pumas, the green-and-white ones that Jacob nicknamed Broccoli.

There were three other women besides Alix, all brunettes with low-slung ponytails. One was significantly heavier than the rest; everyone else seemed to have shed their baby weight at the speed of Hollywood. The facilitator was less well-maintained, though younger. She looked to be in her mid-twenties, and I wasn't sure if her complexion was always so shiny or if it was nerves. I was getting the impression this was her first job since getting her license by the way she announced pertly, "I'm Geri, MFT. That's a licensed marriage and family therapist."

The room was small and overheated, decorated with what I thought of as office-park art, framed pictures of flowers that neither offended nor inspired. The skinny women kept their sweaters on as the heavier brunette and I were shucking off layers. Everyone wore vague smiles that asked what was to come, except for Alix. It was her self-possession that rankled. She looked like she'd never had a moment of uncertainty. I found myself hoping that her husband was fucking someone else, and that she'd find out about it on a national holiday.

It was quickly clear that I wasn't going to get the vulnerability and honesty I'd been looking for in that room. I blamed Alix. Who'd admit to fear and self-doubt with her there? It wasn't that she was nasty, or even particularly dismissive. She nodded just as much as the rest of us. But somehow, she dominated the room. When she spoke, it was with authority. She knew the best way to do everything, it seemed. While Geri, MFT, tried to get the conversation to go deeper ("Has anyone worried about how having a baby will change her marriage?" "Where did you get your ideas of what it meant to be a good mother?"), the group mostly stayed determinedly on the surface, exchanging practical information and product recommendations.

At some point, it came to me that we were all really

asking the same question: "Am I going to fuck my kid up if I do [x, y, or z]?" For Skinny Brunette #2, for example, it was formulated in terms of whether her failure to play classical music (she hated the stuff) would harm her child (i.e., make him stupid), and underpinning that was the question of how much we should sacrifice of ourselves, our own preferences, our own nature, for the betterment of our kids. Only in my case, the questions were in a whole different league: Was I going to fuck my kid up more by keeping Jon out or by letting him in half-heartedly? By going back to work after three months of maternity leave instead of figuring out a way to extend it? By being the kind of mother who *wanted* to keep her husband out, who *wanted* to go back to work after three months? Would I hurt Olivia by simply being me? As the discussion around me meandered from breast-feeding to formula to nap time to nappies, I felt incredibly alone because I had the distinct feeling that I was the only one wondering that.

I didn't think the group helped, except that Alix gave me the names of some day care providers, and I was sure they were the best. But maybe fully formulating those questions in my mind gave me some clarity, because later that afternoon, as Olivia was breast-feeding (with Jon's e-mail open on the screen in front of me), I came to a decision. This couldn't go on any longer.

Jon was coming over after work, so I set Jacob up with a video, put Liv down for a nap, and waited. I was working out my nervous energy in the kitchen, scrubbing the counters, and I didn't hear him come in. "Hello?" he called tentatively from the doorway.

"Hello," I said, my tone opaque. I did one final swipe, rinsed the sponge, and then turned to him.

He hovered, waiting for a cue, as he always did when it was just the two of us. He didn't know what to do with his body, or with his eyes. When the children were present, he made a beeline for them. I couldn't blame him for hungering for a love that was uncomplicated, unsullied. I felt it, too. How could we feel so many of the same things and be so separate?

I sat down at the kitchen table. There was a plastic place mat in front of me with the whole world on it. I ran my hand along it, feeling the finest of crumbs, like silt.

Jon sat across from me. "How was your day?" he asked.

I nearly winced. It used to be the rarest of questions between us. It used to be that he would come in and launch into a story, or ask me something specific like, "How was your meeting with the ESL student?" But hearing him, I knew I was doing the right thing. I felt sturdy in my conviction.

"I want the separation to be official. I want to stop this," I said.

Jon looked stunned. "What did I do?"

"Nothing. You've done nothing."

"Meaning, I haven't done enough to make things right?"

"No. I mean, you've done nothing wrong." But that was just ridiculous. "Nothing new, I mean."

"I thought we were working on things. I've been spending a lot of time here. As a family."

"And it's not working. You can tell that, can't you?"

"It's going to take time."

"But it's not getting easier. Just look at us. Doesn't it make you sad, standing in the doorway like you do, waiting? For what? What are you even waiting for?"

He closed his eyes, and rubbed his forehead. It took him a long time to answer. "I'm waiting for you to look happy to see me."

I felt the tears. "I've been waiting for that, too. We're waiting to be what we were."

"Well, how do we get there? There's got to be a way." He was looking at me intently now.

"I've been thinking a lot today about that Doris Lessing quote I used to love. Do you remember it? I came across it in my Twentieth-century Women Writers class, and I thought it was the greatest thing."

He shook his head. "I remember you used to highlight novels. I never knew anyone else who did that."

We both almost smiled, remembering. Then I continued. "The quote went, 'What's terrible is to pretend that the second-rate is first-rate.' "

"You think we're second-rate?"

"If you're honest, you do, too. And it seems like as long as we don't name it, we can keep living this way, with second-rate. But I can't pretend anymore."

"How do we get back to first-rate?"

"I don't know. But we can't get there from here."

"Let's start therapy, then."

"I knew you'd say that," I burst out in sudden frustration. "I'm so tired of that being your mantra. You're barely doing one therapy, now you want to do two?"

"How do you know what I'm doing in therapy?"

"I know the bits you tell me. We need to be apart, Jon."

He was staring past me, to nothing. "What about Jacob and Liv? Have you thought about what this will mean to them?"

"Of course. I think they're better off seeing us first-rate, even if it's apart."

"We can get back there, together. You just need to give us more time." He reached for my hand, and I let him hold it. "See? The way you're touching me, that's the problem."

"I'm the problem?"

"You're not open to me at all. Do you see that?"

"I've tried. Laney did damage. *You* did damage. Do you see that?"

He released my hand, and looked away, obviously trying to reel in his emotions. "I see that. Do you see anything but that?"

"Maybe I can't."

With a sigh, he said, "Well, then, I'm going to get an apartment. Much longer with my mother and I'm going to—I don't even know what I'd do."

I shouldn't have, but I felt stung. He must have been thinking already about getting an apartment. And what could I do but agree? I nodded, not trusting myself to speak.

"Month to month," he added. "I'm not giving up on us."

The declaration was so dramatic that I remained speechless for a second. "Good" was all I came up with.

What I didn't say was *Maybe we never were first-rate.*

Maybe you *never were first-rate.*

Or maybe I *never was.*

Making the separation official kicked off a fresh round of grief. I mourned for what Jacob was losing, for what Olivia might never know. My insomnia rivaled the first month after I'd found out about Laney.

Jacob hated the visitation schedule even more this time around, and while Jon and I presented a united front like the parenting books advised, Jacob's sense of betrayal centered on me. I thought about reversing my position, but in my heart, I didn't believe that was best for anyone. If Jon and I ever got back together, it needed to be real. But when Jacob would barely look at me over the breakfast table or threw a tantrum at night, I questioned myself all over again. I tried not to show it, though. That would only scare him more.

I found myself wishing Thanksgiving had never happened. I liked to think Jon would have come to his senses after Olivia was born and ended things with Laney on his own. If he had, I would never have been the wiser. I would never have had to rethink my entire relationship with him. I wouldn't have lost my best friend, my family.

But once you know there's no Santa Claus, you can never convince yourself otherwise.

Lil said that a trip to the Japanese baths would do me a world of good, and she seemed so certain that I gave in. She firmly believed that happy mothers are better mothers, which allowed her to have all sorts of me-time and me-procedures. After years working in the ER, now she worked at a medical spa, where she got cosmetic procedures at a deep discount. As a result, Lil looked like she was in her late twenties, tops. She was definitely sexy, though her features were several notches away from pretty. She had the slightest gap between her front teeth and had flirted with veneers before deciding, once and for all, that the space added character.

I'd grown to rely on her more and more. She was non-judgmental and optimistic, qualities that took her from being a casual friend to my closest in record time. After making the rounds to tell people Jon and I were officially separated and seeing face after face full of compassion (with just the *slightest* tinge of disapproval, the unspoken "But can't you just suck it up for your children?"), there was nothing more winning than the way Lil simply nodded and said, "Well, you never know where life's going to take you," as if I were going on an adventure.

Meanwhile, the distance between Tamara and me had only increased. It came out that she was the reason Jon showed up in the delivery room. She'd apparently cracked and confessed to Clayton, who immediately called Jon. At her weepy apology, I forgave her. I understood why she'd been conflicted, and besides, I was glad I didn't have Jon's missing the birth on my conscience forever. The real issue with Tamara and me was that when I was with her, I could tell she thought the problem with my marriage was *me*. She — like so many people who've never been profoundly betrayed — seemed to think that once someone expressed contrition, the onus was on the other person to forgive and forget; if I couldn't do that, I was in the wrong, not Jon. She never said it directly, but it was always there between us.

So it turned out Lil was right: the spa was a revelation. We'd split up for massages (mine Swedish, hers Shiatsu), and an hour of lying facedown in a darkened room while a tiny but eerily strong Japanese woman kneaded my body had left me nearly dazed with calm. The whole place was a serenity shrine: Dimly lit with sconces throughout, there was a subdued color palette of grays and greens and the occasional pop of orange or red, strategically placed bonsai trees, and the faintest scent of sandalwood. (Or was it jasmine? Lavender? Like I said, it was faint.) Lil and I met up in plush robes to drink cucumber water in the lounge.

"Well, don't you look relaxed," she said, smiling.

"I am. I feel like Gumby."

She laughed. "I don't know if I mentioned this, but it's women's day at the baths. Men and women alternate days. I think one of the days is coed."

"You didn't mention it, but that's good news."

"Oh, come on. You have to get back out there. Mingle a little."

"I'll mingle with my clothes on, thank you." I was nowhere near ready to do that, either. I hoped she'd drop the subject.

"Ready to go in?" she asked.

I nodded, and we entered the communal baths. The term conjured images of a dank, subterranean space populated by obese Eastern European women with garlic emanating from their pores. Instead, we found ourselves in an airy room with slate blue walls and a tiled floor the color of sand, recessed lighting, and a few ornamental Japanese lanterns. There were two large round pools, one hot and one cold. Along the sides of the room were showers (we'd been asked to shower before entering the pools), a sauna, and a steam room. There were sleek deck chairs made of bamboo next to the pool, and a woman was lying naked on one of them, eyes closed, her body taut and glistening. I'd never had muscle tone like that, even before the children. I wondered if that was how Laney looked. Even though Jon had never done anything with her, he probably fantasized about her a million times. He could have been fantasizing about her when...

"I'm taking a shower," I said abruptly, and as I washed, I tried my best to shake myself free of Laney and Jon. I was in there a long time.

Afterward, Lil and I went to the sauna. We could hear women's voices as we pushed open the door and were rewarded with the robust smell of cedar.

"...he actually gave me a copy of that book, *He's Just Not That into You*. I mean, instead of telling me he's just not that into me," said one naked woman to her friend. I couldn't help casting a furtive glance to see what he wasn't that into. She looked better than I did, but not by much. Her breasts were high and firm, but overlooked a somewhat paunchy midsection. Her face was understandably flushed, and her hair hung dark and limp to her shoulders. "Hi," she said to us, with a somewhat embarrassed laugh.

"Hi," Lil and I said. "I hope you weren't that into him," she added. It was the kind of remark I would never make to a stranger, but somehow, with Lil, it always came off well. She butted into people's conversations, and they liked her for it.

Case in point, the woman laughed. "Three dates."

"Three dates and he's buying you literature? See, you must be hot shit." Lil gave one of her engaging smiles, and both strangers laughed with her.

We all settled into companionable silence, and when the women got up to leave, covering themselves with the towels they'd been sitting on, they said good-bye to both of us, but mostly to Lil. "Good things are coming your way," Lil said by way of farewell. "Really, I'm very intuitive."

The stringy-haired woman said thanks, and they shut the door softly behind them. "So you're a psychic now," I teased.

Lil shrugged, her eyes closed. "You don't have to be Miss Cleo to see that after that guy, there's nowhere to go but up."

"At least he was honest."

"Yeah, an honest coward."

"I guess I mean, she's better off knowing sooner than later."

"Let me take a wild guess here, and say that you're really talking about Jon. The whole if-I'd-known-then-what-I-know-now game." She made eye contact, albeit sleepily.

"It's hard to play that game once you have kids. I mean, you can't truly regret the relationship that gave you your kids."

"Sure you can. I do." She shifted her position, and I looked away, but not before I noticed she was completely shorn down below. Utterly bushless. She'd had a child, and now she was a child again herself, in a manner of speaking. The result was shudderingly graphic.

"You do? You regret Patrick?"

"When I bother to. It's not the same as regretting your kids. Separate Jon from your kids and I promise you, you'll sleep better." She did a full-body yawn, without a trace of self-consciousness. "I'm ready for the pools. How about you?"

After the spa, Lil and I had a late lunch at one of my favorite restaurants in the city, a great little bistro with buttery walls and mahogany accents. I had wine with my cassoulet, and wondered if I'd be struck down for such decadence, for drinking in the middle of the day, for this glow that had nothing to do with motherhood or men. I loved that Lil thought guilt was a useless emotion that she refused to indulge. The implicit permission to be just me was the best part of being with her.

But my mood changed rapidly during our car ride back to the suburbs. I felt like stamping my feet and shouting, "But I don't want to!" I didn't want to return to the land of cleanliness and thirty-year-old architecture, where you drove everywhere and pretended you could control everything. As we passed through downtown, I eyed the crowds of people who looked like they were leading a thousand different kinds of lives; I didn't want to return to where there was only one. On my block, everyone had children, and conversations about children.

I missed living among artists and students and child-less couples and lesbians. I missed all the paper: flyers stapled to telephone poles, the bulletin board at the Laundromat, even litter in the streets. I missed the detritus of real life, the reminder that life is messy and exciting.

I knew I was romanticizing it. I knew why Jon and I had made the choice we'd made. But I couldn't feel it just then. All I could feel was that I was stuck in that house, and Jon was going back to the city. Jon would be the one to live in its vibrancy.

I found myself imagining his apartment in bitter detail. It would probably be in the Haight or the Mission or maybe in North Beach. It would be small, a studio, but it would have an eat-in kitchen. He would rent it furnished, so it would be nondescript at the beginning: a pullout couch, maybe in imitation leather, a kitchen table, an end table. But then he'd give it character. He'd go into the neighborhood shops every few days and find little gems, like etchings or lamps or a funky cabinet to hold the wine collection he'd start. He'd buy lots of glass because he wouldn't have to worry about fingerprints or kids knocking things over. There would be nothing from Ikea. He'd have a favorite café. He'd walk everywhere. He'd meet his neighbors. Maybe he'd start dating one of them. Or maybe Laney would fly out, and this time, they'd do what they'd both wanted to do the first time around.

"Hey," Lil said. "What's eating you?"

"I just miss the city."

"That's your nostalgia face?" she asked, not buying it.

"I was thinking about Jon renting an apartment in the city."

She nodded. "Enough said."

As we pulled up to my house, I said, "I just wish I could hold on to a good mood longer."

"But it was fun while it lasted, right?"

I reached over and hugged her. "It was," I said, squeezing. "Thanks for everything."

"No problem. Now get in there and greet your monster-in-law."

I was laughing as I got out of the car, though there was nothing funny about seeing Sylvia. We'd had little contact over the past months, as Jon had been in charge of her time with the grandkids. My antipathy toward her had dimmed a bit because she'd done something completely unexpected: she'd shut up. No visits, calls, or even letters to tell me that I was ruining my family—her family — and when I called her the other day to suggest she watch Olivia during my day out, she didn't make a single judgmental statement. On the contrary, she seemed appreciative that I was giving her the opportunity for extra time with the grandkids. That morning, when she showed up at the house, she was more than civil, verging on pleasant.

Still, I was wary as I opened the front door. I followed the sound of Jacob's voice and the smell of unfamiliar cooking into the kitchen, telling myself to breathe, that she was on my turf.

You wouldn't know it, though, from the way she'd taken over the kitchen. She was standing at the range, spatula in hand, as Jacob sat at the kitchen table, action figures in front of him. Olivia was lying in her Moses basket on the chair next to Jacob, sleeping soundly.

"Mommy!" Jacob said, noticing me. He clambered down from his chair, and I was relieved that he seemed happy to see me. I hugged him extra long. Then I kissed the top of my fingers and placed them lightly on Olivia's head, wanting to have some contact with her, but not wanting to wake her up.

"Hello, Eve," Sylvia said, shooting a quick glance in my direction before opening the oven and peering inside. Then she added brightly, "We're having latkes. And kugel for dessert."

Give her an inch, she moves into your kitchen and makes a traditional Chanukah dinner. "We might be all out of ketchup," I said.

"Latkes are best with sour cream and applesauce. I

brought some." Sylvia beamed at Jacob. "How was your day, Eve? Jacob was just telling me about his."

"It was good."

"I've never been to a spa myself." Sylvia flipped the latkes carefully but expertly. "I thought we'd all have dinner together." She looked me full in the face with nervous expectation, and I suddenly got it. With Jon leaving the house, his position uncertain, hers was even more precarious. Maybe she thought I'd try to keep her from her grandchildren if she didn't turn us into family quickly. Ten years of being with her son, and she'd never wanted to be my family.

I didn't know I could still be hurt by Sylvia after all this time. "I'm not hungry," I said, getting to my feet before she could see the tears in my eyes. "Enjoy your dinner."

Once behind my closed bedroom door, I curled up in my bed, trying to block out the smell of the latkes. The phone rang, but I didn't answer it. After four rings, Tamara's excited voice filled the room.

"Eve, Eve, are you there? Oh, I was hoping you'd be there. I have some news. Some fantastic news. I'm getting married! Clayton did the greatest proposal. He got my last-period class in on it. All the girls were swooning. Call me as soon as you get this, I want to tell you all about it. Well, maybe not tonight, actually. We're going out to dinner to celebrate, but I had to call you first. It's just, like, holy shit! Now I have to plan a wedding. What do I know about planning a wedding? Okay, I'll stop going on now. Call me!"

It wasn't so long ago that nothing could have kept me from picking up the phone. It wasn't so long ago that

Tamara and I were like sisters, and that I had every reason to believe in marriage.

I didn't feel up to calling Tamara back, but I dove for the phone when I heard Charlie's voice through the machine. We'd barely said our hellos before I was blurting, "Jon and I are officially separated."

In the pause, I could picture Charlie's face, the different expressions passing over it before he settled on a response. "Is that good?" he finally asked.

"It doesn't feel good, but I think it's good."

"Huh. I never see things like that."

"I'm lonely, Charlie. You have no idea how bad it is."

"You miss Jon?"

"I don't miss how we are together now."

"But you miss him."

"I've had him with me for a long time."

"Half your life," Charlie said.

I couldn't help but laugh. "Where'd you learn to do math?"

"I never did cotton to your book learnin'," he said, in a put-on hick accent.

"So what about you? Have you gotten a job yet?"

"These things take time. You can't rush perfection."

"Oh, you've got big plans, have you?"

"I've decided not to make a move until I know it's the right one."

"So you're standing still," I said.

"Pretty much."

Then it came to me. "Since you were so good at the avuncular thing last time you were here, what do you think about doing it full-time? Just for a little while," I added quickly. "I'm headed back to work, and I looked at a few day cares, but none of them felt quite right, and it'd be so much better for Liv to be at home, with family." I was thinking of Jacob, too, how much he loved Charlie and how good it would be for him to have a man around more of the time.

"You want me to be your nanny?"

"I prefer the term 'uncle.' Listen," I said, warming to my own idea, "it'd be so good for me to have the company, and for Jacob, too. This is a better place than Mom's to figure out your next step, and just think of all the women who'd be attracted to a sensitive uncle like you."

"So you're saying I can date? I'd get my nights and weekends off?"

"I'll come right home from work every day. And you don't need to do any cooking or cleaning or anything."

"Gee, thanks."

"Come on," I wheedled. "It'll be fun. Liv's absurdly cute. We can just try it for a while, and if you don't like it, no harm done. I'll just get her set up in day care."

"I need to think about it."

"Since when?"

"Is this going to be one of those times when you're completely sure you're right, and you won't give up until you get what you want?" He was smiling, I know he was.

"What's your problem with this, Jon?" I said, cradling the phone between my chin and ear. Olivia was against the opposite shoulder. "We don't even have to pay him."

"That's not the point. He's never taken care of a newborn."

"She's three months old." I patted her back and she let out an obliging burp. "Good girl," I told her.

"That's still pretty newly born." I could hear him take a deep breath. "I thought we were going to look at day cares together."

"No. I was going to look at them first, and then when I'd narrowed it down, I'd tell you to go look at them."

"Are you planning to just cut me out of major decisions from here on out? I mean, I only made it into the delivery room by the barest of margins—"

"Hey," I said. "You can't do that. You can't just use that against me forever."

There was a tense pause on the line; then he said, "Sorry. You're right. That's a separate issue."

"Well, what's the issue here? Charlie's going to do a great job with Olivia. He's reading baby-development books, he's taking this really seriously. Frankly, I think this is going to be good for him. And the fact that he won't let me pay him is a godsend. I mean, we could really use that money for your apartment."

The conversation skidded to a halt. We'd avoided mentioning the apartment outright for the past few weeks. "I know we could use the money," Jon said. He sounded tired. "I just wish we'd had a conversation about this sooner. I mean, he's moving in tomorrow."

"He's not moving in, exactly. It's a trial arrangement. If it doesn't work out, he leaves and she goes into day care. I didn't think there was really a downside. You saw how he was with Jacob on the last visit. He's really taken to this child-rearing thing."

"I just feel a million miles away."

"Well, when are you moving back to the city? Did you find an apartment yet?" I asked, choosing to take him literally.

"That's not the kind of distance I was—" He stopped himself. "The funny thing is, I've been dragging my feet because I wanted you to come see the places with me, as if you're going to spend any time there. The whole point is for you not to spend time there."

"I'm sure Tamara or Clayton could give you a second opinion."

"I'm sure they could. Look, it's fine about Charlie. But in the future, if you're going to make any big plans for the kids, could you discuss it with me first?"

"Yes. I'm sorry I didn't tell you sooner."

"Okay. Good night."

"Good night."

In the ensuing moment of silence, I realized we were both waiting for the other to hang up first. It held a strange intimacy; then I heard the click.

"So this is how you treat guests," Charlie said, staring down at a crying, squirming, naked Olivia on the changing table.

"You're not a guest, you're family," I said. I proffered the box of baby wipes. "Now clean your hands with one of these."

"You mean you're not going to demo it first? You just want me to dive into the deep end of the pool like that?"

"It's not that bad. Really." I shook the box, and he tentatively reached for one. "Now you just need to grab her by the ankles and lift her up."

"Are you serious?"

"If you don't lift her up, how are you going to clean her off?" I gave him an encouraging smile. "Come on. Think how strong you'll feel, lifting her up with just one mighty hand."

"Should I use my left hand or my right?"

I considered. "Since you're left-handed, use your right."

He did as told.

"Now, with your left hand, fold the used diaper underneath her so we don't have to look at the crap anymore."

"Hallelujah," he said as he followed my instructions.

"Next, take another baby wipe and wipe her from front

to back. Always from front to back. Don't be shy, there's plenty. We want to get her really clean down there."

He eyed me. "What am I, a frigging au pair?"

"Uncle," I said with a laugh. "We call it being an uncle." I handed him a fresh diaper. Olivia was still dangling by her ankles, but she'd stopped crying and was instead looking up at Charlie with curiosity. "Swap out that dirty one for this, lay her back down, and fasten the tabs."

I watched the careful way he put on the new diaper, and how gently he set Olivia back down on the changing table. "Hello," he said in a soft—though still adult—voice. (Babyese was outlawed in my house.) "Look at you, all clean there."

I wanted to tell him I loved who he was becoming when he was around Jacob on the last visit, and now Olivia, but I thought it might sound condescending. Instead, I said, "Now just put the old diaper in this plastic bag, and then it goes in the trash. And she's all set."

"You're all set," he told Olivia, still just above a whisper. He smiled at her, and she smiled back. "She's smiling!" he announced to me.

Olivia wasn't quick to smile, and especially not with new people. Maybe that was why when she did, it felt so wondrous. Olivia's smiles were a sun shower. You felt you'd never seen anything so perfect; surely, never felt anything so perfect.

"It's one of the best parts of being her mom," I said. "And her uncle."

Charlie and I were still mirroring her smile when her face shifted into a familiar configuration. I laughed. She had timing, my kid. "Looks like you're going to get a chance to practice this again soon. See that face? That's her crapping face. You'll get used to it."

I'd thought I was ready to go back to work, but when I saw Charlie standing in the doorway with Olivia, his hand lifting hers in a wave, my eyes welled up. She'd survive without me, I knew that. Charlie would take great care of her. But no one could love her the precise way that I could, the way that I did.

With Jacob, I'd stayed home the whole first year. He'd gotten both of his parents, in one house, loving each other. But what about Liv?

On the drive to work, I thought about going to Melinda and asking her to extend my leave. She was a little younger than me, a type A workaholic who didn't have kids, didn't want any, but I suspected whether she understood it or not, she'd do it. If she resisted, Dyan would convince her for me.

I wasn't sure if that really was the best thing for me or for Liv, but knowing it was possible soothed me. My eyes were dry as I pushed open the Student Services door and saw a WELCOME BACK banner taped to the wall behind Chad's desk. Dyan, Melinda, and Chad were in a conversation that stopped abruptly as they noticed me. "Surprise!" they shouted, with even more vigor for having been a few beats late.

"Thanks, guys," I said, going to hug each of them in turn. They were so sweetly, entirely predictable. I knew they'd do something to celebrate my return. I'd call Charlie to check on Olivia just as soon as I got in my office, but for now, I was glad to be there in the company of adults.

"How great does she look?" Dyan asked the group. "Three months after giving birth!" While Chad and Melinda had no choice but to nod in agreement, Dyan really believed there was nothing wrong with some "extra junk in the trunk," as she put it; after all, she carried her own. She liked to cite studies about the difference in body image between African-American teenagers and white teenagers—the former being much more comfortable with their bodies no matter what the size—not to mention the statistics on how much more prevalent eating disorders were in the white population. At fifty, married since she was twenty, Dyan was fully comfortable in her skin.

There was a brief discussion about whether there should be singing. Dyan was for it, Melinda was preoccupied with what song would fit the occasion, Chad was willing to go along with whatever decision was made, and finally I took a stand against singing and for immediate eating. It was nine in the morning, and chocolate cake couldn't have sounded better.

I wasn't going to lose the pregnancy weight anytime soon with the way I was going: late-night ice-cream binges that I persisted in calling snacks and round-the-clock snacks that I was calling bites. The funny thing about my doublespeak was that it was occurring exclusively in my own head—no one was asking me to justify my eating. Charlie had always had a sweet tooth and a high metabolism and he wasn't keeping an eye on my waistline. Last night, while watching a movie, we each ate through an entire bowl of peanut butter drizzled with hot fudge sauce, and it was just like the childhood I was denying Jacob.

But Dyan was right about white girls and their weight, or at least this white girl and her weight. Most of my life, I'd been thin and self-critical. My eyes had always gone right to my flaws. When I wore a tank top, I noticed the loose flesh just outside my armpit that pushed against my bra straps, the slight saddlebagging of my thighs, or the fact that my belly wasn't an entirely flat plane. I spent much of my life hiding behind oversized clothes. I remember when Jon first took off my shirt, I averted my eyes and he said, softly and with evident pleasure, "So that's what's under there." Gradually, as the years passed and I saw myself more through Jon's eyes, my clothes started to fit.

After I had Jacob, I went from my lifelong size 6 to between an 8 and 10. My mother sent me magazine clippings with various cockamamie diets. Jonathon hated those clippings. He thought I should just accept the weight gain as a sign of what my body could do: "You pushed out a person! What are a few pounds compared to that?" I figured I'd just try a few more diets, and if they failed, then I'd work on acceptance. It was while I was on the cabbage diet—cabbage soup for breakfast, lunch, and dinner—that I snapped. I was having mood swings, and one night, I woke up at three AM practically in tears. I'd purged the house of all junk food a week before, and now all I wanted was Twinkies. No, I wanted Twinkies, Ho Hos, ice cream, maple syrup, doughnuts, and a big bowl of Apple Jacks. At first, Jon thought I was being hyperbolic, but I truly wanted all of those things, as passionately as I imagine some women want babies.

Jon didn't want me leaving the house in that state of delirium, so I wrote out a list and he trudged out into the night. When he came back, we laid everything out on the table. He had a doughnut, and I had everything else. I remember that as I binged, Jon just sat there and smiled at me. There I was, sometimes doing a two-fisted stuffing into my mouth, powdered sugar on my chin and on my nightgown, and he was smiling at me. He told me later that I seemed so joyful—there was such relief and pleasure in my every gesture—that I struck him as tremendously beautiful. He said there wasn't a trace of self-consciousness about me, and it was something I wouldn't have shown anyone else in the world.

Between that ice pick of a memory and being away from Olivia, I knew this was going to be one long day.

After the party ended, I kept my door closed, not sure I was fit for human interaction. At two-thirty, Dyan knocked and pushed it open, a wide smile on her face. "Can I sit with you awhile?" she asked.

"Sure," I said.

She sat across from me in the ugly gray armchair that looked like it was upholstered with cast-off felt from a children's art class. "You've been cooped up in here all day. What's that about?"

Only Dyan could jump in like that and seem inviting rather than meddling. The kids loved her. They used up boxes of Kleenex every week talking to her. I didn't have any Kleenex on my desk, so I considered my answer carefully. "Just catching up on all the work I missed."

"With your door closed?"

"I wanted to stay focused."

At that, she actually snorted. "Eve, let's be straight with each other. If you don't want to talk about it, tell me that. But don't sit here spinning silliness."

I looked up at her with a rueful smile. "I don't know if I want to talk about it. I feel like I've already tried that. A lot."

"Well, you haven't tried talking to me. I'm a trained professional. Really, I've got the moves and everything." She shifted her position in the chair so that she was leaning forward just slightly, her eyes limpid and subtly inquiring.

I laughed at first, like it was a party trick. But as she held there, her gaze unwavering, I realized it was working. I wanted to tell her everything.

I started out somewhere expected (missing Liv, but thinking she could use a break from all my fears and anxieties), but was surprised by what surfaced over the next hour, with me talking nearly continuously and Dyan saying so little. As I told her about Jon's affair, how he almost missed the birth, my failed attempt to look past everything, and now the official separation, she made noises of empathy, but I couldn't tell what she really thought about it all. I realized how attuned I'd become to other people's signals of late, how I subconsciously tried to give them the version of my life that would be most palatable. Talking to Dyan was freeing, so much so that it let me get beyond Jon to me.

I found myself saying how I'd never really built a career, that I'd been feeling around for one when I got pregnant with Jacob (in what was a happy accident, I assured Dyan, who didn't seem to need the assurance). Then somehow—I certainly didn't know how—I'd become one of those people who seemed to equate kids with a sense of purpose. I'd tried to pretend motherhood was enough, and it wasn't. It wasn't just that I didn't have Jonathon, that I might never have him again, but I didn't have me. I'd never even expected to be a mother—how could I have expected it to be enough once I was? I'd never meant to have this life, not even a part of it. Laney might have fit this life—hell, Laney might have truly loved it, but I'd never—

Dyan leaned in with an intensity that startled me, interrupting me with her eyes, and in the silence that followed, she said, *"This is your life.* Now, what are you going to do with it?"

Just then, I knew what she wanted from me. She wanted me to sit up straighter and own this life of mine. But I couldn't. I shrank back in the chair.

I thought I could feel her disappointment, but she only said, "There's time." Then a second later, "Just don't take so much time answering that you forget the question."

CHAPTER
16

It was the night of Tamara and Clayton's engagement party, which made it precisely the wrong time to look like shit. It was the first social event Jon and I were both attending since the separation. I was already nervous to face Clayton, whom I hadn't seen in months (since Thanksgiving, to be exact). I could tell that Tamara thought I hadn't squealed enough in excitement over her engagement announcement, while I felt the octave I raised my voice should have sufficed, given my own circumstances. I thought of explaining that it wasn't her and Clayton I was dubious about, but marriage itself, and decided against it. It seemed like there was so much she and I couldn't say to each other anymore. Our silences were more meaningful than our words these days.

Charlie was in support of me biting the bullet and facing the music, since now was as good a time as any—in other words, he had a whole host of clichés that meant seeing Jon would suck, but was inevitable. I didn't think my friendship with Tamara could survive my skipping this party, so I had to agree with him. Fortunately, he'd offered to go with me. It wasn't entirely selfless, since he loved parties and recreational drinking and I was the one driving.

Half my wardrobe was piled on my bed, and I was trying to convince myself that a strategically placed scarf could cure all ills. *Laney wouldn't need a scarf,* I found myself thinking. Her name still ran through my head in all sorts of contexts: *Laney probably has a career she likes. Laney's stomach isn't convex. If Jon and I never get back together, women like Laney are going to be my competition.*

I was slumped on the bed in my bra and panties when I heard the doorbell. It had to be Lil. She'd agreed to watch Jacob and Olivia, though mostly it would just be Olivia because Luke and Jacob would keep each other entertained. They'd been looking forward to their Saturday-night play date all week. I could hear the two of them tearing through the house, and I waited for Lil's knock on my door. Finally I pulled on a robe and went down the hall.

Charlie and Lil were in the living room, talking animatedly at closer proximity than seemed customary. When they noticed me, Charlie said, "Hey, shouldn't you be dressed by now?"

"Sorry I was late," Lil said. She leaned in and gave me a hug. "I thought you'd have been ready for a while."

"I've been trying for a while." I didn't like the whiny quality in my voice. Something about their shared good spirits rattled me.

"Do you want some help?" Lil asked.

I glanced at Charlie, who was watching Lil. His attraction to her was obvious. "Some help would be great," I said.

"Well, you girls do your thing," Charlie said. Then he reddened. Lil was making him nervous, and when he was nervous, he got corny.

She didn't seem to notice, and we went back to my bedroom. Once inside with the door shut, she started sifting through the clothes on my bed. Fingering a flutter-sleeved blouse, she asked casually, "Would you mind if I fucked him?"

I stared at her, floored. Oblivious, she continued to paw.

She held up a silky top for inspection. "Maybe this?" she asked.

"Are you serious about my brother?"

"No, I wouldn't be serious about him at all. It would be entirely unserious. He doesn't even live here permanently. That's where you get the best stuff."

"Ew! I can't even think about my brother having sex."

"But he does, right? I mean, there's no way that guy's a virgin." She extended the shirt toward me. "Try that on, okay?"

"I already tried it."

"It seems like it'd look good with your skin tone."

"My blotchy skin, you mean." I looked at myself in the mirror above the bureau, more despondent by the second.

"I'm great with makeup. When's the last time someone did your makeup?"

I thought about it. "My wedding."

"I could really make your eyes pop." She stood behind me and smiled at my reflection in the mirror.

I tried to smile back. I wished I didn't feel so disturbed by the thought of her and Charlie, especially since there was no way I could stop it. He was a grown man. If he wanted to be with Lil, it wasn't really my business. But I was glad when she didn't press me again.

The party would have been Jacob's dream: Up on the roof, lit by candles, surrounded by thousands of bubbles. And people. Jacob loved to be surrounded by people. He already had a well-developed group persona, a willingness to let his voice carry to a crowd, and an innate ability to feed on their appreciation and go one step further. I once asked my mother if I was that way when I was a kid and I'd lost it, or I'd just never had it. She said she didn't know, we didn't spend much time around groups. I thought her answer explained it all.

But somehow, Charlie had it. You know, *it*. Charisma: a way to instantly and unselfconsciously generate goodwill even in places that, at a glance, you'd say he didn't belong. He was the one who greeted Tamara and Clayton first, beaming at them both, thrusting out a hand to Clayton and saying, "You must be the lucky guy."

Tamara looked radiant in the most literal sense, as if she were lit from within. She wore a filmy blue dress that brought out her eyes, and her blond hair was in a carelessly careful upsweep. Clayton had a look that could only be described as satisfied, like he'd found his place in the world. Standing there—a beer in his hand, a cocktail glass in hers—it seemed like they both had. If you could flash forward ten years and they still looked that way, no matter what the world had brought me, I'd have no choice but to believe again in marriage.

"I'm so glad you're here!" Tamara said.

"Me too." I hugged them both, one after the other. "Congratulations!"

"Thanks," Tamara said into my hair; I could smell the purple orchid that was in hers.

"Jacob inspired the bubbles," Clayton said. "When we were planning the party, we happened to notice he'd left some of that bubble stuff behind." He and Tamara exchanged a smile, as if remembering, *What an enchanted moment that was.*

"There's something pretty cool about a bunch of adults standing on a roof blowing bubbles," Charlie said. "I don't know which I want to get my hands on first, a bubble blower or a drink. Which one's in shorter supply?"

We all laughed. "I think there's plenty of everything to go around," Tamara said.

We stood surveying the party. The act of blowing bubbles had everyone feeling loose and uninhibited, and there was something magical about watching the bubbles fly off into the night, as if we'd all been a part of their liberation.

"It's a great party," I said.

"You have to say that." Tamara was smiling like she knew it was true.

"Are any of your students here?" I asked.

"I thought about it. But I figured if I invited one, I'd have to invite them all."

"Mmm, coeds," Charlie said, in the way Homer Simpson would talk about doughnuts. I swatted at him, but everyone laughed. I thought how Charlie and Lil really did have a lot in common, chiefly that they could get away with saying things that from anyone else would draw an offended silence, or worse.

"So you're back at work now, right?" It was the first thing Clayton addressed entirely to me, and I couldn't help noticing the forced warmth in it.

"I've been back a few weeks now."

"How's that going?" He was terrible at feigning interest, but there was something sweet about the attempt.

"It's going..." I hesitated, then said, "Boringly. It's just a boring job, let's face it."

The shared laughter felt good. It felt like the old days, with Charlie acting as a stand-in for Jon.

As if on cue, Jon appeared at my elbow. "Hey, guys," he said. He was holding a glass with what looked like whiskey in it, and he looped his other arm around Clayton, doing a manly, sideways squeeze. Then he pecked Tamara on the cheek. "You look beautiful," he told her.

"Thanks." She shot a quick glance my way. I could feel that my cheeks were hot.

"Hi, Charlie. Eve." Jon bobbed his head at us in turn, flashing a smile. "Great party."

"What do you do for an opening line when you're at a lousy party?" Charlie asked, trying to smooth over the obvious discomfort. "The kind of party where no one's talking, and some girl's crying in the bathroom because her boyfriend's an asshole, and there's vomit on the floor. What's your opening line then?"

"That's when I always break out the bubbles," Clayton said. We all smiled at his effort.

"Bubbles are the new monkey," Jon added. We looked at him quizzically. "You know that old saying, 'everything's funnier when there's a monkey'?"

"Must be before my time, man," Charlie said. His delivery was affable enough, but there was something undeniably stinging in the remark. Before Olivia was born, Charlie had been pulling for a reconciliation, but I'd noticed that since he'd been living at the house, he seemed more in favor of me moving on. I wasn't sure why he'd changed, and he never said anything explicitly. Usually I could read it in his body language and in the expression that crossed his face when Jon's name was mentioned. I hadn't expected him to make such an overt dig.

The awkward silence was broken when a couple came to greet Tamara and Clayton. I realized that the vast majority of attendees were coupled. There were larger groups, but they were just couples coming together. The principal unit of the party was definitely a dyad.

Ignoring Jon, Charlie said to me, "We could go meet some people."

Jon was looking around, trying to seem casual, but I could see the tension in his jaw and neck. Somehow I felt like I should rescue him. I at least had Charlie to take the edge off; Jon had no one.

"How are you, Jon?" I said.

He turned to me gratefully. "I wish I knew."

I smiled. "I know the feeling."

"It's funny, all the things I wish I could tell you and then you're here and I've got nothing."

"You could just start somewhere, and see where it goes." I didn't know what I wanted to happen, just that I wanted him to keep talking.

"Why don't we start with how great you look tonight." His eyes lingered on my face, and I had to look away. "Really great."

"Thanks."

"Can I tell you the truth? It feels ridiculous to stand here with you and tell you anything else." When I nodded, he continued. "I've never felt this heavy in my life. It's hard to walk sometimes, I'm so heavy."

I'd forgotten Charlie was even there—he'd been trying to give us privacy, I guess, by looking around at the party and pretending not to listen—but he suddenly broke in angrily, glaring at Jon. "What are you doing?" he demanded. "Trying to make her feel guilty?"

"Charlie," I said, "that's not how he meant it."

"How'd you mean it, Jon?" There was no mistaking the challenge in his tone.

Jon shook his head, suddenly exhausted. "I'm walking away. Okay? Have a good night, Eve."

"What was that all about?" I asked Charlie. I was watching Jon retreat.

"He bugs me, the way he was looking all hangdog. He made his bed, Eve."

"What's with you and the clichés tonight?"

He grinned. "Right now, I've got bigger fish to fry than you and your ex. Where's the bar?"

                    *   *   *

I wanted to put in an appearance and go home, but I'd
promised Charlie a night out and I could see how much
he loved being there. He came alive among people who'd
never heard his stories; his discomfort was in being
known too well. I was the opposite. Being truly known
seemed like the point of everything.

I pretty much hitched my wagon to Charlie and relied
on him to steer. He was a dynamo, moving from couple
to couple and group to group with a simple, "Hey, can I
cut in?" He was egalitarian, spending no more time with
the few single women than with the obviously attached.
It was connection he craved, but the fleeting kind. He
was good at making people feel listened to in a minimal amount of time; if you asked them later whether he
had a short attention span, they would most likely have
answered no. But I could see it. I could see the moment
he was done with them and thinking only of a grace-
ful escape. Between conversations, he'd ask me if I was
okay, if I needed to go home, and I said no, I didn't need
to. I figured this night was the least I could do for him.

But it was hard being on the same roof as Jon. I was
terribly conscious of where he was and whom he was
talking to. At one point, we were standing in the same
general area, talking to different people, and I was eager
for the gaps in my conversation that would allow me to
catch some of his. I had the feeling he was acutely aware
of me, too, and while that's a sexy feeling when you first
meet someone, it's just depressing after a marriage and

two kids. I thought of approaching him, but I wasn't sure what to say. I just wanted him to have the chance that Charlie had taken away earlier, the chance to start talking and see where it went. But I figured that if he wanted that, too, he'd be brave enough to come back over. He wasn't.

The irony was, Jon and I had so much in common at the party that night. Neither of us was sure exactly what people knew. It was clear that some already knew about the separation, but how many knew the reason? And if they knew the reason, whose side were they on? Was I an overreacting, heartless bitch, or was Jon a lout? The threat of shame hung over every conversation. I was sure Jon felt it, too. I could see it in the sheepish expression he frequently wore.

When I wasn't watching Jon or Charlie, I was watching Tamara. Sometimes I watched her watch Clayton. It was transfixing, the love they clearly felt for each other. I realized they hadn't looked that way at Thanksgiving. Being engaged seemed to have unleashed something inside them, and between them. Maybe it was that now when they looked at each other, they let themselves say "forever." I remembered what it felt like to let go of everything that's previously held you back, the abandon of saying, "The hell with self-protection, this is love!" I wanted to tell her to save some of it, someday she might need it. But on a night like this, she'd be crazy to listen.

CHAPTER
17

It wasn't entirely unexpected when Jon called later that week to ask me out on a date. You know someone long enough, you get a sense about these things. Of course, these were strange times, but just by the law of averages, my instinct had to be right eventually.

My optimism was so cautious that it verged on the superstitious. As I got ready on Sunday, sorting through necklaces and earrings, I noticed my wedding ring in the jewelry box. I felt its weight in my palm for just a second before laying it back down on the plum velvet. Removing a pair of teardrop earrings, I closed the box.

I went down the hall to Olivia's nursery. She was napping, but she stretched and let out a little cry when I approached. I kissed my fingertips and laid them on the top of her head as she settled back into sleep. Her hair was light brown, just as Jon had predicted. It was too thin and wispy for curls, though.

She'd been blossoming under Charlie's care. While she was still more watchful than Jacob had been, she'd begun to smile and laugh with much greater ease. Sometimes I was jealous that Charlie was such a natural—why hadn't she been so lit up when I was with her all day long? — but mostly, I was grateful. Jacob, too, seemed much happier now that Charlie was here. I'd done that much right.

I glanced at the clock. Charlie should have been home by now. Actually, he should have been home way before.

His first "date" with Lil had been the night before. She'd invited him over for a late dinner, after Luke was in bed. I'd assumed he'd come home late last night, or first thing this morning, but I hadn't seen or heard from him. He knew about my date with Jon, and that he was supposed to be watching Jacob and Olivia. I tried to quell my annoyance as I dialed his cell phone.

He answered on the fifth ring, just when I feared I was going into voice mail. I could hear a child's laughter in the background. I stifled my surprise. Lil didn't usually let her men spend time with Luke. Maybe she'd made an exception, since Charlie already knew Luke through Jacob.

"Hi, Charlie," I said, carefully keeping my tone light. "It sounds like you guys are having a good time."

"We're not just having a good time. We're having an excellent time," he boomed. "Aren't we, Luke?"

I cringed a little at his seeming desperation. "Are you in the car?" *Headed home,* I added silently.

"No, we're at the zoo. We are, more specifically, at the — Hey, Luke, where are we? What's that animal right there?" He paused, and I could hear Luke saying something. "That is absolutely right. We're looking at meerkats. Alert little sons of bi —" He stopped himself, then laughed heartily, apparently at something Luke had said.

"You were supposed to be home by now. Jon and Jacob are on their way here."

"We must have lost track of time."

"Well, can you leave now?"

He lowered his voice. "I'm kind of in the middle of something."

"Charlie, you were supposed to be back by five."

"So I'll be late." He said it louder, defiantly.

"You're already late."

"Then I'll be later."

"Don't be an asshole. I'm just asking you to do what you already agreed to."

"And I'm asking you to cut me some slack. How many favors have I done for you lately?"

I tried to control my temper. "You've done a lot for me. And I appreciate all of it. But this is a pretty special night for me. So I'm asking you to please honor your commitment."

He dropped in volume as he said, "This is a pretty special day for me, too."

In some ways, he was just a kid, aching to impress a girl. Anger was replaced by resignation. "Well, how much longer do you need?" I asked.

"Thanks, Eve." He paused. "How about if I leave here in a half hour?"

"Okay. But a half hour really means a half hour. That's a half hour in Eve time, not Charlie time."

He laughed. "A half hour is sixty minutes, right?"

"Don't fuck with me. You'd better be out of there in thirty."

"You got it. And look, I'm sorry. One of these years, I'm going to get that whole time management thing down."

"See you soon," I said, hanging up.

Ten minutes later, Jon and Jacob arrived. "Mommy!" Jacob threw himself at me, hugging me with an over-the-top enthusiasm I hadn't felt in a while.

"Well, hello there!" I laughed, then looked up and met Jon's eyes. He was smiling. "Hi," I said to him.

"Hey," he said. "Jacob, are you forgetting what's in the backpack?"

Jacob released me and opened his backpack excitedly. He produced a bouquet of bright yellow daffodils.

"Jake and I discussed it, and we decided that the point of flowers is to make people happy. And of all the flowers we saw, he was convinced that daffodils would make you the happiest."

I took the bouquet, moved into silence.

"Because they're like the sun," Jacob said. "And when you're happy, you feel warm."

"That is very good thinking. I love them." I looked back up at Jon. "Really, I love them." I stepped back from the doorway. "Come on in. We've got a vase somewhere."

Jon and Jacob followed me into the kitchen. Jacob was chattering away. I had to tell him to be a little quieter because Liv was sleeping, and he complied for just a few seconds before his voice rose again. I realized how long it had been since he'd been able to talk to Jon and me at the same time. ". . . and we went to this museum, I forget how to say it. How do you say it, Daddy?"

"The Exploratorium," Jon supplied.

"The Explor-a-tor-i-um," Jacob drawled in an effort to commit each syllable to memory.

I bustled around the kitchen, checking the cabinets. "And what did you see there, Jake?"

"We heard a lot. Did you know you can't listen and talk at once?"

"That sounds like a good rule of thumb," I said, finally seeing the vase way up high in a seldom-used cabinet.

"It was an exhibit on hearing," Jon said. "Do you want me to get that for you?"

"That'd be great," I said. "Now I just need to remember where the scissors are."

"Why do you need scissors?" Jacob asked.

"To cut the stems off the bottom of the flowers."

"Why?"

"Oh, no, we're back to that phase again!" Jon joked. He'd put the vase on the counter and now he sat down in a chair and pulled Jacob toward him. "Do you remember that, Jacob? When you used to ask 'why' all the time, but you didn't really want to know why?"

"No. Why would I do that?"

Jon started to tickle Jacob, and Jacob collapsed against him, giggling. The ease between the three of us almost felt like before Laney had entered our lives. All these months later, and I could barely make it five minutes before her name recurred. I turned away, and started looking through the drawers for the scissors.

"I bet they're in that drawer with all the coupons and delivery menus," Jon said. "Underneath."

He was right. As I cut the stems, filled the vase with

water, and arranged the flowers, I explained that Charlie was running late. "Is that okay for the surprise?" I asked. "Can we get there later?"

Jacob looked from Jon to me and back again. "You're doing a surprise for Mommy?" he asked.

"We're going somewhere, and Mommy doesn't know where just yet."

"I'm not going?" Jacob said.

"No, it's just for Mommy and me," Jon said.

"Is it something I'd like?"

"I don't know. But I'm hoping Mommy will like it."

Realizing we needed to divert Jacob before he got upset about what he'd be missing, I said, "So, Jacob, why don't you pick something we can all do together for a while? Any game you want."

"We'll all play?" he asked, breaking out into a big smile.

I looked at Jon, who said, "All three of us."

Jacob charged out of the room, and Jon and I laughed at his energy. I sat at the table across from Jon, leaving the seat between us for Jacob. It was our most common configuration during Liv's first few months, like there was a force field between us.

"So you think I'll like the surprise?"

"Like I said, I'm hoping. There's nothing sexier than a man with hope. I hope."

I laughed as Jacob returned and plopped down between us. He put a boxed puzzle on the table. "It's going to be Spider-Man," he said. "And it's going to glow in the dark."

"We won't have time to finish it," I said. "But we can get started, and then maybe Uncle Charlie can take over."

"Uncle Charlie sucks at puzzles."

Jon and I both tried not to laugh, and I said, "That's not a very nice thing to say."

"But he said it first."

Jon and I let ourselves laugh then. By the time Charlie walked in, we had the perimeter about half-completed. He groaned. "Not a puzzle."

"Hey, when you're home on time, you get to pick the activity," I said.

"Yeah, yeah," Charlie said. He turned to Jon. "Hey, man, how's it going?"

"We've got the corners," Jon said, smiling. They were both trying, but there was residual tension from their exchange at the party.

"Well, we should go," I said. I stood up and ruffled Jacob's hair. "You take it easy on Uncle Charlie."

Jacob looked over at Jon. "Do you have to go? Both of you?"

"Don't you remember? I'm surprising your mom. If I don't go, how will she get there?"

"When are you coming back?" he asked Jon.

"You've got the calendar, buddy. You can look at it with Charlie." I could practically see the lump in Jon's throat. "Okay, give me a hug."

They hugged, and then Jon followed me toward the front door. "Could you just give me a minute so I can look in on Liv?" he asked.

"Of course."

I got my jacket from the front closet and waited by the door until he came back down the hall. Then, as the door closed behind us, Jon said, almost more to himself than to me, "I just can't look back. Every time, I know that if I look back, I'm going to lose it." He walked straight to the car, where he unlocked the passenger side for me.

Once we were both inside, I saw he was taking deep breaths. "Are you okay?" I asked.

He tried to smile, but succeeded only in looking more pained. "It just gets me, you know. No offense to your brother, but you don't know what it's like having to leave my kids there with another man raising them, having Liv respond more to Charlie's voice than mine."

"It's not permanent."

"Sometimes it feels like a preview. You know, if I can't make this work" — he gestured between us — "eventually there'll be another man raising my kids."

I didn't know what to say, and he started the car. "So where are we going? Maybe just one hint?" I said with forced brightness.

Jon tried to play along. "How about — it's something living?"

"Something living," I mused.

He gave me more clues and I continued guessing, and the time passed pleasantly enough. Finally we arrived in the Richmond neighborhood of San Francisco, sometimes called New Chinatown. The streets were packed, signs were multilingual, and the air smelled like a fish market.

"I give up," I said. "Where are we going?"

He smiled and said, "Follow me."

I did, and soon we were standing in front of what, on the outside, looked like just another market. But I read the sign (in English), and it was an aquarium.

"There's that wall in the bedroom that would be perfect for a tank," Jon said. "I thought maybe we could find some circling fish. You could give them names. I remember it always bothered you that those fish died without names."

I looked at him sideways for a long moment; then I started to smile. He grinned back.

"Let's go inside and see what they've got," he said. "It said on the Web site that they've got twenty thousand gallons of water in there, whatever that looks like."

The aquarium was narrow, but extended much farther than you would have guessed from the outside. There was a strange blue cast to the light. It was slightly lurid, like we were on the set of a low-budget horror film. Closest to the door were shelves with clear plastic cups, each containing one fish.

"I wonder why they're in cups like that, instead of the tanks." I leaned in for a better look.

"Maybe they're fighting fish," Jon said, "and they can't be kept together. Or maybe they're just the ones that sell the fastest." The sign above informed us they were $2.99.

"This one's pretty." I pointed to a sleek purple fish, and he darted away violently enough to shake the cup. "A little skittish, though."

We walked along the side of the store slowly, gazing in

at the tanks that were embedded in the walls, like *Hollywood Squares*. "These are cool," I said, pointing at a tank full of black fish that each had about three white spots apiece. "They're sort of elegant, like Audrey Hepburn, if she were a fish."

"They're a little high society for me," he said. "But hey, they're your fish."

I peered into the various tanks. One was filled with "Upside-Down Cats": fish that were swimming with their fins on top, eyes on the bottom.

"Those are some confused fish," Jon said. "Ever felt like that?"

I laughed. "Never."

"Me either."

Jon was trying out tricks on the fish, and his favorite was to close his fist, move it close to the tank, and then open his palm suddenly. The more nervous fish immediately scattered to the back. We noticed that the Bala sharks (in three different tanks for small, medium, and large) ran away according to size, with the largest holding their ground.

I spied a tank of small red lobsters. Not much bigger than clams, I didn't realize the red would look like caviar attached to an otherwise ordinary lobster.

"It's like someone went crazy with the BeDazzler! Beads, sequins, you can do it all from home," I intoned like a commercial announcer.

Jon laughed, then seized upon the green spotted puffers, fish that appeared to be wearing green leopard coats. "PETA would throw paint on these guys."

Meanwhile, I'd fixed on the balloon molly fish. They were tiny, half the size of my thumb, and some were gold, some black, and some iridescent, with diaphanous dorsal fins. They all seemed friendly, hovering at the very front of the tank, their goggle eyes seemingly trained on me. They waggled their bodies rapidly while their mouths hung open, like a gossipy sewing circle.

"They seem sort of taken with themselves," Jon commented. "Like a bunch of fat bankers."

"I guess that's what's cool about fish. You can project all sorts of stuff on them."

We continued to move down the row of tanks in a leisurely way, commenting on fish with funny names (like the bubble gum cichlids, in lime, lemon, and orange) or interesting behaviors (the blue torpedo sharks that were nosing their way slowly up and down the sides of the tank as if blind). Lost in the activity, we relaxed with one another. Now, this, I'd missed.

But we didn't see any fish acting as the circling fish had; we didn't see any plain silver fish at all, in fact. In the back were large, freestanding tanks. There was one filled with the showstoppers: clown fish, butterfly fish, and angelfish, darting here and there, in electric colors (orange, purple, yellow) with distinctive patterns (stripes, polka dots, zebra). They never paused in their swimming to regard us.

"These must be the popular kids in school," Jon said.

"Yeah, they don't seem to care that we're here."

"So I guess the question is, are you picking your fish for beauty or love?" When I didn't answer immediately, he added, "If I had to guess, I'd say you're in it for love. I'd say you're going to bypass these guys."

He was right, but I didn't answer immediately. It was a charged moment, which he broke by moving toward the next tank. I felt how much I wanted to stay close to him in that second, so I joined him, and there we stood in horrified, paralyzed fascination. Inside were the XL clown trigger, Miniata grouper, and Mappa puffer. There was something terribly engorged about them, as if the smaller fish they used to be were inside wanting to get out. They were like fish wearing fat suits, and all three of them were pop-eyed and yearning. The Mappa puffer was a bloated creature, black-and-white flecked, with a great yawning mouth. The Miniata grouper was a pale salmon and white, with what looked like four grotesque incisors that he exposed constantly. And the clown trigger was the pièce de résistance: mostly black, a mishmash of stripes, dots, and leopard, with a mouth that was ringed in bright yellow and then further outlined with white. But the minute they saw us, they all rushed forward (in so far as they could rush, given their girth), mouths opening and closing like Beaker's from the Muppets. We moved, they moved. There was no mistaking it: they were into us.

"With these fish, it's all about the personality," Jon said.

"Definitely." I finally turned away from their imploring faces. Do fish have faces? Maybe I wasn't ready to be a fish owner.

After a cursory examination of the entire wall of goldfish, various in their shapes, sizes, and colors, Jon said, "We've been through the whole place. Are there any you really want to take home?"

"No, I guess not." I felt disappointed. I'd wanted to fall in love.

"We didn't see the circle fish. Maybe they can special order them or something. Do you want me to ask?"

"This was a nice idea," I said, reaching out and putting my hand on Jon's arm. "It's okay if we don't actually get fish."

He looked down at my hand, then into my eyes. "I want you to have them."

"I guess there's no harm in asking, then."

He flagged down one of the workers, a young Asian guy with a blocky build and a flattop haircut. "Hey. What do you need?" he asked, bored but not unfriendly.

"We're looking for these fish we used to know," Jon started. "We don't know what kind of fish they were. They were sort of long and thin and silver, or maybe gray, and they just circled each other all day long." Jon glanced at me. "Did I get that right?"

I nodded, loving the "we" and that he'd remembered the details so many years later. It felt like confirmation of something.

"Huh," the guy said. "You're saying they *circled* each other?"

"One would sort of hang there in the water," I said, holding one hand straight out like a shelf, "and then the other would circle." I rotated my other hand around.

He laughed. "Weird. I don't know any fish that do that. Unless they're dying."

"But they did it for months. Could they be dying for months?" I asked.

"Well, either that or mating."

"For months?" Jon said.

"Like I said, I've never heard of it." He shrugged. "You looking for anything else?"

Jon turned to me. I shook my head no. "Thanks for your help," Jon said.

I felt deflated. It was like I'd started to believe that if we found the fish, it would be a sign.

Sensing my mood shift, Jon said, "We can try another aquarium. I mean, we know those fish exist. How old was that guy? Twenty-two? We'll find some old guy with whiskers and a T-shirt that says 'Fish are my life,' and he'll know."

Before I could stop myself, I'd leaned in and kissed him. It took a second for his surprised eyes to close, but it was the first legitimate kiss we'd shared in months.

I backed away, and he said, "Did you really just do that?"

I gave a shaky laugh. "I think so."

"I knew it! All the girls melt for aquariums." We both laughed. He took my hand. "You want to go get some dinner? Now that I'm here, it seems sort of evil, but I'd planned to take you to this really good seafood restaurant with an ocean view. We can go somewhere else, if you want."

"Maybe I'm evil, too, but that sounds really good."

We started reminiscing during the ride to the restaurant, and once we were seated at a table overlooking the water, the conversation was smooth as rails. We shared a bottle of wine, and I felt myself giving way to him. I could practically see my love for him resurrecting, taking on color and dimension right there in front of me.

I wasn't used to much alcohol anymore, and maybe Jon wasn't, either. As we were sharing a chocolate torte with raspberries, gazing into each other's eyes, and I was thinking how long it had been since I'd had sex and how that might soon be changing, I found myself saying just what I meant: "Tell me you never loved her."

Jon froze, with his fork halfway to his mouth.

"If you never loved her, I want you to come home with me tonight."

He looked down at the table.

"I really need an answer."

"It's not that simple."

"Oh, my God. I think I might be sick." I leaned my forehead against the heel of my hand.

"Eve, please. Don't do this tonight. Not tonight. I love you. Do you hear me? I love you."

"But you love her, too." When he didn't say anything, I could taste my shrimp scampi. "At least therapy's made you honest. You wouldn't admit that before."

"It's a different kind of love that I feel for Laney. Felt for Laney," he corrected himself.

"How is it different?"

"You're my wife."

"I think you only love me because you have to, because I'm the mother of your children. I think that if everything else was equal, you would be with Laney."

"That's not true."

"Do you love me like you used to, Jon? Like when we first met?" I hated how desperate I sounded.

"You don't love me like you did when we first met."

"No, I love you more. Do you love me more than you used to?"

He was starting to sweat, never a good sign. "I love you differently, but just as much."

It felt like the equivalent of saying, *I don't like you, but I'll always love you.* "How's it different?"

"A lot's happened. It's been a long time."

"Yeah, Laney happened."

"I never slept with her. She wanted to, and I didn't do it. Why doesn't that count for anything?" he said, frustration rising. "I could have had an affair and I didn't. But that doesn't seem to matter to you."

"You did have an affair. And you just admitted you don't love me like you used to. Why, Jon? Why don't you love me like you used to?"

He slammed his hand down on the table in an uncharacteristic display of anger, and I jumped along with the silverware. Until then, we'd kept our voices low so the surrounding tables would have known something was wrong only if they'd really paid attention. Now people glanced over, but Jon didn't seem to notice. "It's because of scenes like this, Eve. Okay? You want to know why I don't love you like I used to? It's because you put me through shit like this. We were having a great night, and I was enjoying you, and I wanted to take you home and make love to you, but you had to ruin it."

I realized I was crying, I didn't know when I'd started. "I want to go home now."

He didn't respond right away, and I could tell he was trying to regain control of himself. "I'm sorry I said what I did. I understand why you're still upset about Laney. Maybe I was just trying to move too fast. The thing is, a lot's happened for both of us. We just need to start over. We need to have more dates, just enjoy each other's company, start to trust each other again. Okay? Can we do that?"

I shook my head. "I can't. Not after what you just told me."

"I love you, Eve. That's what I told you."

But that wasn't what I'd remember.

CHAPTER
18

I wore sunglasses to work that Monday, since my eyes were swollen and sunlight hurt. I forgot to take them off before entering the building, which led to Chad deadpanning, "Where's the paparazzi?"

I waved a hand at him wearily, a gesture that split the difference between "hello" and "whatever," and went into my office, shutting the door behind me. I sank down into my chair, startled to find my descent interrupted by a pile of books.

There were four of them, dog-eared, moderately stained, with titles like *Perfect Match: The Right Job for Your Personality* and *Find A Career in Ten Steps*. Dyan, of course. She'd been loaning these out to students for years. They'd been pawed by myriad twenty-two-year-olds who felt they had their whole lives ahead of them. The books were absolutely filthy with hope.

Since my talk with Dyan, I'd done everything I could to distract myself from her question. But she was right, it needed to be answered. This was the life I had, so what now?

I tossed the books on the floor.

*   *   *

"He still doesn't get it. He still doesn't even think he had an affair," I said.

"You were both a little drunk, it was the middle of an argument." Lil took a sip of her paper-cupped latte and grimaced. "This is some foul shit."

"Well, you can't have everything. Look at this ambience." We were sitting at a table in the center of what passed for a food court at the community college: a Chick-fil-A, an Orange Julius, and a coffee cart called Espress Yourself. "I mean, I can't believe he said that."

"I guess he thinks he should get points for restraint," she said. "He only saw her that day at the baseball game?"

"That's what he says."

"America's pastimes: baseball and adultery."

"All these months of therapy, that stupid fucking book he read, and he still thinks it's not an affair." I took an angry swig of my coffee, burning my tongue. "Shit."

"Maybe the two of you are just calling it by different names. Do you think he knows it was wrong, what he did with her, even if he's calling it something other than an affair?"

"I'm sure he thinks it's wrong, just not as wrong as having sex with her."

"A lot of people think that," she said. "No one at this table, but it's a pretty widely held opinion."

"You know what bothers me? It's that he gets to think he's still a good guy. It's like, he can write to her for a year, he can tell her every fucking detail about his life and his marriage, he can call her, he can smuggle her into town, and as long as he doesn't cross that line, he's a stand-up guy. He gets to feel superior to all those other guys who go through with it. Maybe it's not that he has better morals than those guys, just less guts."

"Cheaters aren't really known for their bravery, Eve."

"He was in love with another woman. What could be worse than that?" I asked, suddenly tearful.

"He told you that?"

"No, I—" I realized I knew only because I'd read his e-mails. "I just know he was. He practically admitted it last night. I think some part of him still thinks I'm overreacting, that he's the rational one and I'm the irrational one."

"So what are you going to do about it?"

"I don't know. I want to say that's it, last night was the last straw, I'm done, but until that argument, I was feeling in love with him all over again." I stared at the table miserably. "It's like, I can't get in and I can't get out. I look at my kids, and I see him there, and I want to keep loving him. I think, 'What if I'm robbing them of their dad the way I was robbed?' I know it's different, because Jon would always be a part of their lives, but that doesn't mean they're not still losing."

"Kids are resilient. They compensate. You did."

Sometimes I wasn't so sure.

"And you really didn't see any change in him over the past year?" she asked.

I shook my head.

"Then either he's a really good liar, or..." She clearly didn't want to continue.

"Or what? Come on, or what?"

"Or you weren't too observant."

"Well, I shouldn't have had to be. I trusted him. This is my thanks for trusting him?"

She didn't say anything, just fidgeted with her cup.

I checked Jon's e-mail every day that week to see what he thought about our date. There was no mention in the few superficial e-mails he'd written. I didn't know if that meant he was trying not to think about it, if he was too upset to write about it, or if it hadn't made a dent at all. It was hard to imagine that last one could be true, but it surfaced in my most self-pitying moments.

A week later, I got this e-mail:

> Hi, Eve. I wanted you to know I found an apartment.
> It's a studio in Nob Hill, just abutting the Tenderloin.
> I've heard people call it the Tender Knob. Some call it
> the Knoberloin. Whatever you want to call it, here's my
> address...

He listed his address, signed his name, and that was it. There was no reason to expect more. But somehow, I did.

I tried to divert myself in all sorts of ways, the most embarrassing being my new preoccupation with my skin. Considering my battered self-esteem, the increasing likelihood that someday I would have to reenter the dating world, and Lil's encouragement, it was only a matter of time before I wound up at her medical spa.

I followed the directions I'd printed out, but arrived in a no-man's-land of warehouses and fluttering garbage instead of in the chichi enclave where the medical spa was located. By the time I got to my appointment, I was sweaty, red-faced, and sputtering apologies. The glowing blonde behind the desk smiled at me beatifically and said, "You're only a few minutes late, don't worry about it at all. Can I get you some water? Still or sparkling?"

I breathed deeply, then smiled. "Still, please."

She rose and walked toward a closed door. I glanced around. The walls were a soft white, as was the lighting. One wall featured artfully arranged products from floor to ceiling, and the waiting room of tasteful modern furniture was decorated in white and gentle blues. A woman in expensive loungewear with startlingly dewy skin was perched on one of the chairs, reading a magazine. That was encouraging. I told myself the spa had created her.

The blonde returned with a small bottle of water. She handed it to me, along with a clipboard of forms to fill out. I settled across from the success story (or was she a plant?), took a swig of water, and began to read. The questions were typical medical history, except for the fill-in-the-blank *My number one dream would be to fix my _____.* It was a tantalizing phrase. I was a girl with a dream, and it was to fix my _____. My what? My marriage? My fear that I didn't measure up to some woman in Chicago I'd never even seen? My poor judgment for possibly eating into my children's college funds just to fix my _____?

I went with *redness. Also, my acne.* (I always have between one and four pimples. Clear one up, and there's another on the way.) It wasn't the severity of my skin's problems, but the unpredictability that vexed me. Maybe today, I could get control of something. More or less satisfied with my answers, I turned in the form and waited.

It wasn't long before I was ushered into a private room. There was something comforting about the fact that despite some flourishes (the room's oceanic color palette, dimmed lights, and music that could have been the soundtrack of *Crouching Tiger, Hidden Dragon*), it was basically an exam room. While I don't dismiss Eastern medicine, I tend to be a devotee of Western. It's what I know. If someone's going to laser my face, I want to know they have all the credentials the Western medical establishment can bestow, and I don't want said lasering to take place in, for example, a gently undulating pool meant to evoke the sense memory of being in the womb.

Dr. Klinger was Western all the way. Lil told me she trusted all the doctors there, but she hadn't told me anything specific, like that he'd be so young. Well, youngish (thirty-five? forty?); it was hard to tell given his poreless, wrinkleless complexion. He had sandy hair, hazel eyes behind stylish glasses, well-pressed clothes, and my favorite bedside manner: good-humored, informative, and gracious. He was in no rush, even though I wasn't paying him, which sat well with me. Of course, every free consultation was a potential gold mine in future procedures, none of them covered by insurance and, thus, completely at his discretion. But I saw no need for cynicism.

"So we'll tackle the acne first," he said.

"Well, I thought maybe we could do it all together?" I asked hopefully. "One procedure takes all?"

He laughed. "Acne's sort of a stand alone, unfortunately. Let me just look at you under the light." He moved toward me and turned on the light above my head, its brightness roughly the equivalent of a solar eclipse. Weirdly, when I looked at him also bathed in that light like some sort of angel, I still couldn't detect a single pore. Then I realized how my searching gaze might appear to him and I looked away.

He snapped off the light and returned to the seat opposite me. "Here's what I propose for your acne," he said. "We could start with a salicylic acid peel, really get a deep clean, and then there's a regimen my patients have had great results with..."

I was more disappointed with each word. He was talking about a long-term commitment. I wanted a quick fix. "But couldn't we try one of those newer treatments? I was reading on the Internet about how pulsed light can really help acne."

"I tend to be a little conservative with the procedures. I actually talk people out of more than I perform, to be honest." He paused, perhaps sensing my mood. "I really think the best thing is to start with the salicylic acid peel. It's the cheapest procedure, and it's likely to be the most effective, in conjunction with the daily regimen I'd recommend. And to be honest, there's not all that much to suggest that the pulsed light or the lasers improve acne by very much and the treatments are really expensive."

I was sitting there, ready to be bamboozled, and he wouldn't do it. All he'd give me were realistic expectations and a goddamned salicylic acid peel.

"You know," I said, "what I really want to fix is my redness. My cheeks and my nose seem a lot redder than they used to."

"We could do the peel today and you could start the regimen and then come back in six weeks. If the reds aren't getting any better, we could talk about maybe doing a series of laser treatments to cauterize your blood vessels."

Now he was talking my language. Except—did he actually say "the reds"?

Next up was the aesthetician, Julie. She was another blonde with good skin, though not quite as enviable as the receptionist's. I noticed she had several grooves in her forehead. I felt another twinge of disappointment that this was no miracle factory, and then I recognized the absurdity of having allowed myself to believe it could be. Now I was lying there, and Julie was dabbing the acid on my face, which started burning instantly. Well, of course it did. But somehow, I hadn't expected that, the feeling of someone holding a tiki torch to my face. Tears sprang to my eyes. I gritted my teeth.

Noticing my reaction, Julie nodded sympathetically. "I know. It burns." It had been mere seconds, and it was inching toward intolerable. "If you really can't stand it, we could put a fan on you. But you'll get better results if we don't. So you let me know if you need it, and we'll use the fan."

I didn't want to be a wimp, I didn't want to jeopardize my results, but for criminy's sake, we've got a face on fire here. Perhaps sensing my quandary, Julie started madly fanning me with her hands. I'd have to ask Lil if that was standard operating procedure.

Ultimately it was on for less than five minutes. For the last thirty seconds, as Julie sweetly counted down like it was New Year's, I felt like crying not because of the pain but because I had become a woman who would lie on a table and burn her face off while feeling just the teensiest sense of achievement at not having needed a fan.

When I emerged from the room with what could only be called the crimsons, the incandescent reception-ist lined up my products on the counter, described my "regime" in detail (complete with a pantomime of exfo-liation), and gave me the tally. It came to $507, much less than the price of lasers, but still somehow more than I'd expected. I handed over my credit card numbly, and she ran it through, only to whisper a minute later, "It's not going through. It says to call this number."

My first thought was that Jon had cut me off; my second was that he'd run the card up to its limit buy-ing plane tickets and gifts for Laney. My third was that doing this wasn't going to change anything for me, noth-ing that mattered. But the receptionist had already dialed the number and handed me the phone. A woman answered with a chipper "Fraud services."

"This is Eve Gimbel," I said in a low voice, watching the receptionist busy herself by straightening the already meticulous product display. "My marriage is in the crapper, and I'm trying to spend my way out of it. Can you make a note on the account? I might not be done yet."

I got lost driving home.

That night, Jacob noticed that my face "looked funny, like after the beach," but when I said, "Sometimes Mommy's face will do that," he didn't press further. He was eager to get to reading time, anyway.

We'd developed a ritual where I sat on the floor in Olivia's nursery with my legs wide apart, Jacob sat inside the created triangle with his legs similarly arranged, and Olivia leaned against him. As I reached around both of them, holding a book and reading aloud, Jacob took his job of holding Olivia upright very seriously.

Jacob liked for it to be the same book every time, Shel Silverstein's *Where the Sidewalk Ends*. Dyan said I shouldn't be concerned that he liked to hear his two favorite poems over and over: "For Sale" (about selling a sister to the highest bidder) and "Dreadful" (about doing away with a sister by eating her). As I read the poems and he chimed in with the parts he remembered, he seemed to like cuddling Liv, kissing the top of her head, watching her clap her hands and squeal with delight. It was the juxtaposition that disturbed me most: him enjoying the fantasy of getting rid of Liv, while being so affectionate toward her. "Some ambivalence is normal," Dyan assured me, but I still worried. Maybe he was going to turn into a sociopath. I thought about how his dad had left the house so soon after Olivia's arrival, what that might have done to his psyche, and I worried what would happen when Charlie returned to Orange County, if Jon stayed gone, and it was just the three of us for good.

"Read it again!" Jacob said. He pecked the top of Liv's head, and she cooed in response.

"How about a new one?" I suggested. "How about 'The Land of Happy'?"

He wrinkled his nose. "I don't think she likes that."

I tightened my arms around them both. "Let's just give it a try."

CHAPTER

19

Hello?" Since Charlie was closer, he was the one to answer the phone. He paused, then said, "Sure. Will do." He hung up and turned to me. "Jon's going to call back so he can get the machine."

"He didn't ask for me?" I said.

"No. He said he wanted the machine." Charlie looked back at the TV as the phone began to ring. I dashed down the hall to my room as he said, "You married folks are crazy."

I was in time to hear the beep, then Jon's voice. "Hi, Eve. I haven't done one of these in a while. I don't know if you're there. If you are, hello, in real time. To be honest, I don't really want you to pick up. But you're on my mind, and I wanted you to know that. I don't know what to do about it, because every time I try something, it seems to go wrong. I don't know whose fault that is, if it's anyone's fault. I think we're two good people who've loved each other a long time. But man, we're off track. I know I am. I just started taking antidepressants. There, I said it. My name's Jon, and I take Wellbutrin. It's not doing anything yet, not that I can feel.

"I'm not saying this so you'll feel sorry for me. Tell Charlie that, so he won't try to kick my ass next time I pick up the kids. So why am I saying it then? I don't know. I'm one confused man, Eve. I'm like those fish swimming around upside down. And occasionally I'll be offering you a drunken dispatch from here in the Tender Knob, if you're okay with that. I just don't want to be forgotten." There was an ambiguous noise, and I thought maybe he was crying. Another few seconds, and the message stopped. I wasn't sure if he'd been cut off by the machine or hung up himself.

I didn't know what to make of Jon's message. I'd never expected to be drunk-dialed by my own husband. It's not like I was in a position to help him sort out his life when mine was one big question mark, if that was even what he'd been asking.

Tamara suggested I focus on finding a career; Lil thought I should focus on other men, as if they were lining up around the block or growing from the tree in my front yard. Lil had recently started pushing to meet Tamara, thinking it would be good for all of us to be friends. I'd been stalling. I knew Tamara wanted me back with Jon, and Lil wanted me to explore my options, and I'd started wanting both in equal measure—despite the fact that they were diametrically opposed—so I thought if we all met, my head might explode.

I figured it couldn't hurt to read the career books Dyan had left in my office. I was secretly hoping that they'd talk to me in an Old Testament sort of way, like the burning bush spoke to Moses, but it didn't happen. After paging through lists of jobs, and reaching no epiphany, I turned to the tests. I answered a hundred questions about my preferences and skill sets and, somehow, seemed no closer.

While the personality tests didn't seem likely to find me a job, either, they were enlightening in their own way. The Myers-Briggs classified personality types along four continuums: extroverted vs. introverted, sensing vs. intuiting, thinking vs. feeling, judging vs. perceiving. Without conscious thought, I found myself trying to figure out Jon's personality type alongside mine, in the way old married couples instinctively read each other's horoscopes. I was on the line between extroverted and introverted, with a nod toward introverted, and I suspected Jon was the same. But on all the other measures, Jon and I were opposites. He got information from his senses, from facts and figures, while I was intuitive; he was a thinker (calm, detached, objective—*infuriating*), while I was a definite feeler; and I was a classic judger (liked to schedule and plan, needed closure) while he was a perceiver (comfortable with waiting and seeing, liked to keep his options open—*did he ever*).

When I told Dyan that I'd read the books but remained clueless, she suggested I go down the list of jobs and mark anything that wasn't an absolute, unequivocal no. Then I could rank that smaller number, and talk to professors who'd worked in my top three fields. Public health was number three, but since the Intro to Public Health class started just as I was finishing work, there I was.

I blamed Lil for the bizarre reaction I was having to Professor Ray Dubrovnik. She was the one who had me thinking about other men, and since so few crossed my path, maybe I was trying to make the most of them. Ray Dubrovnik was five foot eight and stocky, with what could easily be two fake moustaches pasted where his eyebrows should be. Not since Dukakis had lost his bid for the presidency had I seen the likes of those. He was leading a discussion about the relationship between communicable diseases and meth use, and why it's a particular problem in San Francisco — you'd be hard-pressed to find a less erotic topic, really — and I was sitting in the back row, feeling a stirring that I couldn't believe was sexual, only it was.

I stopped following the discussion and just stared at him, trying to find justification for the attraction I was feeling. His nose, for example, was actually pretty nice. Straight. No one ever talks about twinkling brown eyes, but his did. Maybe it was that he was so confident, he eschewed fashion completely, enough to wear one of those khaki vests with all the pockets that are normally the province of fishermen or nature photographers. All that, plus the man was a dynamo. He loved his work, and he wanted his students to love it, too.

What felt strangest was that I was presumably allowed to do something about this attraction and this guy was in my league, with his naked ring finger and my spare tire.

I was the only one in the room anywhere near his age, which I estimated to be mid-forties.

Class was wrapping up, and he was at the lectern, packing up his notes. His bag didn't seem to go with the rest of him. It was sleek, made out of some shiny material, like the kind favored by bike messengers.

"Professor Dubrovnik?" I said timidly.

He looked up. "Hello, unannounced visitor," he said, smiling.

"I'm sorry. I probably should have cleared it with you. I actually work on campus in Student Services."

"Drop-ins are fine. Uncommon, but fine. What can I do for you?"

"I'm shopping around for a new career, and I wanted to get your opinion about public health."

"Teaching it, or working in the field?"

I'd never considered teaching that or anything else, but I found myself answering, "Both."

"You want the unvarnished truth?"

I nodded.

"You know that saying, 'Those who can't do, teach'? Well, in my case, it's 'Those who are burned out, but still believe in the mission, teach.' Wordy, but true."

"I wouldn't have guessed you were burned out from the way you taught."

"Oh, I'm not burned out on teaching. I'm passionate about getting these kids to be passionate about the thing I had to leave behind for my own sanity. I take that very seriously."

Was he serious? He was half-smiling. I didn't know

what to say, and we stood there for a long, uncomfortable minute.

"Public health is a great field, don't get me wrong," he said. "For me, it was time to do something else, so here I am."

"But now it seems like a trick."

"What does?"

"Being inspirational. You're inspiring them to do something that drove you crazy. It seems—unethical somehow."

"Look, I was them twenty years ago. I got a good twenty years—well, fifteen years, those last five were rough—out of public health. Who's to say they won't get forty? Who's to say they won't be on their deathbeds saying, 'If I'd only created one more needle exchange program...'"

There was nothing unkind in his smile; on the contrary, there was something disarming about it. But I felt unsettled, and I realized what it was: He was talking straight to me because I wasn't young and impressionable anymore. The kids, they wanted to be dazzled. That's what being twenty was all about, believing you could do anything and be anything and that the world would bend to your will. Then you got kicked around and you learned better, but you needed that initial dreamy padding. Man, I felt old.

"I feel old," I said. I had no other response at the ready, and I didn't want to stand there mutely for another second.

He laughed. "What are you, thirty?"

I winced. I hated people guessing right.

"So you're looking for a second career? Third career?"

"It's more like a first career. I've just been killing time, really."

"You have a family?" he asked.

"I have two kids. I'm separated."

"Recent?"

I wondered what gave it away. I nodded.

"I'm sorry," he said, and I believed him.

"Thanks."

"So now you have to support your kids on your own?"

"No. He still supports us."

"Good man."

I didn't understand the turn the conversation was taking. Was Ray attracted to me? Pitying me? Was he attracted to me because he pitied me? None of the above?

"So you came here for some information, and I'm sitting here asking questions that are none of my business. Do you have time to get a coffee? I'll tell you everything I know."

It was the best offer I'd had in months. That was not a cheering thought.

Ray had done it all: He'd worked with drug addicts, domestic violence offenders and victims, the homeless, people at risk for or having already contracted all manner of diseases. He'd been on the front lines, educating and empathizing and getting people the services they needed. He'd been behind the scenes, developing and evaluating programs. He'd worked for the city, the county, the state. And if anything was clear by the end of our conversation, it was that he felt no one should do that sort of work if they couldn't give it everything. He'd seen too many people half-assing it with other people's lives, and when he saw he was about to become one of them, he'd gotten out. At first, being a professor felt like being a traitor or an imposter. Even though the community college was about as far from the ivory tower as you could get, it still felt uncomfortably close for Ray. That is, until he saw that he could inspire the students with his experience and his candor. He never made the life out to be anything other than what he thought it could and should be: noble work, undertaken by dedicated people who knew their hands would get dirty and that there was never, ever time for complacency.

I was, in a word, spellbound. This was a man who lived by his convictions. This was a man who would leave his pregnant wife rather than live in deception.

Not that I was comparing him or anything.

"So you want to karaoke sometime?" he asked.

It seemed that abrupt to me, too. "Karaoke?" I repeated.

"On Wednesday nights. There's this great dive in the city. Some nights you hear one too many drag queens performing 'Goodbye Yellow Brick Road' but mostly, it's a good time."

"I thought they loved 'Candle in the Wind.'"

He grinned broadly. "That too. You haven't lived until you've seen some doll of a tranny crying her way through it with a tiara perched on her wig."

I laughed. "So, Wednesday."

"Wednesday."

Charlie was staring critically at the shirts hanging up in the guest bedroom closet. Finally he turned toward me with a sort of childish helplessness. I got up from the futon to stand next to him.

"Which of these do you think she'd like best?" he asked.

He and Lil were having another "date" after Luke was asleep. Lil was picking up the wine; she knew she couldn't trust him with that. He still bought Pabst Blue Ribbon because it tasted good. He affectionately called it PBR. They'd been seeing a lot of each other, and I'd caught him doing things like surreptitiously sniffing his armpits before going to see her. For Charlie, this was serious.

"Just wear what makes you most comfortable," I said. Jesus, I really had turned into a mom.

He cast me a glance that said that very thing.

"Okay, this one." I reached out and touched a black T-shirt. T-shirts were my only option, and at least that one didn't have anything written on it.

"Are you serious?"

"What's wrong with it?"

"It's kind of boring."

"It's your shirt."

"I'm just saying, Lil's not boring. She's hot."

She's old, I wanted to say. It still seemed strange that

Lil was having sex with my kid brother. Repeatedly. I had adjusted somewhat, but much preferred not to think about it. I'd be remiss, though, if I didn't ask, "You always use condoms, right?"

"What the hell, Eve!" A grimace crossed his face.

"I'm just saying, you should."

"Nice. Real nice."

"With anyone, I mean. Anyone you're going to have casual sex with."

"You hang out with the public-health dude one time and you turn into—Are there any famous public-health dudes?"

We both laughed, grateful to dispel the awkwardness.

"It's kind of weird for me to think of you having a date with Grizzly Adams," he said. "I mean, you've been with Jon forever."

"He doesn't look like Grizzly Adams. He doesn't even have a beard."

"Just the brows."

"You don't even notice them after a while. He's really got presence. He's one of those people who just means what he says, you know? It's sexy."

"If you say so." He was fingering other T-shirts in his closet speculatively. "I can't believe I'm taking this long to pick a fucking shirt. What's up with that?"

I didn't answer. I was thinking about Ray. And about Jon. It was true that I found Ray sexy, but the thought of actually having sex with him currently held no appeal at all. Not just because of his potential furriness—which was a concern—but because of his un-Jon-ness.

Ray was what Jon would call "a real character." I had the quickest flash of an impulse to call Jon and describe Ray, with his centipede eyebrows and his rechanneled passion, and then to say, "Maybe I'm going to find something to do with my life, something I can talk about the way Ray talks about his work. Like there's honor in it." And Jon would say in his "you and me against the world" voice, "Yeah, let's make that happen."

CHAPTER
20

It was only a split second, but I saw it. Just before Tamara smiled and told Lil how great it was to meet her, there it was, a look in the eyes that said *so this is why I hardly see you anymore.* I knew this wouldn't go well.

"It's really great to meet you, too!" Lil's sincerity was palpable, and painful.

We seated ourselves at the table, and I said (with way too much compensatory enthusiasm), "I love sushi!"

"It's good," Tamara said. She reached up to smooth her hair, which was pulled into a messy bun. She glanced surreptitiously at Lil as she did it. I couldn't help noticing how distinctly unpolished Tamara and I were in comparison with the perfectly accessorized Lil: we were the work casual chinos to her ultra–low-rise skinny jeans, the Dansko clogs to her Jimmy Choos.

Glad for the prop, I consulted the menu. "How do you guys feel about unagi?" I asked.

"That's eel, right?" Lil said.

"It's one of the cooked ones."

"That one's okay." Lil began to scan the menu. "It

seems like if you're going to do sushi, you should do it raw, you know?"

"I'll split the unagi with you," Tamara said quickly.

"Oh, I'd split it." Lil smiled at us both. "I just think we should get a good balance, you know?"

Two "you know?'s" in a row. Now that Tamara was here with us, I found myself critical of Lil, then guilty for feeling that way. Lil was a wonderful person. She'd stood by me like no one else lately.

No, that wasn't fair. Tamara was doing her best. She just wasn't as open-minded as Lil was. Truthfully, neither was I. That was why it had taken me so long to like Lil this much.

The next few minutes passed in semiawkward negotiation. Sushi for three wasn't my brightest idea. Finally the food was ordered and we were sipping our sake, smiling with nervous anticipation.

"So you're a teacher," Lil said.

"For five years now. Some days it seems so much longer."

"How old are the kids?"

"It's high school." Tamara lifted her cup to her lips.

"I think that's going to be my age," Lil said. "You know how every parent has an age where they're really great with their kids? Mine's going to be high school."

"You seem pretty great with Luke now," I interjected.

"Oh, I'm good now. I'll be great then."

I could see that Tamara was jarred by Lil's confidence, and unsure how to respond.

"I wonder what my age will be," I said.

"Eleven," Lil answered immediately.

"Eleven? I only get to be at my best for one year?"

"Oh, it'll be more than one year. I see you being really good with the tweens."

"I hate that term," Tamara said. Then realizing she might have sounded harsh, she added, "It's like an advertising demographic, not a stage."

"I kind of like it." Lil smiled benignly. "You know, it's when they're in between. Not totally kids, not totally teenagers."

"I understand it," Tamara said, and I stiffened. I wished she would let the subject go. "It just seems a little made-up, like how Hallmark invented Mother's Day."

"I like Mother's Day, too." Lil laughed. "You will, too, someday."

Eager to change the trajectory of the conversation, I blurted out, "I had a date."

Tamara turned to me, mouth slightly agape. Lil nodded encouragingly, ready to hear the details. Unlike Tamara, she already knew of Ray's existence.

"When did this happen?" Tamara asked, trying (and failing) to sound casual.

"I met him last week, and we went out last night."

"You didn't even say anything," she said. "We talked over the weekend. Just for a few minutes, but..."

"He's a professor," Lil said. "At a community college, but still a professor. I've always thought those tweed jackets with the elbow patches were kind of sexy."

Tamara ignored Lil and stayed focused on me. "Was it a real date?" she asked.

The question was harder to answer than you'd expect. Ray had offered to come and pick me up, but I'd declined. Part of it was that I wasn't ready for the formality of dating (the pickup, the drop-off, the good-night kiss, maybe); part was that I wasn't ready for the intimacy of anyone seeing where I lived; and the rest was that I didn't want Ray the Urban Warrior to drive up to my suburban house in my suburban neighborhood and pass judgment. That's what dating was: It was one person's expectations, associations, and preconceived notions colliding with another's. It was an act of hope.

I'd met Ray at the karaoke place. It was indeed an old-fashioned dive bar; by which I mean, it wasn't some hipster construct, but was genuinely run-down. The neon lights on the sign behind the bar were flickering because no one could be bothered to get them fixed; the exposed brick wall was crumbling for the same reason. The battered wood floor looked like people had been aggressively moving furniture across it since San Francisco was a gold rush town.

"Well, hello there!" Ray said. He was at the bar, drinking something amber from a highball glass. He spun toward me on his stool, but didn't stand or make any move to touch me. I leaned against the bar next to him, hoping the maneuver had a glint of sexiness to it. I felt ridiculous. It didn't help that a man who looked homeless was at the front of the room mumbling his way through the Beatles' "Money (That's What I Want)." A dozen patrons were scattered at the tables facing him, paying no attention.

Following my eyes, Ray said, "It'll fill up later. I don't like to get up there until there's a crowd. I feed off the audience."

I smiled politely. The notion that he and this audience would reciprocally generate some sort of electricity struck me as absurd. I felt like jumping in my car and speeding home. If I left right then, I could be the one to give Olivia her bath instead of Charlie.

I forced myself to say, "The only time I've ever done karaoke, I was a backup singer. I shared a mike with three other girls."

"The harmony." He nodded seriously. "Harmony's the backbone of music."

Lil cut into the story. "He's adorable! I mean, not necessarily physically, but I like this guy."

Tamara just waited for me to continue.

Ray and I got a table — "Not too close, but not too far away from the action," he said. His unwavering belief in "the action" might have been delusional, but I had to agree with Lil: there was a certain charm in it, the same indefinable charm that had worked on me in the classroom and then at coffee. It had to be his charm, because it wasn't his wardrobe. He was wearing a short-sleeved shirt with pictures of hula girls printed on it, and a few wiry chest hairs sprouted from the top.

"My God," Tamara said.

"Hipsters in San Francisco wear that kind of stuff," Lil rejoined.

"He's forty-four," I said.

"Aging hipsters," she amended.

"My God," Tamara said again. "It's like he's wasting away in Margaritaville."

What I didn't say—because I didn't want to even say Jon's name in front of Tamara—was that at least Ray was dressed with a point of view. Whatever else you might think about Ray, he was undoubtedly a man with a point of view. It was so refreshing that I was able to overcome my visceral distaste for the hula girls and start telling Ray everything.

I know that's not a recommended dating strategy. But when presented with a sympathetic, interested male ear, something happened to me. I didn't do it right off the bat; I mean, I didn't sit down and say, "So my husband was having an affair." There was a period where Ray did standard first-date patter, told engaging stories, and I laughed in what was going to have to pass for flirting, at least for that night. I was enjoying myself, particularly his anecdotes about the karaoke regulars (complete with impressions that sometimes veered into serenade). Ray had a surprisingly mellifluous voice.

Then, I don't know, he asked me how long I'd been separated, and what my marriage used to be like, and there was something about that unexpected question (and the Rusty Nails we were drinking) that opened the floodgates. I told him about my vacation theory, and how maybe that was where things went wrong, and then the MC called Ray's name—

"What vacation theory?" Lil interrupted.

There was something just the tiniest bit triumphant

in the glance that Tamara shot Lil. "It's her theory about how vacations trick us."

Lil looked to me for amplification.

"I think vacations warp the mind," I said. "You know how if you have a really amazing vacation, you think it's telling you something important about the relationship? And then if you have a bad vacation, you think that's telling you something important, too?"

"We've tracked it," Tamara said with authority. "We know tons of people who've moved in together or gotten engaged because of a good vacation, and people who split up after a bad one."

"It doesn't happen right away," I said. "It's just like, the seed gets planted and suddenly you start to see things differently. For better or for worse."

"Okay." Lil seemed unconvinced, but was ready to get on with the story.

So Ray got up and went to take the mike. He'd been coy about what song he was picking, as he didn't want his selection to be compromised by my reaction. When the first notes rang out, I wanted to cover my face. It was the Eagles' "Desperado." I wasn't an Eagles fan under the best of circumstances, but that schmaltzy mess of a song? I looked around, sure everyone in the place must be sharing the sentiment.

I know I keep saying this when it comes to Ray, but something happened. He was up there, all earnest brio, and the whole audience felt it. It was like he said: He was feeding off us, we were feeding off him. And I tell you, where normally I'd be rolling my eyes, I had tears in them. The crowd started holding up lighters and swaying back and forth.

"Must have been a lot of smokers," Lil said.

"Well, no wonder you were all teary. There's that whole 'You've got to let somebody love you' line," Tamara said. "It's just so obviously manipulative."

I shook my head. "I don't think so."

"You wouldn't. You're vulnerable. That's what he's smelling."

"None of us know what he's smelling," Lil said. "He could be smelling a newly single woman, ready to—"

"Can we stop talking about my smell now?" I asked. "Yeah, the parallels between 'Desperado' and me are striking. You can never get me because I'm always out ridin' fences."

"It's metaphorical." Tamara waved a hand. "I don't trust him, that's all."

"Well, you shouldn't trust any of them." Lil poured another round of sake for the table. "But so far, this one's no worse than the rest. Who knows, maybe he's better."

When Ray finished to thunderous applause—he was right, the crowd had quadrupled in size—he came back to the table, wiping sweat from his brow, reseated himself, and prompted, "So you and Jon were in Mexico?"

I found I didn't want to talk about Jon and the vacation theory. I didn't want to say that Jon and I had been together less than a year and we'd been having a blissful time in Mexico and then I got food poisoning and needed an IV and Jon sat by my hospital bed, and even though we both knew I wasn't going to die, there was something about the love and need and fear I saw in his eyes that told me I could count on him forever. I felt my defenses crumble completely—it was like I'd been wearing armor, only to finally realize there was no battle to fight—and I let myself say, "I love you, too." I let myself feel it in every bone and in every pore. That trip changed everything.

I didn't say that. I said, "Why 'Desperado'?"

We talked for hours, tuning in only occasionally for the very best and the very worst performances, though we debated which was which. There was a woman who brought the house down with the Kinks' "Lola," and a person of indeterminate gender who slayed us with Britney Spears's "Oops!...I Did It Again." Ray was an impassioned talker—whatever the subject—and I was shocked to find it was already midnight.

He walked me to my car, and I was relieved that he didn't move in to kiss me. I wasn't sure if I was feeling an absence of desire, or just of sexual confidence. What was disconcerting was that I didn't feel any longing on his part. He hugged me, waited on the curb while I got in the car, then patted the door frame before moving back into the bar.

"He went back to the bar?" Tamara asked suspiciously.

"That doesn't mean anything," Lil said. "It could be that he wants to take his time with you because he likes you, and he just wants to get his rocks off with some girl from the bar. It shows respect."

Tamara and I stared at her.

"The point is, we just don't know," Lil continued. "You don't know this guy yet, so watch out for him like you should watch out for all guys. Just see how it goes."

Neither of us could really disagree with that, though I was still mildly disturbed by the suggestion that Ray had gone back inside to pick up some other woman.

"It's the not knowing that really stinks," I said. "I mean, I used to think I knew, and now I'm back to wondering."

"You always had to wonder," Lil said. By now, the food had arrived, and she was mixing generous amounts of wasabi with soy sauce.

"I just don't go in for that 'all men are pigs' stuff," Tamara said. "And I specifically know that Jon isn't a pig."

It was the first time either of them had mentioned his name. They both waited for my reaction. I exhaled, then said, "I don't want to talk about Jon tonight." I determinedly picked up a tuna roll with my chopsticks.

"I can understand that," Tamara said, "but I still see Jon. I see how he's suffering when you're out dating."

"You think I haven't suffered?" I glared at her. "You think the fact that I had one date means I'm not suffering anymore? Are you fucking kidding me?"

Lil put her hand on my arm. She was trying to keep things even-keeled, but Tamara must have seen it as Lil asserting our closeness. She turned to Lil and said, "I don't even think she'd be dating if it wasn't for you."

I could not believe this. I was thirty years old, the

mother of two, and was possibly going to be both the object of and the participant in a catfight.

Lil stood up. She said, "There's a lot of history and a lot of emotion between you two. It's got nothing to do with me. So I'm going to go." She looked in her purse. "Shit, I don't have enough cash to cover my part. Could you let me know what I owe later, and I'll pay you the next time I see you?"

She was being so adult that both Tamara and I felt chastened. "I'm sorry," Tamara said. "It's a touchy subject, but you're right, it has nothing to do with you. I'll leave. Besides, I have cash." She got to her feet and started rooting in her purse.

"This is silly!" I said. "I don't want anyone to leave. I just want to restart this night. I want to restart this year." With both of them towering above me, I felt like kids must when they watch their parents argue.

Tamara and Lil looked at each other. Lil was the first to smile. "How about," she asked, "we both sit back down on the count of three?"

Now we all laughed eagerly.

"One . . . ," I said.

CHAPTER

21

Charlie was waiting up for me. It wasn't hard to do, since I was home by nine-thirty, but I could tell that was why he was positioned on the couch, idly flipping through TV channels. His eyes loped over to me and then back to the TV, and he said, "Oh, hi." The "Oh" was the dead giveaway.

"Oh, hi to you, too," I said, sinking down on the couch next to him.

"It's not like I'm not glad to see you. I'm just tired. I was helping Jacob with his homework."

"He's five. How much could it tax you?"

"He's almost six. They grow up so fast these days." He grinned at me. "How was your dinner?"

"Complicated." I reached down and undid the sensible T-strap on my shoes. Sensible or not, my feet ached. "Everything okay with the kids?"

"No problems. I've got this child raising thing *down*." He took a swig from the beer can which was resting on the coffee table. "So tell me about your dinner."

"Let's just say Tamara's not a fan of Lil's."

"What's her problem?" There was no mistaking the defensive tone in his voice.

"Like I said, it's complicated."

"Lil's a good person. What's Tamara got against her?"

"It was just a vibe I got. It's fine. There won't be any more group dinners, that's all. I'm more of a one-on-one person anyway." If you looked past the outright hostility early on, it was just a vibe. Once Tamara and Lil sat back down, we all made a concerted effort to talk about neutral subjects and laugh whenever possible, but it just never coalesced. They weren't each other's type.

"What did you guys talk about?" Charlie asked, pretending it was offhandedly.

"We talked about Ray for a while. I told them about the date."

"What did they say?"

"They both said not to trust him, but with Lil, it was more of a general rule, and with Tamara, it was more specific. She saw evil in his song selection."

Charlie laughed. "I saw lame in his song selection."

"I told you, the audience loved him."

"Right." He furrowed his brows slightly. "Lil has a general rule about not trusting men?"

"Yep."

"So she doesn't trust me?"

"It's safe to assume."

"She's been hurt pretty bad, huh?"

"I'm neither confirming nor denying. She'll tell you what she wants you to know."

"Oh, come on," he wheedled. "What's the good of dating your sister's friend if you don't even get the inside track?"

"There's no good in dating your sister's friend."

"So you've got a problem with Lil, too?"

"No, I don't. But I'm not giving you any insider information."

"So you won't tell me what she said about me tonight?"

"No, I won't." I got to my feet, picking up my shoes.

"Aha!" he said victoriously. "So she did say something!"

The truth was, Lil had said two things: "He's cute" and "He's young." You've got to give it to her, the woman's discreet. It seemed like Charlie was a whole lot more invested than she was, which would have been a greater source of concern right then if I hadn't been dead tired. Two nights out in a row was a lot for me. Two nights away from my babies, whom I suddenly ached to smell and touch. And instead of Jon here to ask about my night, it was Charlie, pumping me for information on Lil.

For about the millionth time since I'd first found out about Laney, I felt the sudden, sharp pain of *How did we get here?* No one had ever told me that "How did we get here?" was an emotion, but it is.

"I'm neither confirming nor denying," I repeated. Better to let him go to sleep believing everything was reciprocal. What did I know, maybe it was.

"You want to hear something?" he asked.

"Can you say it fast? I'm about to collapse."

"Mom's with someone, and it sounds like he's actually good for her."

"Based on what?"

"She said it. I guess they've been together a few months, but she didn't want to tell anyone until it seemed to be going somewhere."

I shook my head in disbelief. "Where would it go? She doesn't know anything about relationships. Why do you think mine's so fucked up?" When it came to my mother, the things that came out of my mouth always surprised me. I sounded like such a victim.

"Well, everyone gets it right sometime."

"Do you really believe that?" I asked.

I could see in his face that he did. He hadn't been able to keep a job or a relationship, and now he actually seemed to be putting his eggs in Lil's basket—clearly a grievous error in judgment—but at least he was capable of misplaced optimism.

"I'm going to kiss my kids," I said, heading for the hallway.

"Make it a double!" he called after me.

That night, I dreamed about the circling fish. Only Jon and I were the fish. The circling was making me dizzy. It wasn't romantic or pleasant or intimate, like I'd always imagined; it was actually quite nauseating. Because we were fish, I couldn't tell him to stop circling me, and I couldn't seem to stop myself from circling him. It was like being trapped on an amusement ride long after I wanted to get off. I was grateful to wake up, even if it was hours until dawn.

Charlie's always been a heavy sleeper, but this was the first time since he'd been staying with me that I crept into the guest room and turned on the computer. I hadn't checked Jon's e-mail in weeks (I wasn't finding anything useful, anyway) but that night, the compulsion was so strong it felt psychic.

The password still worked, but there was nothing new in his in-box or his Sent folder. A chill went through me. Maybe he knew I'd been in this e-mail, and was carrying on all sorts of relationships from a new account. Or maybe he was so depressed that he wasn't communicating with anyone.

Reading Jon's e-mail had given me a false sense of control. I thought that I could at least be prepared for whatever was coming next, and now my anxiety was running wild. It was bouncing between the poles: At one end, Jon was already back together with Laney or in love with someone new. At the other end, he was so depressed he could barely make it through another day. My rational mind would have admitted other possibilities, but I didn't have access to it just then.

Olivia was crying. I needed to pull myself together and go to her. She needed me to soothe her, and in this condition, I'd only make her more upset.

One way or another, I told myself, *it'll be okay.* But as I held Olivia, telling her the same thing, she just cried and cried.

CHAPTER

22

─────────

I couldn't exist in this middle ground any longer. The lack of a definitive was driving me crazy. Either Jon and I were going to move forward, or I was done. So the next night, after I put Jacob to bed, I told Charlie I'd be going out. I didn't want to say where, but he guessed. "You know there's no shame in visiting your own husband, right?" he asked, seeing my guilty expression.

The Tender Knob was pretty rough, more Tenderloin than Nob Hill, for sure. My image of Jon walking his neighborhood like life was an episode of *Cheers* was immediately dispelled. It was obviously a neighborhood where most commerce was illicit, and I felt sad that Jon had been relegated to this. I bet Ray had done a lot of work here in his day.

I located Jon's building (midway between a liquor store and a flop hotel), and when I couldn't find parking within a few blocks, I decided to spring for the lot across the street. It took effort to get out of the car, and not just because the darkened lot was spooking me. It was entirely possible that this was a big mistake. Things were at a more or less peaceful stalemate. They could certainly get worse. I didn't want things uglier; I wanted them cleaner. In the best-case scenario, I'd know that he finally understood just how wrong his affair with Laney was, he'd admit to everything that I already knew, and he'd profess to loving me above all else (excepting Jacob and Olivia, of course). I wasn't sure what the worst case was.

I forced myself to go to his building. There it was, our last name written in Jon's scrawl next to the buzzer. It's funny, the things that can knock the wind out of you just by confronting them in some new, unexpected way. Every day when I went home, I realized Jon wasn't there. Logically, it followed that he was somewhere else. But seeing the evidence—feeling it, all through me—that this was, in fact, where he lived...

I pressed the buzzer and waited. After a reasonable interval, I went ahead and pressed again. Jon's voice crackled through the intercom.

"Hello," he said, sounding half-asleep.

"Jon, it's me."

I was about to repeat it when he said without inflection, "You didn't call."

"I guess I wanted to surprise you." I added weakly, "Surprise!" A second later, I asked, "Can I come in? It's kind of...seedy out here."

A loud noise rang out. It took me a second to realize that in lieu of an answer, he was buzzing me in. I reached for the door, but by then, the buzzing had stopped. Feeling a little foolish, I pushed the button next to his name, and this time, when he buzzed, I was ready for it.

Inside was more promising than outside. There was a long corridor with a marbled floor and a faded Persian-style carpet runner down the center. An aged crystal chandelier hung from the high ceiling. I walked down the hall until I found Jon's apartment and knocked hesitantly on the door.

When he opened it, he was wearing an untucked T-shirt and jeans; his feet were bare. He had five o'clock shadow and an expression of wary embarrassment. As he stepped aside to let me in, I saw why.

The galley kitchen had dishes piled high and crumbs and spills on the countertops. In the main room, there was an unfolded futon with rumpled covers, facing a TV. A crib for Olivia was pushed against one wall. There were two large windows with heavy damask drapes in front of them, and the whole place had that too-lived-in smell. The ceilings were high and wainscoted, and the floor was refinished oak, and I could see that it would be a nice apartment if it weren't so obviously inhabited by a depressed person.

He turned and surveyed the kitchen. "I've been working late a lot," he said. "I always clean up before I bring Jacob and Liv here."

"It's not that messy in here, really."

"I'll make up the futon. There's no place to sit otherwise."

"Do you want help?" I asked as he started to pull at the frame.

"No, that's okay."

I stood by until the couch was ready, not sure where to look. He gestured toward it.

"If I'd known you were coming over, I would have...," he started to say once we sat down, but he didn't finish the sentence.

"I should have called. I'm sorry."

"I just don't know what to think about you being here. Why are you here?" He looked directly at me for the first time since I'd arrived.

"I don't know," I said. "I guess I wanted to see how you're doing."

He shook his head, a bemused smile coming over his face. "You came here to gloat? Because you've got somebody and I can barely do my dishes?"

"Is that really what you think of me?" Clayton the carrier pigeon strikes again.

"I don't know," he said.

"Were you drinking?"

"I've had *a* drink. One."

"Sorry. It's not my business."

"Is it to hurt me, Eve?" he asked. "Is that why you're dating so soon?"

"I didn't even want you to know about it."

"Well, there's an irony for you. You're keeping things from me now."

"We're separated. Are you seriously going to tell me there's no difference between my having *a* date—one— and you falling in love with another woman?"

"Why are you so convinced I'm in love with Laney?"

"The things you wrote to her—" I stopped, my face suddenly warm.

"How do you know what I wrote to her?" he asked, his tone suspicious.

It occurred to me that I could get out of this. I could say something like "I can imagine the things you wrote"; I could get accusatory as a way to deflect and camouflage. I'd known Jon a long time. He was a fundamentally trusting person, and he fundamentally trusted me. But I didn't want to keep the lies going any longer. If I told him I'd been reading his e-mail, I'd never be able to do it again, and maybe that would free us both.

"When I first found out about Laney, I wasn't in my right mind," I said. "And I think if I hadn't started then, I never would have started."

"Started what?"

"Reading your e-mails behind your back."

He was clearly stunned. "Are you fucking kidding me?"

"No."

"Which e-mails?"

"All the e-mails you wrote to Laney and all the ones she wrote to you."

It took him a minute to find a reply. Emotions dawned over his face in rapid succession (confusion, disbelief, shame, fear, anger). He rested with anger. "What did you think you were doing?"

"I was trying to get the truth."

"By sneaking around behind my back," he said. "For how long?"

"I started Thanksgiving night."

He was shaking his head in disgust.

"Hey," I said, "I didn't know if I could believe anything you said. So I was checking."

"Checking," he repeated, his voice like flint. "And what were you checking for, Eve?"

"I was checking for all sorts of things. I was checking to see if you still loved me. I was checking to see if you loved her. I was checking to see if she was better than me, if she was funnier, prettier, smarter. I was checking because I didn't understand why you wanted her in your life when you had me. I didn't know why I wasn't enough. I was trying to find out who you were, Jon, because the man I married wouldn't have had Laney in his life."

"What did you find out? What kind of man am I?" He was practically sneering.

I shook my head. I still didn't know.

"What kind of person are you, that you'd spy on me for months?" he asked. "And the whole time, you're pretending you're better than me."

"I never said I was better than you."

"Like you haven't spent months being self-righteous." He got up and strode around the room, trying to get himself under control. But I could see the second when he said, *Fuck it, I'm just going to let her have it.* "All this time, I've let you treat me however you wanted, like I deserved it. I let you have your way. I let you have your anger. I let you kick me out of the house. I let you invite me back in, but not really. I let you sentence me to this. How do you like the neighborhood, Eve? Great place to raise kids, isn't it? But wait, you're the one who's raising the kids. You're the one who's got the house, and your brother as a nanny, and a new boyfriend." Now he was yelling. "You're the one who's reading my fucking e-mail, because you get to do whatever the fuck you want!" He picked up a glass from the counter and, to my shock, hurled it at the wall with enough force to shatter it.

"You're scaring me," I said.

He didn't answer, just stared at me with something akin to hatred in his eyes.

"I can't talk to you right now." Numbly I reached down to pick up my purse. "I need to leave now."

"What's wrong, Eve? You can dish it out, but you can't take it?"

He was taunting me like we were in a schoolyard. I was more frightened for him than me. "I don't know if I should leave you like this, but I don't think I should stay."

"Don't treat me like I'm crazy!" he shouted. "I'm pissed off! I have every right to be pissed off! What's crazy is that I didn't do this a long time ago."

If this was a schoolyard, he thought I was the bully and he was just turning the tables on me. "I'm going now," I said. "Take care of yourself, Jon."

My head was spinning as I scurried out, and then as I drove home, and it hadn't stopped by the following morning. All through the day, I had flashbacks to his angry face, his mocking words echoing in my head.

By way of exorcism, I called his voice mail. "Hi, Jon, it's me. I know you're at work. I just wanted to say that

I'm sorry for the e-mails. I knew all along it was wrong, but you have no idea what it feels like to find out you've been lied to for months. You do things you never thought you would. I'm not trying to defend myself or say it was okay; I'm just saying I was in a lot of pain, too. I don't know if it would help for us to talk more right now, or if you just need time, but I want us to talk again. You just didn't even seem like you last night and I'm—" I broke off. "I hope you're okay. I'm sorry."

All night, I hoped Jon would call back. Ray called, but I didn't pick up.

I opened my e-mail and started typing.

Clayton,
I know we haven't been close for a while now, but I want to ask a favor. It's actually more for Jon than for me. I went to see him last night, and he was so angry. He was like a different person. I know he started tak-ing an antidepressant, but I don't know if he's still in therapy, or if he's talking much to you or to anyone else about how he's feeling. I hope so. Please do what you can to help him. And if possible, don't mention me.
Thanks,
Eve

I'd sent the e-mail and was staring blindly at the screen when the phone rang. It was just after ten, the witch-ing hour for people with kids. Hoping that it was Jon, I answered without checking the caller ID.

"Hello?" I said too loudly, like a person woken up from a nap.

"Eve! You answered." My mother sounded pleased. She was used to being screened.

"Hi, Mom."

"How are you?" she asked, lowering her voice the way you would when asking that question of a cancer patient.

"I'm fine."

"You don't sound all that fine."

"Well, it's sort of a generic answer."

"How are you really?"

"I think Jon and I are over. For good."

"Oh, Eve!" My mother's disappointment was palpable. "That's terrible!"

I should have tried it out on someone else first, someone like Lil or Charlie. Unfortunately, they were both unavailable at the moment. Otherwise engaged, as the phrase goes. "It could be worse," I said without conviction.

"Of course," my mother agreed immediately and unconvincingly. "It could always be worse."

"I could have a disease."

"That's true. You could."

"I don't know if there's too much to say about it right now. I just have to get used to it."

"Are you sure there's no chance you two could work it out? He really loves you."

"As it turns out, he really doesn't. Let's not talk about this."

"I just feel like if there's even the tiniest chance, it's worth it. For Jacob and Liv—"

I felt something white-hot inside me. "How can you say that? What about my father? And Charlie's?"

"I would have tried. They didn't want to."

"You said they're bastards. Both of them."

"They are."

"But you would have tried."

"Absolutely."

At that second, I felt sorrier for her than I did for myself. Which was saying something. My anger evaporated. "There's no hope here, Mom. Let's talk about something else."

She was quiet; then she said, "I'm sorry, Eve. I know how you've always felt about Jon."

I nodded, feeling the threat of tears.

"The reason I'm calling is because I wanted to come see you. And Charlie. I've missed him. He's a pretty good roommate, isn't he?"

"He actually is."

"And I'm dying to see Liv for the first time. Phil and I are doing a road trip up the coast. Can you believe my entire life I've never been through Big Sur?"

"Oh, right. Phil."

"Charlie told you I was seeing someone?"

"He mentioned it. He said you sounded happy."

"I am happy. And I'm finally going to see Santa Barbara. Remember how we used to watch that soap opera together when you were little? Remember Cruz and Eden?"

She sighed, I suppose at the memory of the star-crossed lovers. "No couple should have to overcome so many obstacles."

"Unless there's a team of writers, no couple ever does."

CHAPTER
23

For the first few days, I didn't tell anyone what had happened with Jon, because it would have meant admitting I'd spent months reading his e-mails. But the thought of him hating me was so awful that I couldn't bear it alone. I decided to confide in Dyan. Lil was a close second, but Dyan was actually trained to withhold judgment.

"What were you expecting?" she asked, a touch judgmentally, I thought.

"For him to act like Jon."

"Nobody goes through something like this and stays the same. He's getting in touch with his anger." She shifted in my visitor chair. "Damn, can't Chad order you a new chair? I feel like 'The Princess and The Pea' over here."

"I don't think it's in the budget."

She waved a hand dismissively. "I'll work it out for you."

"So, is that it? Is that all you've got for me?"

"Now you're even, you and Jon. He lied to you for months, you lied to him. You're still not over what he did, but you expect him to be over what you did in three days?"

"I only did it because of what he did."

"Two wrongs make a right in your book?"

"Remember how you talked to me when I first got back from maternity leave? What happened to that?" I asked.

"I was sitting in my therapist pose then." She shifted into it, then back again. "See the difference?"

"Any last advice?"

"Settle in for a long wait. Work on you."

I didn't have long to wait, actually. Jon left me a message a few days later. "Hi, Eve. I'm still pretty angry, but my therapist thinks this is a good time for you to join us for a session. I'm not sure if it'll do any good, but it's Tuesday at six-thirty." He gave the address and hung up.

Louise looked like the quintessential San Francisco therapist (in her early sixties, her long silver hair pulled back in a low ponytail, wearing a linen tunic and loose-fitting pants) and her office completed the picture. The walls were soft yellow with Japanese watercolors on all except the one directly behind her, which displayed her pedigree (Stanford). Between her upholstered white chair and the couch where Jon and I sat was a coffee table, which held a clear glass bowl filled with multicolored rocks, a small bubbling fountain, and a box of tissues. Thanks to the fountain, I had the continuous sensation of needing to pee. Jon's body was tense next to mine, and his face gave away nothing.

"I'm so glad you could join us today, Eve," Louise said. "Jon and I have been talking for a while about inviting you in." She paused and looked at me expectantly.

Not sure how to respond, I came up with "It's good to be here," as if I were a guest on a talk show.

"I know it's not a comfortable thing, coming into a session when I have a preexisting relationship with Jon. I'll try to be mindful of that." She was shifting her eyes equally between Jon and me as she spoke. It had a practiced look that I didn't like. But then, she was a professional. A professional with my life in her hands. Jon trusted her, it seemed, and he definitely didn't trust me. No matter what she said, her allegiance was to him, not to me or to our marriage. Who knew what she was thinking about me, especially in light of the e-mails? "Let me just start by asking you, Jon, what you'd like to get out of today's session. I'll ask you the same question next, Eve."

"I'd like to feel less angry about her reading my e-mails," he said. "Every time I think about it, I get furious all over again."

"Good. What about you, Eve?"

"The reason I went over to Jon's apartment the other day was to try to get a handle on things. I wanted to know if we were ever going to try again, or if we just need to move on. I feel like I have my answer, but I don't want Jon hating me."

"So your goal for this session...?" she prodded.

"I guess I have the same goal. For Jon to stop being angry with me. I don't want him smashing any more glasses."

Jon snorted. "Right. I'm the one with the anger problem."

"So we're agreed on our goal," Louise said quickly.

"Jon, what thoughts and feelings have you been having since Eve told you about the e-mails?"

"Like I said, anger."

"Drill a little deeper, Jon." She leaned in almost imperceptibly. "We've talked about how anger can cloak the more vulnerable emotions underneath. Emotions like sadness, disappointment, fear. Why don't we look at those? Maybe if Eve can address those, you'll find it easier to forgive her."

"Maybe I don't want to forgive her," he said. "Maybe I've been too forgiving for our entire marriage."

"Go with that," she said.

"She's been making all the decisions for months— years, really—and she comes to my apartment supposedly to decide together about our future. But first, she's got a bombshell to drop."

I wasn't following his logic. I looked at Louise for guidance, but she was nodding slowly, as if he'd unlocked some great secret vault.

"So her reading the e-mails...," Louise began.

"Yes, it was all about her," Jon said. Oh, good Lord, they were finishing each other's sentences. Yet another woman Jon was more intimate with than he was with me. "She wanted to know things, so she was entitled to get the answers by any means necessary. She's got no respect for me. And when I look back at how I've acted in this marriage, I've got no respect for me, either. How can you have a marriage without respect?"

Louise looked at me. "What's your reaction to what Jon just said?"

I was caught off-guard. I hadn't expected my turn to come so soon. It seemed like a good time to showcase my listening skills. "Well," I stalled, "I guess Jon feels disrespected."

"Does he have reason to feel disrespected?"

"Yeah. I mean, yes, I read his e-mails. It's pretty disrespectful behavior. But it's not fair to say that I've never respected him. There were pretty extenuating circumstances here. He'd just admitted he was involved with another woman—"

"But you read the e-mails for months!" Jon said.

"And you'd lied to me for months," I countered. "I didn't know what I could believe out of your mouth. So I figured the e-mails were the truth."

It felt like we were two children squabbling, waiting for a parent to intervene.

"So you felt you couldn't trust Jon," Louise said.

Oh, Stanford must have been proud to graduate a genius like her. "Yes."

"Jon, what's your response to Eve? Try to really consider from her perspective here."

"I guess I can see why she wouldn't trust me. Not immediately. But what makes me so mad is that she didn't give me a chance to earn her trust back. Even when she let me hang around more after Liv was born, she was so closed off." He was addressing only Louise, as if I weren't even in the room.

"What Jon's forgetting is how devastated I was," I said to Louise. "I mean, he seems to think the affair isn't that big a deal because he didn't have sex with Laney. But what about everything he told her about me and about our lives? What about how much he just plain wanted her? I mean, reading about him in that hotel room made my stomach churn. It's like, Laney was his fantasy, his perfect woman, and I was just his reality. Does he have any idea what that did to my self-esteem? To my view of our marriage? I was terrified to let him back in."

"Tell him," Louise said.

I turned to Jon, but I couldn't muster the same energy. I felt a little silly as I repeated, "I was terrified."

From the look on his face, nothing I'd said had penetrated. "That doesn't excuse what you did. All those months, you were treating me like shit for being dishonest when you were being dishonest yourself. You were being a hypocrite."

"Don't throw stones, Jon. I didn't treat you like shit for being dishonest, I treated you like shit for having an affair."

The words hung there between us. Then Jon said softly, "So you admit it. You admit you treated me like shit all those months. You were claiming you weren't punishing me, but you were."

"I guess I was," I said, defeated.

After a silence, Louise said, "That's a big admission, Eve. I give you a lot of credit for being able to own that. Jon, what does that mean to you?"

"I don't even know anymore." He was staring dispiritedly into the bowl of rocks.

"When Eve said how devastated she was, did you really hear her?" Louise asked.

"It's hard for me to hear her right now," he said. "I'm still too mad. She just sat there and made excuses for reading the e-mail. She made it my fault."

"Jon, focus on the hurt instead of the anger and speak directly to Eve. What hurt you about Eve reading the e-mails?"

He turned to me, his face creased with effort. "What hurts me the most isn't that you read the e-mails, it's that you just assumed all sorts of things from them and you never even asked me anything. All that stuff you said, about how she was my perfect girl and you were just my reality—you just assumed all of that. You don't know how I felt while I was involved with Laney, or how I've felt since you kicked me out. This whole time, I've been waiting for you to ask me questions about Laney and the affair, but you never did. I felt like maybe you didn't even care. And then I find out that you didn't ask me because you were reading my e-mails. But what I wrote to Laney wasn't the whole story." He swallowed back emotion. "Fuck, I would have read the e-mails with you if you'd asked. But you never did."

"How could I have known that?" I said. "I always thought you were the most honest, decent person I'd ever met, and suddenly I find out you had another woman. I mean, the first time I read your e-mail, I wasn't doing it to catch you; I was doing it to prove that Laney was nothing to you. And in those first conversations we had, you kept pretending she was nothing, but I knew you were lying."

"I was scared. I didn't want to lose my family."

"I was scared, too. It doesn't make your lying okay."

"It doesn't make yours okay, either."

We turned to Louise helplessly.

"This is good," she said. "You're both being honest. That's the first step toward forgiveness." She seemed to expect us to ask what the next step was, but we didn't. "You really love each other, or you wouldn't both be this hurt. But you need to decide if you want to move beyond that. You created this relationship together, and you can re-create it. It wouldn't be easy and it wouldn't be pretty, but you could, if you both wanted to."

Jon and I looked at each other. Neither of us spoke.

I figured out which Saturday Jon had spent with Laney. He'd laid the groundwork all week. The Monday before, he told me he'd just been assigned a bear of a project and that it had to be done by 9 AM the following Monday, no excuses allowed. He donned a worried expression, made it sound like his job was on the line. He said he didn't know how much of the weekend he'd have to work, but it would be at least Saturday. Obviously, he'd been leaving his options open. If Saturday had gone differently with Laney, I imagine he would have told me he was working Sunday, too. Maybe they would have spent the weekend in her hotel room. Who knows?

Having no reason to doubt him at the time, I told him he should do whatever he needed, pull an all-nighter if he had to. Seeing how nervous he was, I reassured him that he was good at his job and that everyone there loved him. I asked him what I could do to support him through the weekend; whatever it was, I'd do it.

If I'd had a different reaction, if I'd acted, say, annoyed at the disruption, maybe he would have gone through with it. Maybe he would have thought he was entitled to sleep with Laney, that he deserved it for putting up with someone like me. That was all it might have taken to send us over the edge, the wrong word at the wrong time. There was no sanctity in that.

After the therapy session, I thought about creating a new relationship, but that memory just kept tripping me up. I pictured Jon feigning job insecurity, and I saw myself going along with him, taking for granted that what he'd said was the truth. I couldn't imagine ever feeling that type of innocence again. I'd always know that Jon was a person who could concoct a scheme to see his mistress, who could come home and put on a performance, and all the while, perhaps even in his own mind, deny that she was anything more than a friend.

It seemed I wasn't ready to forgive just yet. But I'd try to move on.

Lil assured me that the best thing would be to keep seeing Ray. Since he was still calling, it seemed like the path of least resistance. We had a few chaste dates. He was in no rush to get physical, which wasn't doing much for my confidence, but at least it was giving me time to clear my head.

I was finally letting him pick me up at home. Maybe that would remind us both that this was actually a date.

I was in Olivia's room and had just finished breast-feeding her when the doorbell rang. "Charlie!" I called. "Can you come and take Liv?"

He poked his head in the door. "No, I'm going to answer that and meet your gentleman caller."

I stood up from the rocking chair and Olivia immediately burst into tears. "Charlie, sit down and rock her."

"You rock her an extra minute. I need to have a little talk with Ray. Find out his intentions, his prospects…" He was grinning.

I wasn't. I jiggled Liv, hoping she'd stop crying, but it wasn't working. "Seriously. Please take her."

"Seriously. I want to meet your guy."

"You'll meet him next time. Please." The doorbell pealed again. I hated to leave her when she was crying.

"Fine." Charlie took Liv from me, sat down, and began rocking.

"No, that's too fast. She likes it slower." I straightened my shirt and touched my hair.

"Hey, Liv and me have our own system." He maintained his pace and her sobs started to fade out. He patted her on the back. "You're cool, little one," he said softly.

"Okay, I'm going." I kissed the top of Liv's head.

"Don't forget, Lil's coming over tonight."

"If you do it in my bed, you're both dead."

He laughed. "At least one of us should be getting some."

I hurried down the hall and yanked open the front door. Ray looked just as he always did—poorly dressed, smiling warmly—but there was something transformative about having him on my doorstep. It was the first time it had been so apparent that this was a man who was here for no one but me.

As if to confirm the change, he leaned in and kissed me on the cheek. "You look lovely," he said.

I touched my hair self-consciously, but instead of protesting that *no, I didn't, I'd been breast-feeding five minutes ago,* I smiled and said, "Thank you."

"You ready?" he asked.

"Let's go."

I followed him to his car, parked behind Charlie's Datsun. I was surprised to see it was a relatively new, nondescript sedan. I'd pictured him in something with more character. This car fit in just fine in my neighborhood.

He opened the passenger door for me, and I got in and thanked him. Once he was in the driver's seat, I said, "Sorry I was late. Olivia was crying, and it's hard for me to leave when she's like that."

"That's what I figured. I could hear her from outside."

"Wow, really?"

"She's either got a hell of a pair of lungs, or your house is made of plywood."

I laughed. "You know, I've never trusted suburban construction."

He nodded mildly. It was one thing for me to knock where I lived, another for him to do it, and I appreciated that he got the distinction.

"Which neighborhood do you live in?" I asked.

"The Mission. Not too far from the park. I've been in the same apartment for about ten years."

"Has the neighborhood changed much?"

"Like everywhere else in the city, it's gotten hipper and richer. But you can still get the best burritos this side of Mexico. Do you like burritos?"

"As long as they're not too spicy."

"I know just the place. Next time." He reached across and squeezed my wrist. It was unexpected.

"Next time." I didn't know if I found his confidence off-putting, or his certainty that he wanted to see me again flattering. But I was smiling, so that meant something. "You should take a left here."

He nodded. "I memorized the route."

"From my house to the theater?"

"It's only a few turns."

His preparedness was peculiarly touching. I thought about squeezing him back, but where? His wrist seemed too copycat, his forearm was just weird, and his leg seemed too forward. By the time I'd run through my options, we were pulling into the parking lot.

There were a number of stores sharing the parking lot with the theater, and I glanced at the Bed Bath & Beyond. A young couple was exiting the store, laden with bags. It seemed obvious they were just moving in together, or maybe just married. He was clowning, putting a laundry basket on his head, and she was laughing in that "Oh, stop!" kind of way. Someday, I thought, you'll really want him to stop.

"It's pretty crowded tonight," Ray said as he looked for an open space.

"Saturday night," I said distractedly, watching the couple cross the lot toward their car.

"I can't remember the last time I went to a Saturday-night movie. We should go out afterward and get a milk shake. One milk shake, two straws, I'll tell the waitress, for me and my girl."

Startled, I looked over at him. He was still scanning the lot. I didn't know if he was mocking the idea of me being his girl, or was trying to let me know that he wanted me to be.

"Ah," he said, turning on his blinker and pausing to let a car back out of its space.

The ticket line was long, and I felt disoriented. I didn't know what Ray was trying to tell me, or what I wanted to happen. Jon was off with Jacob, Charlie and Lil were probably screwing on my couch, Olivia was asleep in her crib, and here I was, waiting to see the new Hugh Grant movie when I felt like there was nothing romantic or comic about love.

"Why did I want to see this movie?" I asked Ray. "He's just going to play the same character he's played twenty times already."

"He plays it well, at least. Isn't it good to know there's something you can count on in this uncertain world?" He was smiling at me. "There's Hugh Grant, death, and taxes."

He launched into a story about seeing a Hugh Grant movie in Indonesia, and I'm sure it was a good one, but I was only half-listening. It wasn't Jon holding me back anymore, just me. I tried to focus as Ray was wrapping up: "Sometimes, when you're traveling for a while, just knowing what you're going to get and then having that expectation fulfilled is the greatest thing. Then you can go back to the unknown, fortified."

"I can see that," I said. I could, I just couldn't think of anything to add. My last vacation had been to Disneyland. How strange, to know that Jon could now take the kids for a week and I could go anywhere I wanted.

Tickets in hand, we went inside the theater. The lines for the concession stand were formidable. "Can I get you anything?" he asked.

I shook my head. "Movie popcorn is like two days' worth of saturated fat."

"If that's your only argument against it—"

"No, my big argument is that I don't feel like standing in that line."

"Why don't you go ahead and find us seats? I'll stand in line."

"No, that's okay," I said. I did want to get away from the smell of the synthetic butter as quickly as possible. There was a banner above the concession stand promoting a new movie with a blobby blue cartoon character whose six-foot-tall cardboard cutouts were standing sentinel throughout the theater, and along the perimeter were arcade games that flashed and rang. Not to mention the throngs of people streaming by, laughing and talking. It felt like sensory overload.

"Is something wrong, Eve?"

I forced a smile. "No."

He looked at me carefully. "That's a little hard to believe."

"I'm a little out of sorts, I guess."

"Are you thinking about Liv? I can't imagine how hard it is to leave your kids behind."

Now I smiled for real. "Thanks."

"So look, if you want something to eat, I'll stand in the line. If you don't, let's go in. Where do I get off eating two days' worth of saturated fat, anyway?"

I wound up glad we didn't get popcorn or anything else that would interfere with Ray's smell. I couldn't believe I'd never noticed it before, this vague but delicious scent of anise and man. It wasn't cologne or soap or food; it was just him. We'd never sat this close, and I found I couldn't concentrate on the movie at all. I was focused entirely on Ray's proximity—when he shifted in his chair and his shoulder brushed mine, his forearm flat against the armrest, whether his head was tilted toward me, how his chest moved when he laughed. It must have been the pheromones. I was chemically drawn to Ray.

I kept trying to position my body in a way that would invite him to put his arm around me, but he seemed not to notice. There was no way he was that engrossed in the movie. Sure, it was passable, maybe even good by Hollywood standards, and Hugh Grant was his usual droll self. But come on.

Right before the third-act complications, I took matters

into my own hands. I plopped my head on his shoulder. There was nothing artful about it, and for the first few seconds, it was merely awkward. But then, Ray snaked his arm around me so that his hand was against my collarbone, and my entire body relaxed. I was surprised there wasn't a *whooshing* sound, the release was so complete.

Neither of us said anything. Every so often, I could tell that Ray was smelling my hair, and sometimes we held hands. We didn't laugh again at the movie, as if we didn't want to jostle each other and ruin the moment. When the final credits rolled, we watched them all the way through, from Hugh Grant to the Foley artist to the film score. As the lights came up in the theater, we turned to look at each other.

"Hey," he said.

"Hey."

We smiled at each other with such naked affection that I felt embarrassed. I didn't want him to see how much I'd needed that: to be close to someone, to breathe him in.

We left the theater and walked toward the car. I thought he might take my hand, but he didn't. Then, once we were in the car, I thought he'd suggest somewhere to go, maybe reference the milk shake again. He didn't.

A few quick turns, and we were back at my house. He was smiling faintly, like he was remembering something pleasant, so that seemed encouraging. I decided to see the silence as companionable.

Once the car was in park, he turned to me. "Good movie," he said.

"It was...just like all the others. Good to have an expectation fulfilled."

He laughed.

I waited for him to move toward me. It occurred to me that he might want me to ask him in, which I couldn't do. Lil and Charlie were in there. What if Olivia woke up? What if, for some reason, Jon brought Jacob home instead of keeping him overnight?

"I wish I could invite you in," I said. "It's just not a good night." But I still wanted to be kissed. I still felt the memory of his body against mine, and now that I knew what he smelled like up close, I could smell it from across the car. I turned toward him in a way that said—unequivocally, in no uncertain terms—*Kiss me.*

He was smiling at me, but he was immobile. I wondered how long I could sustain this pose, with my body angled toward him so obviously. I felt stupid, and undesirable, and, finally, irritated. "Thanks for the movie. Good night," I said, and leapt from the car. I didn't even give him the hug that was our standard.

Once inside the house, I sat on the couch for several minutes, waiting. I pictured him knocking on the door, and when I opened it, he would embrace me passionately. We'd share a first kiss that was worthy of his smell.

I looked out the window and saw he'd driven away. I walked down the hall to my room. Charlie's door was closed, but I could hear the faint squeaking of the metal futon.

I slept badly, and when I woke in the morning, there was an e-mail from Ray. I saw it had been sent the night before. The subject heading was "Will I ever see you again?" and in the body of the e-mail, only the word "Please." I typed back, only "Yes." I was smiling as I sent it.

A few days later, I was reading in my room, with the door closed, when Jon came by to pick up the kids. We'd kept our interaction minimal since the therapy session, and I'd been doing my best to keep him off my mind.

"Eve?" Charlie rapped with his knuckles.

"Come in," I said.

He closed the door behind him and sat on the edge of the bed, his face unusually somber. "Jon's here."

I nodded. "It's his night with Jacob."

"He wants to talk to you."

"Did he say what he wants?"

"No."

I sat up straighter on the bed so that I could see myself in the mirror. I'd hoped my medical spa "regime" would turn me into an "After" photo by now, but I still felt distinctly "Before." How did my hair manage to straddle limp and frizzy at once? Not that it made any difference, really. "Tell him to come on back."

Charlie arched an eyebrow.

"Yeah, it's going to be pretty erotically charged. Somehow, we just might be able to resist each other." The idea

that attraction between Jon and me had become laugh-
able filled me with sudden sadness.

Charlie reached out and patted my shoulder awkwardly. "I'll go get him, okay?"

Waiting for Jon, I tried to smooth my hair. He caught
sight of me from the doorway, and I felt foolish for engaging in such useless vanity.

"Come on in," I said.

He stepped into the room. "Is it okay to shut the door?
I don't want—"

"Jacob to hear," I finished for him. "I know. Neither
do I."

"Not that I'm expecting to yell or anything," he assured
me quickly. "Or break any glasses."

"That's good to hear."

"I'm sorry about that, by the way. I just kind of lost it
that night. No matter how angry I get, I don't want to do
things like that."

"I understand. It was a pretty intense night, to put it
mildly."

He nodded, a grateful look in his eyes. "Well, I'll just
get to what I wanted to tell you. I know you used to say I
was sleepwalking through my therapy—"

"That wasn't what I said."

"It's what you meant."

"Well, yeah."

"You were right. I was sleepwalking. Now that I'm
really doing it, what I'm finding out is that I was sleepwalking through a lot of stuff in my life." He ran his hand
through his hair and fixed his eyes on the book on my

nightstand. "Somewhere along the line, I guess I started to think of you as a force of nature. I thought nothing I did made a difference, that it would just end up being your way so I might as well give in right from the start. I never should have left this house, Eve. I should have fought." He blinked so suddenly that it looked like a tic. His eyes briefly met mine. "And now, I don't even know that I want back in, I'm so mad at you, but I think I might just be mad at me. It's all pretty jumbled at the moment." His laugh was more like a hiccup. "Louise is calling this progress."

"Why are you telling me this, Jon?" I asked gently.

"Because I don't think I was entirely fair to you in our therapy session. I'm not ready to be fair to you yet, but I hope to be someday. Does that make sense?"

"In Louise-speak, you hope to hear me someday?"

He smiled for just a second. "I've been depressed, and I've been angry about a whole lot more than just the e-mails, much as those piss me off. I think I wanted to hurt you like I've been hurting, but there's got to be some other way to deal with it, something other than us shooting each other full of holes."

"I hope there is," I said.

"We're going to be in each other's lives no matter what. Louise says we should think of it as a work in progress."

"I guess you could say that about pretty much anything. Or anyone."

"She does. She uses that phrase three times a session. To be honest, sometimes it drives me fucking bonkers."

We both laughed.

"I should go," he said. "Jacob's waiting. I just wanted to see you face-to-face. You said you were reading my e-mails to figure out who I am; well, I'm trying to figure that out, too."

I was proud of him, and envious, too. He was doing what Dyan had told me to do. He wasn't just figuring things out relative to me, he was figuring them out relative to him. I was running over the same old ground; he was in unfamiliar terrain. Until Laney, I'd assumed that whenever I broke new ground, it would be with him. Maybe no marriage can sustain that.

"You're really doing something, Jon. It takes guts," I said.

A look passed between us of such true understanding that I realized this was the closest I'd felt to him since that day at the aquarium. No, since before Thanksgiving.

"Well, I should go," he said. "Take care of yourself."

"You too, Jon."

My mother and Phil Tibbs were coming that weekend. Charlie and I couldn't resist using his full name every time we referred to him once we found out he was the owner of Phil Tibbs Motors, and we referred to him often. "Do you think Phil Tibbs likes pickles?" Charlie would ask, and I'd start giggling. "Do you think Phil Tibbs will walk around the house wearing an undershirt, boxers, and black socks?" I'd ask, to his amusement. Jacob started getting in on it, too. "Do you think

Phil Tibbs likes math?" he said to me as I was tucking him in. "I don't know, sweetie," I answered, kissing his nose. "Do you want him to?" Jacob nodded. "I want him to do all my math."

Phil Tibbs Motors sold only American cars. Charlie and I made bets on what kind of car he'd drive: Charlie said a Cadillac Escalade (just like all the rappers), and I went with an Oldsmobile, though I wasn't sure they still existed. The car that pulled into the driveway on Friday night was actually a silver Chevy pickup truck, its engine growling loudly enough that Jacob ran excitedly to the window.

"Time to meet Phil Tibbs," I whispered to Charlie. "Will Phil Tibbs like us?"

"Will we like Phil Tibbs, that's the real question," Charlie whispered back.

Jacob had flung open the door and was shouting, "Mom-Mom!"

My mother looked over at Phil, who nodded—in permission?—and then she ran to Jacob and hugged him tight against her. "My baby boy!" she said.

"I'm not a baby!" Jacob protested, but he was still smiling inside her embrace. "Mom-Mom's blond!"

It was true. Mom-Mom was now blond and wearing a colorful scarf like a headband, like she was Annette Funicello from those beach movies. Phil Tibbs's doing?

Phil Tibbs went to grab their bags from the back of the truck; then he strode forward. He was of average height, barrel-chested, with blond-gray hair that had thinned enough to see his liver-spotted scalp through. His face looked equally weathered, though his teeth were straight, and I'd seen worse features.

Putting the bags down on the front stoop, he thrust a hand out toward me. "Phil Tibbs," he said. "Pleased to meet you."

I avoided looking at Charlie, because I knew we'd both crack up. "It's good to meet you," I said. "Come on in."

He entered behind my mother, who was now clutching Charlie. "Do you know how I've missed you?" she told him.

Phil said, affably enough, "Good thing she's got me for company these days." He waited until my mother released Charlie, then shook Charlie's hand, repeating, "Phil Tibbs. Pleased to meet you."

Charlie did laugh then, but somehow he got away with it. He just seemed good-humored. "How was your drive, guys?"

But Jacob couldn't contain himself to wait for the answer. "You have to see Olivia," he said. "You've never even seen her!"

"I've seen pictures," my mother said. "But I would love to see the real thing."

Charlie glanced at the clock. "She gets up from her nap around now. She'll probably have a big old stinky diaper." Jacob laughed. Charlie looked at me. "Maybe Mom-Mom should change it. That's how you greet family, right?"

My mother said to me uncertainly, "I could change her diaper, if you want."

"No, no. That's just how we greet uncles." I gestured

toward the couch. "Why don't you sit down and relax. I'll go take care of that and then bring Liv out."

"We've been on our asses for hours now," Phil said. "It'd be good to stand. Why don't we come with you?"

Before I could decide how to answer, Charlie said, "Olivia can get a little freaked if there are too many people in the room with her. Why don't you follow me into the kitchen, where we can all remain standing just as long as you want. I can get you drinks, some food if you're hungry…"

To my relief, Phil, my mother, and Jacob all followed Charlie into the kitchen. By the time I walked in, holding a freshly diapered Olivia, they were all sitting at the table, except for Jacob, who was jumping around.

"Why so hyper, buddy?" Charlie asked him.

"Mom-Mom and Phil Tibbs are here!" Jacob said.

Charlie openly smirked, but my mother and Phil were smiling at each other and didn't seem to notice.

"She's just beautiful," my mother said, turning toward me. "Can I hold her?"

"Of course," I answered, placing her carefully in my mother's arms. "Here's a cloth. She's a drooler."

"They all are at that age," my mother said.

Jacob came and huddled close to my mother. "I can make her smile."

"I'm sure you can," she said.

Olivia wasn't smiling, though. I wished she would, but at least she wasn't crying. Jacob tried singing little songs, dancing around, but Olivia wasn't in the mood just then.

Phil had shifted his chair closer to my mother and was joining Jacob in moving around and making faces. "Hey, Jake," he said. "Do you know the one about the wheels on the bus?"

"Everyone knows that one," Jacob said.

"You want to sing it with me?"

"Okay." But it was clear he didn't much want to.

"I'll sing it with you, man," Charlie said. "I love that one."

Phil looked at Charlie a bit sharply, as if he thought he was being made fun of. Then he seemed to decide Charlie had good intentions and his face relaxed. "Can I hold her, Eve?" Phil asked.

"Sure."

My mother passed Liv over to Phil, and she made a noise like she was about to bawl, but then, somehow, she went the other way. As Phil Tibbs minced around for her amusement, she actually started to smile, and then to laugh.

"I got the touch," he said.

"You do." My mother gazed at him with such frank adoration that I had to look away.

"Hey, keep it clean, you two," Charlie said.

Phil Tibbs spit when he talked. And he talked pretty much all the time. He was loud, he was abrasive, he couldn't stop saying "ass" in front of my kids, he laughed too loudly at his own jokes. He was sixty, which reminded me that my mother was nearly sixty, which reminded me that she didn't have that many Phil Tibbses beating down her door, and she'd have fewer all the time.

That's why I tried to cast a kind, forgiving eye toward Phil Tibbs. He did seem genuinely taken with my mother. He laughed too loudly at her jokes, too. He patted her arm with a pride of ownership that—while reminiscent of the way he might, say, pat a Buick with low miles—was nonetheless pride; I'd never seen that in her other boyfriends. The night they arrived, I caught sight of her going into the bathroom as he was coming out, and he took her hand and kissed it, slow and sweet, right there in the doorway. I knew, in that second, that if they weren't in love already, they were well on their way.

Not to mention, he was sparing no expense for this trip. They'd stayed in some five-star hotel right on the water in Santa Barbara and drank champagne on the beach. When they left, they were going to continue up the coast to Mendocino, to a lodge with a fireplace and a Jacuzzi. No one had ever treated her like that, not in her entire sixty years.

We were going on the first triple date of my life, and what a motley crew we were: Lil and Charlie, my mother and Phil, Ray and me. Jon had already picked up the kids. While I was in my bedroom getting ready, a note was slipped under my door. In an uneven scrawl, it said:

Eve,
Do me a favor? Meet me in the backyard as soon as posible.
Phil

I decided to pretend that he really did know how to spell "possible" but was just writing fast. I hurriedly applied my lipstick and opened my door. I looked left and right before entering the hallway, like I was in a spy movie. Then undetected, I slipped through the house and out the sliding glass doors into the yard.

Phil Tibbs was sitting on Jacob's swing set, his feet hidden in six inches of grass. Since our yard was barely bigger than the swing set itself, you would have thought I could have kept it up.

"Hi, Phil," I said. "What's up?" I perched on the swing next to him.

"Maybe we oughta wait until Charlie's here," he said. "Is it okay if I smoke a cigar?"

"Well..." I hesitated. "I don't want my hair and my clothes to smell like it. Maybe you could go over to the fence and then point it away from me?"

"Maybe I shouldn't. Your mom doesn't like the smell much, either." He smiled faintly. "I tried to take up pipes for a while. You like pipes?"

We both looked up as the glass doors opened and Charlie emerged from the house, barefoot. He approached and sat on the other swing so that we flanked Phil.

"So what's your deep, dark secret, Phil?" Charlie asked.

Phil looked flustered by the question.

"I'm just kidding," Charlie said.

"Oh. I guess I'm just a little nervous here." Phil cleared his throat. "I've been married before, you know."

"I didn't know," I said.

"Just the one time, you understand. It was a long time

ago, and we didn't have any children. She's a good lady. She got married again, had five kids. Jesus, five kids. Can you imagine?"

"That's a lot of fucking kids," Charlie said.

Phil nodded. "So I'm just saying, I don't have any kids. I make a good living; I've got a nice house; I can take care of your mom."

Charlie and I exchanged glances.

"I think I can be a good grandpa to Liv and Jake. And I know you're both grown, so we could just get to know each other. I'd like to marry your mom—that's what I'm saying."

Charlie and I were quiet; then he started grinning. "Phil Tibbs wants to marry Mom."

I began to smile, too. "Phil Tibbs is going to be our stepfather."

Phil looked like he wasn't quite sure what the joke was, but was trying to be game. "I'm hoping so."

"When are you going to ask her?" Charlie was almost bouncing up and down with excitement. He looked like Jacob.

"I wanted your opinion on that. Do you think she'd rather I asked her in private, up in Mendocino, or at dinner tonight?"

"Dinner tonight," I said.

"Definitely dinner," Charlie confirmed.

I hadn't spent much time in steak houses in my life. My mom couldn't afford them when we were growing up, so occasionally we'd go to a chain restaurant that had an "all you can eat" meat buffet where the price for kids was based on some body weight algorithm. By the time I was eleven, the forced weigh-ins had lost their charm. I resented the way my mother was too busy gorging to even talk, and at the end of the meal, she'd look out over the sea of formica tabletops with a dreamy satiety.

There was definitely no formica in evidence at the steak house Phil had picked. I hadn't known a place like this even existed in San Francisco. Dark wood paneling, mahogany booths upholstered in black leather, plain white tablecloths, TVs (on mute) tucked discreetly into every corner showing sports, no admission of sunlight, not a feminine touch in the house, and an older, mon-eyed, predominantly male clientele that looked like they might have been the masterminds behind Enron—it was like we'd been transported to Texas. Our waiter even had a faint twang, though I suspected it might have been affected to increase his tips. San Francisco reasserted itself only in that there were no stogies blazing anywhere, by force of law.

Phil was doing his best to seem right at home (as if he were some captain of industry instead of just a small-business owner), while my mother looked around with the kind of enchantment that clearly formed the backbone of their relationship. Charlie was sharing her enthusiasm, Lil seemed unusually subdued, Ray head-to-toe amiable, and I was just reeling from the bludgeoning masculinity of the place. *My mother's getting engaged in an old boys' club. And I'm here at the closest thing to a family dinner, with someone other than Jon.*

Ray laid down his menu and found his way into Phil's monologue on the great steak houses of the world. "So you're a traveler, Phil?" he asked.

Phil looked unsure how to answer the question, as if Ray might be putting him on. "I've been around," he said, somehow managing to sound both cautious and slightly challenging.

"What about you, Barbara?" Ray turned to my mother with a friendly smile.

"Would you believe that this trip with Phil"—my mother patted Phil's arm—"is my first time really seeing the coast? When I visit Eve, I always fly or drive the quick way inland. I can't believe I've waited so long. It just takes your breath away." She smiled at Ray, then quickly turned her attention back to Phil.

"Pretty spectacular," Ray agreed. "What about you, Charlie? Do you always take the quick way?"

Charlie laughed. "Oh, no. I take the long way around every time."

"Good man." Ray grinned at Charlie. "So let me get this straight. Charlie and Eve, you both grew up down in Orange County, so you've been Californians all your lives?" Charlie nodded. "And Barbara, what about you?"

"I'm from Kansas originally."

"So you must know your steaks," Ray said.

I glanced at Phil, whose grasp around his glass of bourbon seemed particularly tight. He hadn't decided how to proceed with another alpha male at the table. Charlie and I had been yielding the floor to him all weekend. Until then, I hadn't realized that Ray even was an alpha male. But there he was, directing the conversation, drawing Lil into it, asking where she'd grown up. I felt safe beside him, knowing that everything was in hand. I didn't have to worry about how we'd all get along; Ray would see that we did. I'd missed being taken care of in that way, being part of a couple. The waxing and waning, the give and take, *I'm tired, you take the load for a while.*

I wasn't sure Phil would do that for my mom, but I hoped. She'd been carrying the load herself for so long. No one had ever proposed to her—not even after finding out she was pregnant—and I liked the idea of someone telling her, *I choose you.* I didn't know what would happen afterward, if they'd even go through with the marriage, but that moment would mean something regardless. At least once in her life, every woman should feel chosen.

Charlie was whispering in Lil's ear. Maybe he was telling her about the proposal. Lil nodded and forced a smile. The disparity in their affections was painfully clear.

I was momentarily distracted from my concern by the waiter's arrival. Charlie knew Phil was paying, and was living it up by ordering a twenty-two-ounce Kansas City strip steak. Phil smiled approvingly and said he was ordering the same thing, in honor of my mother. I got the salmon, expecting Phil to protest; he didn't comment, just gave me a smile slightly laced with pity.

After we'd ordered, and Phil had finished his drink, he seemed to return to his usual form. He told stories about the tough climate for American cars, about the tough climate for America in general, and even though I could feel Ray bristle next to me, he maintained a genial expression.

I was surprised when a few minutes later, he took my hand. It seemed so proprietary, right there in front of my mother and brother. We hadn't even kissed, but it felt like some sort of announcement. I got a little jolt as his fingertips lightly caressed my knuckles, and on a purely physiological level, my body knew it was owed a kiss. But then I thought of Jon in my bedroom the other night, of the man he was trying to become, and what I wanted most was to get out of there.

"Excuse me," I said to the table, standing up.

"Excuse me, too," Lil said, to my surprise. "Women in pairs. You know how it is, guys." Once we were away from the table, she took my arm and said, "Let's go outside. I need a smoke."

It was a chilly night, and I wished I'd worn panty hose,

much as I ordinarily hated them. Still, I was grateful to
have a minute alone with her.

"How did you know I needed this?" I asked, rubbing
my bare arms for warmth as she pulled a pack of ciga-
rettes from her purse.

"You?" she said. "Honey, I needed it more."

I had a sinking feeling as I waited for her to continue.

"Your brother's a doll, but he's driving me fucking
nuts." She lit up a cigarette and puffed at it with urgency.

"How?" I tried to keep the defensive tone out of my
voice.

"He's trying to take things too far. I mean, what am
I doing at dinner with your mother? Please. I'm not his
girlfriend."

"I guess he wants you to be." There was no guessing
about it.

"I was clear from the start. These things have a shelf
life."

"Always?"

She looked at me; then her eyes flicked back to the
street. "Look, it would take a lot for me to reconsider once
I decide what a guy's good for." I bristled and she went
on. "I don't mean it like that. Charlie's great. But the odds
are, if we keep going like this, he's going to fall in love
with me. And I'm not going to fall in love with him."

She was trying to sound resolute, but I heard something underneath. A certain catch in her voice.

"How can you be so sure?"

"Because he's obvious. He's young, and I know everything he's going to say and do before he does. And I'm

starting to get that heinous impulse to be his mother. You know, to tell him how much potential he's got, to try to help him figure out what's good for him and how to get it. I don't want to go there." She sucked on her cigarette.

"So, is it that you're not able to fall in love with him because he's obvious, or is it that you don't want to fall in love with him?"

"I don't want to, so I won't." She turned away, exhaled in the other direction. "I'm going to end things. Tonight. Or maybe tomorrow. Soon."

"You're going to break his heart." My baby brother finally puts himself in a position to really care about someone, and what does it get him? What does it get any of us?

"This isn't my fault." She took one final drag, then stamped out the cigarette on the concrete with more force than seemed necessary.

"I'm not saying it's your fault. But is it possible this could really work? That Charlie could get his shit together and the two of you could fall in love?" I thought of how Charlie was with Jacob, and what it would be like if he, Lil, and Luke actually became a family and he lived here for good. Was it really so implausible?

From Lil's face, the answer to that was yes.

I could barely look at Charlie when we reseated ourselves at the table. Ray leaned toward me and immediately asked if I was okay.

I shook my head to say *Not now,* and he nodded. Then he said to the table, "So, have you guys heard the one about the schnauzer who walks into a bar?"

Everyone said they hadn't, and Ray proceeded to tell a bad joke with such obvious relish that we had to laugh. Well, everyone else laughed. I just couldn't bear sitting there, watching Charlie lavish attention on Lil, knowing he was about to get hit by a freight train. There was no warning him, though. Warnings should have come sooner.

But I had warned him. Lil had warned him. Somehow he'd believed that he'd overcome her resistance and make her love him. Maybe it was his hope, his utterly foolish faith—is there any other kind?—that was killing me as I sat there.

I did my best to participate in the conversation, and Ray made it as easy for me as he could, like a boat towing a dinghy. I could tell they all liked him, even Phil. As the dinner plates were being cleared away, I leaned over and said in Ray's ear, "I think Phil's going to propose to my mother soon. Leave gaps for him, okay?"

Ray turned to me with the complete delight that I wanted to feel, that I liked to think I would have felt in the absence of Charlie's impending devastation. He squeezed my shoulder and whispered, "That's good news. They're a good match."

"Really? You think so?" I whispered back.

"She likes to adore people, he needs to be adored."

"That's so cynical."

He shook his head. "No, because he's prepared to earn it. Trust me, it's going to work."

I smiled at him and took his hand.

Charlie was in the middle of a story about his days as a mechanic, imitating the accents of some of his Hispanic coworkers. It wasn't his most politically correct moment, and I could tell Lil wasn't enjoying it. Phil was laughing heartily, and my mother was taking her cue from him.

"That's just what they sound like," Phil said. "Exactly!"

"He's always been a good mimic," my mother said.

"When he was a little kid," I interjected, wanting to move away from that particular impression, "he did the best Kermit."

"And you were Miss Piggy," Charlie said. "She was a dynamite Miss Piggy."

Ray looked from Charlie to me. "There's no way the two of you are getting out of here without doing those."

I felt my cheeks getting pink. "I don't know if I remember the lines."

"You can just say anything." Ray smiled encouragingly.

"Yeah, just say anything." As out of sorts as Lil was, even she couldn't resist.

Charlie—forever the ham—was rubbing his hands together in a pantomime of fiendish delight. "Hmm, which bit should we do?" He appeared to consider. "I've got it! It's got to be 'Together Again'!"

I groaned. "No way."

"I know you remember the words to that. We did it like a hundred times."

"Even I remember the words," my mother said.

"What's 'Together Again'?" Ray asked.

"It's from *The Muppets Take Manhattan*," Charlie said. "Early in the movie, the whole cast sings it and then Kermit gets amnesia and is separated from everyone, and once he and Miss Piggy reunite, they sing it on a carriage ride through Central Park. So Eve and I used to do *our* version of the Kermit and Miss Piggy version. Sometimes we'd get really crazy with it, do a bunch of scat. It was priceless, I tell you, priceless."

Everyone was smiling, encouraging us. Charlie and I really had passed hours that way, and at the memory, a feeling of warmth spread through me. "Let me just say, his Kermit is better than my Miss Piggy. And I'm not doing any scat. I'm sticking to the lyrics."

"Fine by me," Charlie said. "I wish I had a harmonica so I could get the pitch right. But okay, here goes." He whistled the melody, then stopped to address his audience. "Just so you know, Kermit really does start by whistling." When he began to sing, it was in a Kermit impersonation so dead-on you would have thought he'd spent the last twenty years practicing.

Emboldened, I waited for my cue, then took my solo in what I hoped was a passable Miss Piggy. Charlie and I dueted for the chorus, gazing hammily into each other's eyes, and when we'd finished, the table exploded into applause.

Phil actually pounded a fist. Charlie stood to take a bow, reached around to take my hand and pulled me to my feet, with both our hands raised jubilantly à la *Rocky*.

When we sat down, my face was flushed. I liked that our performance and its reception were so discordant with the overall vibe of the restaurant, as if we owned the place and the hell with all of them.

"You're beautiful," Ray said. He didn't even lower his voice.

Charlie was grinning at me before he turned to Lil. She ran her hand along the side of his face in a way that told me she could love him, if she didn't already.

Phil cleared his throat. "Well, it seems like love's in the air. So maybe now's the time." He shifted in his chair to face my mother, taking both her hands in his. "Barb, you're a miracle. You're a goddamn comet, is what you are. I want to give you everything. I want to give you my life, if you'll take it."

My mother's chin trembled as she looked at him, disbelieving.

"I want to get down on the floor here in front of you, but I'm afraid my knees will give out and they'll have to take me out on a stretcher." He and my mother both laughed. "So instead, why don't I just reach in my pocket and you can take a look at the ring I've got in there." He released her hands and pulled out a jewelry box. Tears starting to run down her face, she opened the box. "If you don't like it, we'll change it. That goes for a lot of things. You don't like them, we'll try to change them. So what do you think?" He smiled at her tenderly. "Will you be my wife?"

"Oh, Jesus," she said. "Of course, I will!" Her hands were shaking as she lifted the ring out of its cushioning.

She looked over at me. "I don't even know which finger it goes on! That's how close I've ever gotten!" We all laughed. I realized I was crying. Charlie had the biggest smile I'd ever seen, and Lil was wiping at her eyes.

"It's this one," I said. I pointed at my naked finger, and cried some more.

CHAPTER

27

As we stood outside the restaurant, my head was fizzy with more than champagne. It felt like a contact high. I could see Lil was sharing in the sense that all is possible, all is permissible, there's no tomorrow. She said something into Charlie's ear and he turned to the rest of us. "We're going to Lil's house. Don't wait up," he said. He clasped Phil's hand. "Welcome to the family, man. And thanks for the killer steak."

Phil gripped Charlie's shoulder with his free hand. I saw his jaw was clenched with suppressed emotion. "It's my pleasure."

As Lil and Charlie hurried down the street, I looked at Ray. "Where's your car?" I asked.

If he was surprised, he didn't show it. "A few blocks away." He smiled. "You need a lift?"

I laughed at the perhaps unintentional double entendre, peeking over at my mother and Phil to see if they'd heard. My mother was holding her hand up in front of her admiringly, Phil enraptured by her pleasure. They were consumed.

"Mom," I said, "I think we're going to go out for a

drink." I embraced her, then Phil. "Congratulations, you two. Go home and celebrate."

My mother giggled. "We will."

Ray shook their hands and said his good-byes; I barely heard him, I was so focused on what was about to happen. Every cell in my body thrummed with anticipation.

I took his arm as we walked in desirous silence. When we were next to his car, I couldn't tell who had kissed whom first, only that we'd moved together as if choreographed, tongues in mouths, hands in hair, my back against the passenger-side door. I don't know how long we stayed like that, how many people passed by, but when he stepped back just slightly to look into my face, I nearly collapsed. I'd never before felt literally weak in the knees, like I'd been making out with a matinee idol instead of an aging community-college professor. But we were all aging, really. And holy shit, that was a *kiss*.

"Wow," he said.

I laughed, glad he thought so, too. I'd been a little afraid it had been a figment of my imagination, the product of too many celibate months. It had been months since anyone had touched me sexually. Since Jon had.

"Let's go to your apartment," I said, drowning out my own thoughts.

He hesitated.

"What? I want to. I really, really want to." I pressed my body against his again. I could feel he was hard.

"I know. I want to. But I don't know about tonight."

"What's wrong with tonight?"

"I think you might be—" He stopped himself. "Look,

how about if I make you dinner later this week? You can come over then." He ran his finger along my cheekbone. "I know a good bar right near here. Best dry martini in town."

"Then we go to your apartment?" I hadn't had this feeling in—was it years? Married sex is different—and I wanted to stoke it longer.

"Not tonight, but soon. Pick a night this week."

I thought about my schedule, about the kids, and it was like every horny impulse drained out of my body. I was back to being *her* again. "Maybe you should just take me home."

"Are you mad?" His hand paused, still on my face.

"No." It was the truth. "Dinner will be good. I like dinner."

He pulled me closer. "I'm the king of pasta. A pasta pasha."

My laugh was faintly nostalgic.

I picked the following Saturday. I wanted to be able to stay over after the sex I hoped we'd be having, and both kids were slated to stay over at Jon's apartment that night.

My libido—previously in hibernation—had been reactivated. Lil laughed at me, how I seemed like a teen-ager who couldn't wait to get some. It was true, I didn't want to wait, though the wait was tantalizing. I was having robust fantasies about what it would be like with Ray. I had the feeling he was an experienced lover, and I was eager to experience everything.

Jon had been with only one woman before me, and now that I had enough distance to reflect honestly, sex between us had never been of the "bombs bursting in air" variety. In the beginning, I was so thrilled to be with someone loving that anything satisfied me; I could have an orgasm from Jon bringing me a glass of water. But as the years went by, his repertoire never grew and I suppose mine didn't, either, not even my vocabulary for what I wanted. That's because what I wanted was for it all to be as effortless as it had been, and since I knew that wasn't possible, I contented myself with what was.

Now I didn't have to. I could ask Ray to show me what he knew, and help me figure out what I really liked. Whatever happened with Ray, this was an opportunity. I did my best to banish Jon from my thoughts so I could take it.

Lil seemed to be indulging herself, too. Instead of seeing each other less that week, Charlie was going to her house every night. I thought that maybe she'd changed her mind about him, but when I saw her on Wednesday, she said she hadn't. "I know, I know, I've got to let him go," she said. "But you don't know what it's like. Or maybe you do, now." She gave me a sly look. "Now that you're aching for the professor. Think about what it would be like if you were with someone who could fuck like the professor kisses. Well, maybe you will be. But I am right now." I resisted the image that conjured. "I'm going to end it," she said. "I am."

Every night, I tried to wait up for Charlie, thinking that he might need a shoulder to cry on. But he never came back until early the next morning and he was always in high spirits. It hurt me to see him prancing in, as gleeful as a little boy. He had no idea. He thought he'd won.

On Friday morning, I was lying in wait when he walked in the front door.

"Hi," I said, louder than I'd intended, startling him.

"Fuck!" he exclaimed. He threw himself on the couch next to me. "What are you doing?"

"Just reading." I indicated the magazine I was using as a prop.

His eyelids drooped as he assumed a dreamy expression, as if reliving the night before.

"Here's the thing, Charlie," I said. He rolled his head toward me, eyeing me sideways. "I'm just wondering if Lil is right for you. I mean, since when do you want an instant family?"

"Why are you worried about this all of a sudden?"

"Because you and Lil seem more serious now."

"It's not serious," he said unconvincingly.

"But you want it to be."

"Lil's a great woman, Luke's a great kid. I don't analyze everything like you do."

"I think you're in love with her."

"I think it's none of your business." He stood up. "Are we done here?"

"Does she know? Have you told her?"

"Eve, stay out of it."

I pinpointed the shadow crossing his face. He was afraid I'd tell Lil he loved her, and that would be the end.

So he did know. Deep down, he knew he hadn't really broken through. "She already knows, Charlie."

"She told you that?"

"Not in so many words."

He was quiet, and then a smile came over his face.

"What?" I demanded.

"She knows I love her, and she's inviting me over every night. It doesn't take a genius to figure this out, right?"

Oh, God. Earlier he'd seemed to know on some level that he was on borrowed time; maybe he'd been prepared for things to end. Now I'd somehow convinced him that Lil loved him, too.

He took my silence as confirmation. "Don't worry, Eve. I think everything's going to be fine. I'll even start breakfast. I've got tons of energy."

As he headed for the kitchen, I thought frantically about how to undo this conversation without betraying Lil. There was no way I could protect him now, not that I ever could.

When the doorbell rang on Saturday night, Jacob went running down the hallway, his backpack already on. "Bye, Mom!" he shouted gaily.

"You have to wait. Your dad has to get Olivia and her things, too," I called after him.

He'd already yanked open the front door. "Hi, Daddy," he said. "Let's go."

I caught up with Jacob, and smiled at Jon. "Hi."

As Jon's eyes scanned me appreciatively, I felt myself

blushing. "Hi. You look good." He put his hands up, smiling, and said, "None of my business why you look so good. But you do. You look kind of glowy, if that's a word."

The blush intensified. "Thanks."

"Let's go," Jacob said again, tugging at Jon's jacket.

"We just have to get Olivia and then we're out of here," Jon said.

"Why do we have to bring Olivia?" Jacob was pouting as he looked up at Jon. "Then we can't do a lot of stuff."

"But there's a lot of stuff we can still do," Jon said. He squatted down so he was on Jacob's level. "I got some new games for my apartment. And you know Liv sleeps a lot. There's plenty of time for just you and me."

"It's not enough," Jacob said.

"But you know what's happening tomorrow? There's a Giants game on TV. I bought you one of those big foam hands you like. I'll make you a hot dog, it'll be like we're there."

"It's not like being there," Jacob said, looking at the ground, "because Liv will be there."

"Why don't I go get Liv ready, and you two can talk a little more?" I said.

Jon smiled at me gratefully and turned back to Jacob.

Olivia was drooling more, and she'd be teething soon. I just hoped she wouldn't be too fussy that day, for Jacob's sake. As I gathered her things, I could hear the rise and fall of the conversation in the other room—Jacob protesting, Jon mixing empathy with reality. He'd always been good at that. I had faith that things would be in hand by the time I changed Olivia and brought her back into the living room.

Jon and Jacob were sitting on the couch, and Jon was talking quietly to Jacob, who still looked discontented. "Here she is," I said, kissing her head. "How's everything out here?" Olivia was letting out a low gurgle, but was otherwise calm.

Jacob didn't answer, just stared at the floor.

"We're going to have fun," Jon said. "Why don't we get going, buddy?"

"Fine," Jacob muttered, standing up.

As I handed Olivia to Jon, she let out an earsplitting cry. "I think she might be on the verge of teething," I said.

Jon looked like he appreciated my effort, but that explanation wasn't fooling anyone. I knew it hurt him to be this much of a stranger to Liv.

He put his arm out so I could slip the bag with her things over his shoulder, and in that second, our eyes met. "Bye, Eve," he said, his eyes sad, his smile wistful.

CHAPTER
28

Some nights just can't be salvaged. They start out off-key, and somehow all the good intentions and planning and hope in the world can't dispel the underlying whiff of doom, and at the end, you realize you should have just quit while you were ahead. You shouldn't have suggested going to one more bar, or adding on a cappuccino, or watching the second in a double feature. You should have accepted the simple fact that some nights aren't your night.

But there are those times when, miraculously, it turns around. One of you names the tension, or just starts laughing, and somehow you've done it. You're having a different time than you thought you would, but maybe even better for the intimacy of the near miss. You've dodged a bullet, together.

I was hoping my night with Ray would be the latter. I tried to remind myself that you can't have the latter without the former. If your plane wasn't going down, you couldn't have that glorious moment where it righted itself.

Well, this plane seemed to be going down. I was

shaken by the moment I'd shared with Jon, traffic into the city was bumper to bumper, and parking (even by the standards of the Mission on a Saturday night) was atrocious. I was sweating and sure that I'd forgotten deodorant, and I felt my inner thighs sticking together under my skirt. Why had I worn a skirt? It was a ridiculous choice. I didn't like even thinking about what shirt Ray would be wearing, and how many drinks it might take for me to get beyond it. What were the odds I would recover that sexual feeling from last week? There was no way lightning was going to strike me twice.

After a nightmarish parallel-parking job, where I grazed the nearby bumpers no fewer than four times, I walked the five blocks to Ray's apartment. People who were younger and better-looking than me mobbed the streets. It occurred to me that they might not have actually been younger, but I felt ten years older than them. Which would put me right in Ray's ballpark. I was thirty and dating a forty-four-year-old man. That's like saying you've given up.

Ray buzzed me into his building, and I approached his apartment with trepidation. Who knew what decorating horrors lay inside? I knocked lightly, and when he opened the door, my mouth immediately watered. "What is that?" I breathed.

"Bolognese sauce," he said. He pecked me on the cheek, and I inhaled him, that reassuring scent that reminded me why I'd come.

I went inside, pleased to find that the apartment was eclectic, but by no means repulsive. There wasn't much furniture, just a weathered brown leather couch and matching chair and ottoman. The perimeter of the apartment was what drew the eye: The walls were an unusual fern color, and each one showcased a different interest. There was a wall of music (both CDs and vinyl), floor to ceiling, and a wall of bikes of different types and from different eras that almost seemed like an art installation. "Do you ride all of those?" I asked.

"I take the classics out for a spin every now and again, but mostly, I just ride the newer ones." He pointed to two bikes. "That one's for the city, that one's for the mountains."

I approached a wall covered with framed photos. "Burning Man," he said, referring to the yearly festival in the Nevada desert, where thousands of people gathered to create their own civilization for a week. "It's the biggest ode to self-expression and community in the world. And the drugs aren't bad, either."

He went into his kitchen to stir the pots as I looked at the photos. I'd heard about Burning Man, but never had occasion to go. It was like a dream city that people erected and destroyed in a week's time. They made pagodas out of PVC pipes, lived inside homemade geodesic domes. From his pictures, it seemed Ray was especially taken with the fire art: metal sculptures with flames rising high into the desert night, people dancing with blazing torches. There were day images of the white-sand desert itself, then of groups of people walking across in various stages of dress and undress. One showed a group of men wearing only tulle ballet skirts, engaged in deep conversation. There was one of Ray dressed head to toe in flowing white, like an Arabian sheikh, an expression of contemplation on his face.

"You go every year, I take it?" I said.

"I wouldn't miss it. You've never been, I take it?"

"No."

"Everyone should go at least once."

"Do married people with kids go?" I said, without thinking.

Ray seemed unaffected by my blurt. "Probably. Do you want some wine?"

"That'd be great."

I watched him uncork a bottle of red and pour it into two glasses. He brought one to me. I took a gulp and started coughing.

"Easy there," he said.

"Do you ever get the feeling you should quit while you're ahead?" I asked.

He looked at me carefully, then sipped his wine. "What are you trying to say, Eve?"

"I just have this sinking feeling about tonight. I know I shouldn't say that, but I can't quite shake it."

"I like that you say things you shouldn't say."

"Your turn. Say something you shouldn't say."

He took a minute to consider. "Here's the deal, Eve. I don't want to marry anyone. I don't want to be the father to anyone's kids. I like you, and I'm attracted to you, and I think we can be good for each other right now. And if that's all, well, that's good enough. We don't have to take this so heavy."

While listening to him, my feelings segued from confusion to rejection to relief to excitement. "So you're saying no pressure."

He raised a glass in toast. "No pressure," he said.

This is an opportunity.

Leading me toward the bedroom, Ray stopped and turned back. "Are you sure?" he asked.

"Yes," I said. After trying out a few ways to say it in my head, I went with, "I want to learn from you."

"What do you want to learn?"

"I want to learn about me. What I like. What I'm capable of."

He moved in close and kissed me. It was slower and sweeter than the other night, but just as intense. Yes, I was sure.

Once in his bedroom, he turned on a floor lamp. I was startled by the sudden light, but then realized it was soft and forgiving from the iron-framed bed. "May I?" he asked, touching my shirt.

I nodded, and he lifted it over my head. I tried not to feel self-conscious. I suppose I'd expected to stay dressed until he wanted me so badly that my body wouldn't matter.

I hated that I thought that way.

This is an opportunity.

That I was ruining, in my head.

"Hey," Ray said gently. "Come back." He was tracing my collarbone, then kissing it. "You look perfect."

I closed my eyes and let myself believe it as he kissed

my neck, reaching behind me and unclasping my bra in one expert move. I felt the heaviness of my breasts as he took the bra away, then lightness as he cradled them in his hands. My nipples hardened under his mouth, and I leaned my head back, feeling nothing else.

His hands were still on my breasts, and now his lips were on mine, his tongue alternating in pressure. I reached for the zipper on my skirt and released it, feeling the pleasure of the fabric slipping down my legs. I stepped free, and we moved to the bed.

Ray yanked his head back suddenly. "You're okay?" he said.

The question pulled me out. "Yes, I'm good," I said. I plunged back in, thrusting my tongue into his mouth.

"Good," he said through the kiss. The word echoed through me.

He began kissing downward, from my neck to my breasts to the space in between to my stomach. I giggled as he licked my belly button, then tensed slightly as he continued below. I thought that it had now been hours since I'd showered, and about how long it had been since someone had put his mouth there. It might have been the most naked I'd ever felt, as he paused there.

He began lightly kissing my clitoris, and I immediately moaned and forgot everything.

He went harder, then softer, sped up, slowed down. Every time I arched my back even the slightest bit, tightened my hand in his hair, he responded. I'd never been read so well.

He put his finger inside me, just a little bit, then farther. I missed his mouth; then it returned as his finger continued rhythmically. "Oh, my God," I gasped. He moved his mouth and finger in concert, and I felt myself opening up. Now he had two fingers inside me. I grabbed at the iron headboard, my legs starting to buck involuntarily. I didn't want to come. I didn't want it to end, and I wanted it to end right there. The sensations were too intense. I didn't want to feel the best I'd ever felt with someone I barely knew. It seemed wrong, and then that seemed out-of-this-world erotic.

"Do you want me to stop?" he asked. It was like a dispatch from another planet, I was so far away.

"No," I said desperately.

He started up again with his hand. I looked down and saw him watching himself touching me. He noticed me looking.

"I like to watch," he said. "Is that okay? It turns me on to watch you."

I didn't want to say, *It's too personal.* I didn't want to say, *Jon always had his eyes closed.*

I nodded, closing my own eyes. I wanted to return to before, when it was all sensation. I tried to let go, but I couldn't.

Ray was the one to let go, and he moved so that we were face-to-face. "Sorry," he said. "I didn't mean to freak you out. I'm a visual person."

"There's nothing wrong with it, I get that."

"What turns you on?"

"I don't know," I said. I felt antsy. Too much talk, and I'd never recover that earlier feeling.

"Are you okay with us trying to find out? I mean, it seemed like you liked what I was doing for a while there."

"I loved it. It was a little scary."

He looked searchingly into my eyes in the half-darkness. "You don't need to feel scared with me. The scary thing, I think, is really showing yourself sexually to the person you're spending a lifetime with, worrying that they're going to judge you for what you really want. That's when people hold back. You can just be anything you want in here." Ray paused. "What do you want, Eve?"

I reached for him.

"Like this," he said, taking my hips in his hands and showing me. Then he groaned.

I was on top, and his lower body was lifted off the bed, moving with me. Two bodies of equal force, pressure, intensity. I felt him everywhere. I felt myself everywhere.

"Use your muscles," he said.

"I am," I said. It was a workout.

"No. Down there."

I lost the rhythm for a second, focusing on how to do what he was asking.

"Just grip my cock," he said. "With your muscles."

I never would have expected it, but when he said the word "cock," I just about lost it. Jon had never been a talker.

"Keep talking," I said.

"Grip me, Eve. Hold on to me."

I got what he meant. It felt like I was holding him tight, from the inside. A charge went through my entire body.

"Oh, God, that's it," he said.

"Keep talking," I said.

"You're so tight on me. You're so sexy. Eve, Eve, Eve, Eve, what a beautiful name, Eve..."

I couldn't stand it. I erupted. I released guttural sounds I'd never heard myself make before as I shuddered and collapsed on top of him. I was nearly hyperventilating.

He stroked my hair. "Eve," he whispered in my ear. "Sweet Eve."

I couldn't move or speak. He was running his hands lightly along the sides of my body, and I shivered against him.

After a few minutes, I realized he was still hard inside me. "You didn't come," I said. The truth was, I didn't want to do anything about that. I was spent.

"This was your night. And trust me, I had a time of it."

I slipped away from him, and laughed. "My legs have gone numb."

"You were up there awhile." He grinned at me.

"That was crazy. Just"—I fumbled for a word, then finished—"crazy. I don't know what else to say."

"I saw you. You don't need to say anything."

I felt shy, realizing he'd watched me. Then I said, "How'd I look?"

"Spectacular. You should do that more often."

"Thank you. For everything."

"My absolute pleasure."

Not sure about the protocol, I asked, "Do you want me to go home?"

"No. Why would I want that?"

"We said no pressure."

"Look, no pressure doesn't mean no feelings. I think you're a terrific woman. In love with your husband, but that's a story for another time." He touched my face. "Don't look so stricken. Did you think I was somehow missing that fact?"

I'd just had the most intense orgasm of my life with a man who not only didn't love me, but seemed fine with the fact that I loved Jon. And he was right, it was a fact.

"Can I give you a piece of advice?" he said.

"Sure," I managed.

"Figure out why you're so mad at Jon. It's not just because of this other woman. You've been pissed at him a long time."

"This is the weirdest conversation I've ever had."

"You don't get out enough."

CHAPTER
29

So I had the most amazing, earth-shattering sex of my life," I announced. "And I want Jon back."

Tamara burst out of the dressing room, looking like a half-plucked peacock: one arm in, the other arm out of, an entirely too lacy wedding dress.

"That's not the one," I told her.

"You had sex with Jon!" she squealed.

"No, I had sex with Ray."

"You had amazing sex with Ray, and realized you want Jon back?" she asked incredulously.

"Yes."

"How does that happen?"

"I haven't a clue."

"So you're not going to have sex with Ray anymore?"

"My body really wants to, but no. I love Jon, and I want to try to trust him again."

Tamara plopped down on the raised platform, facing away from the three strategically placed mirrors. She worked her free arm into the dress as she considered her next statement.

"You don't have to be diplomatic. You can be excited. I know this is what you've been wanting," I said.

She cocked her head. "I don't know."

"What do you mean, you don't know? You were against me dating Ray from the start."

"Well, Clayton's always been so sold on you getting back with Jon that I guess I just went along. Not consciously," she added quickly. "You know how it's so easy to get sucked into thinking the same way when you're in a couple?" I nodded and waited for her to continue. "The thing is—and don't take this the wrong way—maybe you and Jon aren't the best match."

One of the few touchstones of my life throughout the past months had been Tamara's certainty about my marriage and her unshakable faith in Jon. It had alienated us, no doubt, but it was an underlying constant. With it suddenly pulled away, I felt like a house losing one of its support beams.

"Say something," Tamara said nervously, plucking at the lace inlay on the satin skirt of her gown.

"I'm just surprised."

"It's like, I'd finally decided to support you in moving on, and now you want Jon back. I feel like I'm always doing the wrong thing by you. And we just get further and further apart . . ." She looked away, trying not to cry.

I sat down on the dais next to her. "I'm glad I'm here today. I wasn't sure you'd still want me to do this with you."

"I'm glad you're here, too." She looked down at herself. "I hate these dresses."

"That's a bad one."

"I hate them all. They're not me."

"No wedding dress is you until you put it on and suddenly see yourself there." I flashed back to my own moment of recognition: that's the woman who's marrying Jon. God, I was thrilled.

"I'm thirty-two years old. I don't want to waste a year planning some wedding that's going to spend our down payment on a house."

"I thought your parents were paying for it."

"They're fighting about it. My mom thinks my dad should pay more than half, since he's got so much more money, but, of course, Trudy is fighting tooth and nail against it." Trudy was her stepmother. "Clayton sees how much I hate the fighting, plus he's got his pride about having them pay for the whole wedding, so we decided to foot most of the bill. But really, my mother's the one who wants it to be some extravaganza to make all her friends jealous." She gestured to her dress. "I mean, this isn't me."

I felt sad that this was the first I was hearing about something she had probably been struggling with for a while. "Does Clayton want a big wedding?"

"Not particularly."

"So don't do it. Have what you want. What do you want? Come on, just say the first thing that comes to your mind, like free association."

"It's easier to say what I don't want. I don't want something formal. I don't want a veil. I want to walk down to Clayton with him looking into my face the whole way."

"That's the advantage of being thirty-two. You know who you are. Do whatever you want; don't do anything you don't." I put my arm through the crook of her elbow and smiled at her.

She smiled back. "I don't want a head table."

"Amen!"

Laughing, she said, "And I'm not going to have place cards. People can sit wherever the hell they want."

"Hallelujah!"

"Only the people who really love us can come. No friends of my mother's that I haven't seen since I was twelve. And I want to wear one of those slip dresses, something simple and silky, and flowers in my hair," she said, warming to the fantasy.

"That sounds beautiful, Tam."

"Now, you just have to help me tell my mother."

I laughed. "Oh, I can do it. I've been standing up to Sylvia—sort of—for years." As I spoke her name, inspiration struck. "What about Sylvia's house? Say, her backyard. Then you wouldn't have to reserve a place way in advance and you could have the wedding sooner, if you wanted."

Tamara's eyes lit up. "Like this summer!"

"Over in Berkeley, it's beautiful in, say, August. Even early September. No fog."

"That yard was gorgeous!"

"There's a clearing between some trees, where you could have the ceremony, with a view over the bay."

"It would be perfect." She looked at me urgently. "Do you really think she'd loan us her house?"

For all Sylvia's faults, I knew she would, and that made me feel a rush of affection for the old broad. It was a good time to have one, since I might stay her daughter-in-law after all.

Not shopping for a wedding dress with Tamara turned out to be the best day we'd spent together in months. We left the store and went out for a three-cocktail lunch. Mostly, we were talking and laughing, but halfway into her third vodka tonic, Tamara told me why she'd been thinking maybe Jon and I weren't made for each other after all.

She recalled times she'd seen me be short with Jon, or blame him for things, and times when he and I disagreed and I just ran him over. Sometimes, she said, I didn't seem to have perspective where Jon was concerned. If something was frustrating me, it was Jon's fault.

I asked why she'd never said anything when Jon and I were together, and she answered that he just seemed to take it in stride. If it doesn't bother him, she figured, why should it bother her? Who was she to criticize someone else's relationship? Besides, a lot of the time, Jon and I looked great together. We had history and in-jokes. A lot of the time, she said, Jon and I were what she and Clayton wanted to be.

Once, she'd gotten a taste of my full-scale anger toward Jon. He was late from work and he hadn't called. Tamara and I were supposed to go out somewhere, and Jacob had been acting up all afternoon, and I was maybe five months pregnant and not feeling good. She said Jon apologized right away, but I said, "Get in here," and indicated that he should follow me to the bedroom. From the living room, Tamara could hear me shouting. She couldn't hear Jon much at all. Then I came down the hall, my face tight, and said, "Come on, let's go."

Was that the night, I wondered, when Jon e-mailed Laney about how I'd acted? Or maybe he'd felt low and called her. Remembering the way I talked to Jon that day—and how I'd thought nothing of it at the time, how I'd felt justified, even—I saw that I had opened the door for Laney myself. I hadn't invited her in; no, Jon had done that. But he hadn't acted entirely alone. In a strange way, it was good to think that there was a reason for Laney. If I wasn't blameless, then there were things I could do better next time, if Jon and I had a next time.

When I got home, Charlie was talking a mile a minute about his future. Normally, I would have been overjoyed to hear him even say the word, but not that day. He was talking about maybe getting his own apartment, whether I'd be willing to pay him whatever the day care places charged, and what rents were like in that area. I asked him if he really wanted to live in the suburbs, and he hemmed and hawed and played coy, but it was clear he was just wanting to live near Lil. His fantasy was getting a short-term lease, with the idea that Lil would ask him to move in with her after a few months. He'd never lived with a woman before, but this could be something great. He said it twice: this could be something great. I bit my tongue, went into my room, and called Lil.

She answered her cell phone on the fourth ring, slightly out of breath. "Oh, hey, Eve," she said.

"Lil, you need to do something about my brother."

"What's with the stage whisper?"

"He's in the other room and I don't want him to hear what I'm about to tell you."

She sighed, and I had a feeling she already knew. "Okay, tell me."

"It's gone on too long. He's talking about getting his own apartment out here. This is the first time he's talked about living anywhere other than where we grew up. This is big. He's talking about his future." I found myself about to cry. "His *future*. He never talks about that. And he thinks his future is with you. You have to tell him that it isn't."

After a pause, Lil said, "I wish it was. It's not easy finding someone as good as Charlie. Just genuinely good. I've never, ever believed anyone before when he said he'd do anything for me."

"Charlie said that?"

"Yes." Lil's breath was ragged. "But I can't put my energy into something that's going to end someday. I can just see it. We don't have enough in common, it'll take years for him to get his shit together, and let's face it, he's got years to burn that I don't."

I'd never heard Lil admit before that aging mattered. "So you need to end it now."

"I know. I don't want to."

"Lil, please. You need to. He's my brother."

Her voice was sadly determined. "I will. I'll do it tonight, so be ready. He might need you."

CHAPTER
30

Charlie didn't come home that night. I waited up, and finally called Lil on her cell phone at midnight. She said flatly, "I did it, he left around ten. I don't want to talk about it." I asked if she was okay, and she said in that same tone that she was. There seemed to be nothing left to say, so I hung up and worried.

He showed up the next morning at six-thirty. He looked like hell, smelled like booze, and he, too, didn't want to talk about it. "I'm going to sleep now," he said.

"If you're not coming home, you need to call me. I was worried all night."

"I thought you'd figure I stayed at Lil's." He looked me full in the face. "She already told you."

"Charlie, it's not like we were colluding or—"

He cut me off. "You get Jacob ready yourself. Knock on my door just before you go and I'll take care of Liv. But I'm not making any promises after today."

"Why are you so mad at me?" I asked his retreating back.

Not turning around, he said, "I'm not mad at you." He

continued down the hall, went into his room, and shut the door.

I was anxious all day at work. Charlie was going to leave. I could feel it. He loved Jacob and Olivia, but they were my life; he'd wanted his own life with Lil. Now that he wasn't going to have it, he'd go back to his closest approximation. Back to loser friends, easy sex, no job, no home of his own, but at least it was his.

I was suddenly terrified. I couldn't imagine being in the house alone. Charlie had camouflaged the reality that Jon was gone; he'd stood in as an adult male voice. He'd been my tag team partner, my confidant. The brother who couldn't have been trusted six months ago to pick someone up at the airport on the right day had become my rock.

I spent much of the day marshaling every argument I could for him to stay, but eventually I had to admit my own selfishness. I wasn't the one to say whether he was better off staying or going. The decision had to be his.

Just before two o'clock, Chad knocked on my office door and stuck his head in. "You've got a visitor," he said with a broad smile.

I flashed on an image of Jon, and my heart surged. But Chad stepped aside, and it was Charlie, pushing Olivia in her stroller.

"I thought I should finally see where you work," he said. He looked around approvingly. "Nice. It could use a window, but nice."

I was relieved to find no trace of anger in him. "It's so good to see you. This morning—"

"It was way too early," he said dismissively.

As he settled into a chair, I greeted Olivia. She gurgled happily. I thought how much she'd changed under Charlie's watch, and I hoped my guess was wrong and he was staying after all.

I sat in the chair next to him, instead of going back behind the desk. "What's going on, Charlie?" I asked.

He smiled at me, but there was something in it that evoked an image of him driving away and me standing by the roadside. It was a good-bye smile. "You know what's going on."

"I'd rather hear it from you."

"It's time for me to take off. We've taken care of each other pretty well these past months, but all good things come to an end, right?" His face was composed, but his Adam's apple was working way too hard.

"Is it just because of Lil? Or was it me, too?"

"I was starting to feel edgy. That's why I talked about getting my own place. I mean, I'm a guy. How long am I supposed to live with my sister and her two kids?"

I nodded. "But if Lil hadn't ended things—"

"They would have ended eventually. It's like you said. What am I going to do, be a husband and father?"

"I think you'd be a great one, actually."

"Someday. That's a good thing to learn about yourself. I wouldn't have guessed it."

"But not now?"

"Nah. Not now."

"So what will you do?" I asked.

"I'm going to live with Mom again. Just for a while. I

talked to her this morning, and then to Phil. He's going to give me a job as a mechanic at his dealership, and as soon as I get a few paychecks, I'll get my own place."

"Is that really what you want to do? Be a mechanic?"

"I don't know. I was good at it, I just screwed off too much." Olivia started crying, and before I could move, Charlie leapt up to check on her. Her teething had started, and he rubbed ointment on her gums.

"Have I told you how proud I am of you?" I said. "The way you've stepped up with the kids, the way you stepped up with Lil. I know it didn't work out, but you really put yourself out there. That's big."

He avoided my eyes as he resettled himself next to me. "Thanks," he mumbled, suddenly shy.

"Don't stay a mechanic if it's not what you want, okay? But don't quit until you find something else."

He did a military salute. "Yes, sir."

"I just don't want you to settle. You've got a gift, and it's people."

He shrugged.

"No, I'm serious. I'm still looking for mine."

"You've got lots of gifts, Evie. But I don't have time to name them. Liv and me, we're going to take a walk around campus." He got down on his haunches by the stroller. "What do you think, girl?"

"I can take my break now and show you around," I said. "Then you'll have time to name all my good qualities. Maybe one of them can give me an actual career."

"This doesn't look so bad."

"I could do worse." I turned to Olivia, and lifted my voice. "You ready to go meet Dyan?"

There was the question of timing. Maybe I shouldn't approach Jon now; maybe he'd think I was doing it only because Charlie was leaving and it was convenient. Maybe I *was* only doing it because Charlie was leaving. But deep down, I'd known before that. I wanted Jon and me to have another chance when we were smarter and stronger. At least, I hoped we were smarter and stronger.

I asked him to meet me at a café in the city, walking distance from his apartment. I had a fantasy about us staring into each other's eyes, wordlessly communicating our desire, then hurrying back to his apartment, fumbling with the locks on the door, then with his belt buckle... Being with Ray had unleashed all sorts of cinematic (at times, pornographic) scenarios in my mind, only starring Jon. I'd been so busy with all the arrangements around Charlie's departure that it hadn't been hard not to call Ray, who seemed to understand the need for distance after getting that close.

I got lucky on parking and tried to convince myself it was a sign. If this had been a Chinese restaurant, I would have been madly cracking open fortune cookies. Instead, it was a loud, bustling café, with a well-dressed crowd (I'd decided to go more Nob than Loin) and energetic baristas shouting out drink orders of such specificity they became parodies of themselves: "Half-fat, light-foam, part-Americano, shade-grown mocha!"

I settled myself by the window with my workaday cappuccino and watched the foot traffic, hoping Jon would also be early. Again, I got lucky and he was.

I stood up as he approached and we shared a quick, strained hug. "Let me get your drink," I said.

"No, I'm already up."

"I'm up, too. And I'm the one who invited you."

"Well, I was up longer, and I'm the one who's late."

"You're not late." Was this banter? Or just bad conversation? I couldn't tell. My palms were sweating.

"Eve," he said with finality, "I'll get my own drink."

I noticed that as he crossed the room to the counter, there was an energy to his step. It seemed positive (for him, if not necessarily for us).

He returned with his coffee, and we sat sipping our respective drinks. "Well," I said, "at least it's not awkward."

"We've got that going," he agreed, smiling.

"I've been doing a lot of thinking, and..." I paused. "Argh. What kind of beginning is that?"

"A thoughtful one?" he suggested.

I laughed. "I'm so nervous, the last thing I needed was caffeine."

"What do you want to tell me, Eve?" he asked gently.

"Okay. I just need to dive in, and if it's messy, it's messy."

"Agreed."

"I just don't know if you're still angry with me. Can I ask you, are you?"

"Sometimes," he said.

"How about now, this minute?"

"Right now, I'm pretty mellow."

"Good. Okay. So... I've been thinking about all that's happened, and about you and me and Laney. I know I haven't always been as good to you as I should have, and that's part of why you were involved with Laney."

He raised his eyebrows, but said nothing.

"I'm not saying that makes everything with Laney okay, but if we both take responsibility for things, maybe we could try again." I realized I'd been holding my breath, and exhaled.

"I appreciate that. But I guess I feel like you've never fully taken responsibility for what came after, for the way you pushed and pulled me, and then for reading the e-mails. It's going to be hard for me to trust you again."

"It's going to be hard for me to trust you again, too. But I think we just need to do a lot of talking, and ask a lot of questions. I was wrong for not asking you more about Laney. I don't want to assume anything anymore, and I don't want either of us to lie, no matter how tempting it is, no matter how much easier it seems like it'll make things." I paused and looked into his eyes. "What I'm saying is that I'm going to do my absolute best to forgive you for Laney and I'd like you to try to forgive me for everything else. I've made a lot of mistakes."

"Part of me is so happy to hear you say that, and the

other part of me just can't believe it took so long. Does that make sense?"

"Yes."

"Therapy's been good for me. I don't feel like the same person I was. I mean, even this conversation—I can feel how different it would have been just a few months ago. I would have jumped at anything you said. But I'm not like that anymore."

"I see that."

"I don't want to become that guy again. I'm lonely as hell, Eve, but I'm a better man."

I saw that, too. "I'm trying to be a better woman. For a while, Jon, I didn't know who we were. I didn't know who this man was who'd betray me with Laney, and I didn't know who this woman was who'd read her husband's e-mails night after night. But I don't think we're those people anymore. I mean, I'm hoping."

He nodded. "I've been wanting to apologize once again for Laney. Because regardless of what you did, that was wrong. And some part of me knew that all along. Otherwise, I would have told you about her when she started taking up more of my time and my thoughts. I rationalized it because there was no sex, but on some level, I knew she meant more than she should." He leaned toward me. "But she never meant more than you. Never. That's the truth."

"How did it happen, Jon?"

"Life was stressful. Sometimes it was boring. You'd heard all my stories; Laney hadn't. Sometimes I felt like a superhero talking to her, like I was a hundred feet tall." He looked away, and I could see that he was trying to decide whether to go on. "But it was more than that. I couldn't stand up to you. I felt like I was no match for your convictions or, frankly, for your anger. Sometimes it seemed like what I felt didn't matter. Sometimes I didn't even know what I felt, I was so used to just sucking it up. I'm not saying this to make you feel guilty, it's what I felt. In talking to Louise, she helped me see that part of why Laney was so dangerous was that she was my release valve. I'd feel down after something happened with you and instead of telling you how I felt, I went to Laney so she could build me back up. I let myself turn away from you, Eve, and that was wrong. It was unfair. And I'm sorry."

Tears pricked my eyes. "Thank you," I said.

He reached over and squeezed my hand, then held it. "I'm going to think about this for a while, what we said here today and where we go next. And it's not because I don't love you. I love you plenty. But I need to know that I'm doing the right thing."

I was disappointed, but I tried not to show it. "I understand. I respect that."

"I love you. But we can't go back."

"I love you," I said. "And no, we shouldn't go back."

"So I'm going to go think." He began to smile, and I did, too.

"Tell Louise I said hi."

"I will."

CHAPTER 31

Jacob and Luke were on the swings, arguing strenuously. I thought we should intervene, but Lil predicted that if we gave them a few minutes, they'd work it out. It was a debate Jon and I used to have. He said I was always too quick to jump in, and I could see now that I'd grown accustomed to overruling him. But he was right a lot of the time, just like Lil was this time. They did work it out, as Lil and I watched from a nearby bench.

"He misses Charlie," Lil said, her eyes on Luke. "Much as I wish it was different, much as I want to be all things, he wants a man around."

I avoided saying that I thought she did, too. Not just any man, but I was pretty sure she missed Charlie herself.

Lil could read my face. "Yes, I miss him, too," she said.

"Phil's giving him a pretty good opportunity. Paying him well, giving him good shifts."

"Here's to nepotism." She raised her bottle of sparkling water to Charlie, then took a long swallow.

"I guess I mean, it's not the worst idea he's ever had."

"How are you doing with everything?"

"Not bad. Olivia's day care provider seems great, and she says Olivia's making a normal transition. I was so relieved, just hearing the word 'normal.' I can tell Jacob wishes Charlie was still here with us, but he doesn't seem angry with me about him going. I think Charlie explained it to him really well, told it to him like a bedtime story, where an uncle who loves his nephew very much has to go on a journey so he can be a better person. Jacob has Charlie's cell phone number, he carries it in his backpack, and Charlie said he can call anytime. They've already spoken twice since he left. Jacob is looking forward to the next chapter in the story."

There was sadness in Lil's face as she listened, but she only nodded. "What about Jon?" she asked.

"I'm feeling weirdly at peace about Jon. It's like, if he gives us another chance, that's great; if he doesn't, I gave it all I had. I took my best shot. Well, I was prepared to take my best shot."

"I'll cross my fingers for you."

"Yesterday I was in line at the supermarket, and this woman was talking on her cell phone really loudly. She was saying how her new boyfriend was such a great catch. She said it like three times."

"She sounds annoying." Lil proffered her water to me, and I took a long swallow.

"She was. But I used to say that about Jon, maybe not three times in a row or so loud that strangers could hear me. But I thought it."

"As if we can catch anybody. You catch a cold, you

don't catch a guy." She shook her head, blond ponytail swaying gracefully down her back. "You can find them, but you can't catch them, no matter what your mother told you."

"You don't want to know what my mother told me."

"But you wouldn't really want to catch them, would you? That term always makes me think of when I was a kid and I'd catch fireflies in glass jars."

"Wouldn't they die?" I asked.

"You poke holes in the lid, and you let them go eventually. But anyway, I think catching a guy sounds like that. You know, trapping someone so he can spend a lifetime forced to blink just for you."

"Ah, if you love someone, set him free, right?"

"That's one way to do it."

Jacob and Luke came running up to us. "We want to get ice cream. Can we get ice cream?" Luke asked. He looked imploringly at Lil, while Jacob cast the same look my way.

"When I'm done talking to Jacob's mom. Why don't you guys go on that spinning-wheel thingy over there?" She gestured.

"We did that last time," Jacob said.

"And you had fun last time." She waved her hand. "Go on, give it a whirl. Shoo."

After a minute more of enervated protest, they did. I always enjoyed Lil's laissez-faire parenting style, and that Luke seemed to understand she was allowed to have a life outside of him. The kids were now spinning happily, but I figured we had another seven minutes, tops.

"So what's your gut feeling? Is Jon flying back to you or not?" she asked.

"I'm really not sure. What's amazing is that I spent so long not realizing he had the free will to leave anytime he wanted. I guess I just thought he was locked in. But it's never really locked in. I mean, you think saying 'I love you' is going to do it; then you think getting married is going to do it; and surely, having kids should do it. But nothing does."

"And thank God for that. Because when you think it's locked in, you get lazy."

"I guess we did. Take our sex life, for instance."

Lil nodded knowingly. "That's how you end up with a Laney, all right."

"But he wasn't having sex with Laney."

"I bet he was having fantasies about her, though."

I knew he had, but even now, I hated thinking of it. "Yeah, yeah, our sex life was a problem."

"Do you mean to tell me you're just now realizing that sex is important in a relationship?"

"I guess I am."

"Well, who was going to tell you? Really, you just had to pick it up in the streets."

We were both laughing as Jacob and Luke made their way back to us.

There was a Post-it in Dyan's handwriting on my computer a few days later: *Have you forgotten the question?* Then she'd listed a few classes and times. They corresponded to

my top two career choices, the ones ranked above public
health. Elementary Nutrition started at four-thirty.

Before I could come up with a reason not to go, I
dialed Lil's number to see if she could watch Jacob that
afternoon. I'd have some time to kill before the class, and
had a good idea of how to spend it.

"So I kind of figured it was over, but it's good of you to
make it official," Ray said.

We were sitting in his empty classroom, side by side,
in chair/desk combos. The night we'd spent together was
just fresh enough that I was glad to have the arm of the
desk between us. On the dry erase board, he'd drawn a
diagram about community outreach, and I kept looking
at it whenever his gaze on mine felt too intense.

"It's not like I didn't enjoy myself," I said. I turned
toward the board.

"Oh, I could tell," he said.

"Jon and I might try again."

He nodded, unsurprised.

"You were right, I'm still in love with him."

"Then it's good that you're trying again. Pull out all
the stops, that's what I say."

"I don't actually know what's going to happen. He's
still deciding whether he wants to try again."

Ray shifted so that he was looking at me directly. "Are
you ending things with me, or asking me to convince
you not to end them? I just like to be clear."

"As of right now, I'm a free agent, I can do whatever I

want. Like I said, Jon's still thinking things over. But if I put my energy into you, it's energy that's not going into Jon. Which was why Laney was so toxic."

"So you're ending things."

"So I'm ending things."

"Fair enough."

"There's something else I wanted to tell you," I said. Then I hesitated. I could see that Ray wanted to get going. He wasn't meant to be my friend, at least not yet. He'd done me a lot of good, and, as he would say, that was good enough.

"What's that?"

"If I remember, I'll come back," I said.

What I almost told Ray was I'd been thinking a lot about what he'd said, why I was so angry with Jon, how far back it went. I kept recalling one moment.

I was already crying from his marriage proposal, and I just kept crying when I saw the pregnancy test. Jon thought they were tears of happiness—I guess he hoped they were—and I tried to let him know otherwise, but it seemed like he wouldn't hear it. "We're so young," I said.

"We have our whole lives ahead of us," he said. "And now we're going to have a baby."

I wanted to feel his enthusiasm; I wanted to follow him anywhere. It was ironic that Jon later became the one who wasn't listened to, because that night, it was me. I was trying to say I couldn't do what he wanted me to do, but he wouldn't hear it.

I wonder now if Jon hadn't been so forceful, so convinced that we were doing the right thing by going ahead with the pregnancy, what would have happened. I think of my dream about Lavender, and I suspect I couldn't have gone through with an abortion. If Jon had gone back and forth with me, if he'd just wavered awhile, if I'd owned the decision to have Jacob, would I still have this anger inside me about the road not taken?

I liked to think of myself as being without regrets. Rationally, I knew they were useless. But I was a person with a thousand "what-ifs." The funny thing is that if you follow your what-ifs back far enough, they become someone else's: What if my mother had been impregnated by someone who actually gave a damn? What if my father had stepped up and decided to be a better man once he knew he was having a kid? That's when you realize just how foolish it is to retrace your steps when all you can really do is take a good, hard look around and walk forward.

I wasn't the tattoo type, but if I had been, I'd have an anklet that read: this is your life, so now what?

CHAPTER
32

Testing one, two, three," Jon said through the answering machine. His playful tone wasn't fully masking his nervousness. "I'm sitting here with a wedding invitation for Tamara and Clayton. Can you believe how fast these kids grow up? And I'm thinking that it would be pretty strange to attend a wedding stag in my own childhood backyard. And it would be even stranger to be there with anyone but you. Tragic, really.

"Louise thinks our best shot would involve a whole lot of work, asking a lot of tough questions, and being brutally (and I mean, brutally) honest with each other. About the only thing scarier than that is the thought of losing you forever. So I want to try this. If you do, too—"

"I'm here," I said.

Tamara got her wish: a small affair, a slip dress, no veil, no place cards, me as her only bridesmaid. She floated down the aisle, orchids in her hair, beaming all the while. Sylvia had declined the invitation, but I saw her peering from an upstairs window. I could have sworn she was smiling. I smiled back, but I couldn't tell if she saw me.

For the newlyweds' first dance, the band played "Wonderful Tonight." Jon and I had never liked it much; Tamara had always adored it. (Was it that line about brushing long blond hair that sold her and alienated me?) Clayton took Tamara's hand and led her to the clearing everyone understood to be the dance floor. I watched for a minute, then wandered to the edge of the yard.

It was twilight, and while the Bay Area isn't known for its sunsets, Tamara had lucked out. We all had. There were swatches of purple and violet surrounding the usual dusky pink. In the distance, the Bay Bridge was partially obscured by the fog of a San Francisco summer, while the Golden Gate was just a faint memory. Below, courtesy of the quickly darkening sky, the water was indigo and appeared motionless, but I knew that was just my vantage point. Everything rushes on. And I'd later tell Lil how the lights in the Berkeley houses spread out before me were like fireflies. I allowed myself a private smile before turning back toward the party.

Jon and Jacob were waltzing together, mocking the serious romantic intent of the song neither of us cared for, as other dancers held each other close and took the song as written. I continued to smile, only it was public now, as Jon caught my eye. He smiled, too, and held out his hand, beckoning. There were still so many questions to be answered, but somehow that made it even better to be chosen. I stepped forward, the night finally at my back.

READING GROUP GUIDE

1. After learning that her husband, Jon, has been emotionally involved with another woman for the past year, Eve thinks, "In all these years, I'd never had occasion to doubt Jon's love and fidelity. It was like suddenly finding out you've been living in someone else's marriage—someone else's bad marriage. I mean, these sorts of things don't happen in good marriages, do they?" Do they?

2. The first time Eve reads Jon's e-mail, she's doing it to prove his innocence. Does that make it less wrong? When she continues to do it, is her behavior justified by circumstance? If not, would it be justified by any circumstance?

3. Psychologist and infidelity expert Shirley Glass has said that there are three main traits that distinguish an emotional affair from an ordinary friendship: emotional intimacy that is greater than in the marriage, sexual tension, and secrecy. Does Jon's relationship with Laney qualify?

4. Eve's friend Tamara thinks Jon's actions are less of a betrayal because there was no sex, while her friend Lil thinks an emotional affair is worse than a sexual one. Which point of view does Eve find more convincing? Which do you?

5. Did you find yourself siding with Jon and/or Eve at different points in the book, and being frustrated by the other spouse? Think of the strongest reaction you had to either Eve or Jon, and what experiences from your own life influenced it.

6. The reader doesn't find out very much of substance about Laney. Why do you think the author chose this approach instead of, say, having Eve call Laney so the reader could get a sense of Laney's voice? Was it the right choice for the story the author was trying to tell?

7. Tamara advances her stuffer theory: men who don't feel comfortable expressing their anger stuff it down until it hinders their ability to love their partners. Do you buy Tamara's theory? And is Jon ultimately a stuffer?

8. If you were to develop a corresponding theory about Eve's anger, what would it be?

9. Eve decides against staying together for the sake of the children. In initiating an official separation, she tells Jon, "I think they're better off seeing us first-rate, even if it's apart." Do you agree?

10. Eve and Tamara are initially much closer than Eve is to Lil. This element changes during the course of the book. Why do you think this happened? Does Eve become more like Lil and less like Tamara?

11. Eve's mother finds love in the form of Phil Tibbs. Though it's not the relationship she would choose for herself, Eve ultimately supports it. Have you had situations like this in your own life?

12. When Eve finally confesses to Jon that she read his e-mails, he becomes uncharacteristically furious, even throwing a glass. Is his response appropriate in the context of what's come before? Could you argue that it represents growth for him?

13. Were you surprised that Eve had sex with Ray Dubrovnik, and that it clarified her feelings for Jon?

14. Ultimately, Jon and Eve both assume responsibility for their own role in what's happened, and try to find forgiveness for the other. What do you think the main offense of each person was?

15. Is it a happy ending?

ABOUT THE AUTHOR

My first novel, *Five Things I Can't Live Without,* was a lighthearted look at the neurotic art of self-sabotage. The central premise was that my character, Nora, was looking for problems where there really weren't any; she was thinking herself right out of happiness. For my second book, I decided the main character might still have a whiff of the neurotic but I'd really give her something to worry about.

When I first sat down, I didn't know what Eve would find out (I didn't actually know her name was Eve), but I knew it would happen on Thanksgiving. An affair seemed obvious (too obvious) until I realized it was an emotional affair rather than a physical one. The reason I'm using language like "find out" and "realized" is because for me, the process of writing novels is like that. There's nothing better than that moment when your character surprises you. For example, I thought Eve was going to decline sex with Ray and then it turned out she was having it. Enthusiastically. Who knew?

Since I'm a practicing marriage and family therapist,

the issues of emotional intimacy and fidelity were close to my heart. The more I thought about Eve and Jonathon—who they were and what they could represent—the more excited I became. I liked the idea of starting with Eve's discovery about Jonathon and then having the book turn into her own journey of self-discovery. I liked that she could be alternately sympathetic and infuriating (or both at once). When we feel wronged, we rarely show our best selves all the time. And writing complicated characters is a lot of fun. They surprise you more often.

Holly Shumas

5 Ways to Disaster-Proof Your Relationship

1 Choose a partner who fits with you on lots of levels. If you're very different people, make sure your differences are complementary.

2 Listen to that warning voice inside your head (and the voices of those who know you best).

3 Recognize that we can never know another person completely. This can be a little scary, but it can be exciting, too. Open yourself up to surprises.

4 Figure out your own triggers. (For example, why does lateness bother you so intensely?) Strong reactions say as much about us as about our partners, so look to yourself first.

5 Remember that even in the best relationships, people lose that loving feeling every now and again. When it happens to you, don't panic; focus on reconnecting. And keep the faith! You chose your partner for a reason, right?